WITHDRAWN FROM STOCK

Pomegranate Soup

Born in Tehran, Marsha Mehran escaped the Iranian Revolution with her family and moved to Buenos Aires, where her parents set up a Middle Eastern café. She has since lived in Australia and New York City and now lives in the west of Ireland with her husband, Christopher, who is constantly called upon to taste her experimental cooking. She is currently at work on her next novel.

Praise for *Pomegranate Soup*

'*Pomegranate Soup* is glorious, daring and delightful. I adored the Iranian sisters, Marjan, Bahar and Layla, who are looking to build a life, start a business and find love in a place so far from home. Ireland has never been more beautiful – the perfect setting for this story filled with humour, hope and possibility'

Adriana Trigiani

'A feast of feelgood!' *Ireland on Sunday*

'Delightful' *Birmingham Evening Mail*

'Beautiful strangers bring exotic recipes to town . . .
Fans of *Chocolat* will savour the tale, not to mention
the 13 recipes, including one for pomegranate soup'
Publishers Weekly

'Wonderful . . . fuses the magical mysticism that
surrounds Croagh Patrick with the exotic Persian
cuisine of Mehran's native Iran . . . Hats off to Miss
Mehran and here's to reading her next novel'
Out of Ireland

'A most unusual and charming novel . . . delightful
and addictive'   *Deseret Morning News*

'A romping tale full of sensuous recipes and gentle
humour . . . Charming . . . You can almost smell how
good the book will be . . . Delicious'
The Free Lance-Star

'Riveting . . . Delectable . . . A mouthwatering tale
with flavours of *Chocolat* and *Under the Tuscan Sun*'
The Orlando Sentinel

'[A book] ready to be discovered and devoured . . .
Marsha Mehran describes the food in mouthwatering
detail – with a dash of magic realism' *Chicago Tribune*

'Refreshing . . . Intriguing . . . Enchanting . . . A
wonderful treat'   *Bookpage*

'Highly recommended'   *Library Journal*

Marsha Mehran

Pomegranate
Soup

arrow books

Published in the United Kingdom by Arrow Books in 2006

1 3 5 7 9 10 8 6 4 2

Copyright © Marsha Mehran, 2005

Marsha Mehran has asserted her right under the Copyright, Designs and
Patents Act, 1988 to be identified as the author of this work.

This novel is a work of fiction. Names and characters are the product of
the author's imagination and any resemblance to actual persons, living or
dead, is entirely coincidental.

This book is sold subject to the condition that it shall not, by way of
trade or otherwise, be lent, resold, hired out, or otherwise circulated
without the publisher's prior consent in any form of binding or cover other
than that in which it is published and without a similar condition
including this condition being imposed on the subsequent purchaser.

First published in the United Kingdom in 2005 by William Heinemann

Arrow Books
The Random House Group Limited
20 Vauxhall Bridge Road, London SW1V 2SA

Random House Australia (Pty) Limited
20 Alfred Street, Milsons Point, Sydney
New South Wales 2061, Australia

Random House New Zealand Limited
18 Poland Road, Glenfield
Auckland 10, New Zealand

Random House (Pty) Limited
Isle of Houghton, Corner of Boundary Road & Carse O'Gowrie
Houghton 2198, South Africa

Random House Group Limited Reg. No. 954009

www.randomhouse.co.uk

A CIP catalogue record for this book
is available from the British Library

Papers used by Random House
are natural, recyclable products made from wood grown in
sustainable forests. The manufacturing processes conform to
the environmental regulations of the country of origin

ISBN 9780099478928 (from Jan 2007)
ISBN 0 09 9478927

Typeset in Goudy by Palimpsest Book Production Limited,
Polmont, Stirlingshire
Printed and bound in Great Britain by
Cox & Wyman Ltd, Reading, Berkshire

Everyone knows,
everyone knows
we have found our way
Into the cold, quiet dream of phoenixes:
we found truth in the garden
In the embarrassed look of a nameless flower,
and we found permanence
In an endless moment
when two suns stared at each other.

I am not talking about timorous whispering
In the dark.
I am talking about daytime and open windows
and fresh air and a stove in which useless
    things burn
and land which is fertile
with a different planting
and birth and evolution and pride.
I am talking about our loving hands
which have built across nights a bridge of
    the message of perfume
and light and breeze.
—'Conquest of the Garden', *Forough Farrokhzad*

Prologue

Dawn rose over Clew Bay and the small Irish
village of Ballinacroagh. Had Thomas McGuire
stopped to admire the fanfare of saffron rays, he
might have missed the beginning of the end of
his rule over the sleepy seaside town. But, as was
often the case with men of his temperament,
Thomas had little time for daydreams. The obsti-
nate businessman had charged out of his hard
bed at five-thirty that morning, determined as
ever to tend to his growing empire of three pubs,
two spirit shops, and one inn on Main Mall.

The Mall's slowly winding medieval street began
with the greasy Blue Thunder chip and burger

shop, and ended with a dusty, fourteenth-century church and monolithic memorial to St Patrick in the town's square. In between lay the usual combination of pubs, Clarks shoe shop, religious relics shop and Aran sweater and souvenir shop that one has come to expect of Hibernian towns situated in the shadows of Mother Nature's handiwork. Unable to rival the glory of millennial sedimentation and ancient Celtic causeways, such places are happy just to exist on the peripheries with a bland shrug to improvement, for why even try? In Ballinacroagh the natural phenomena are dominated by Croagh Patrick, or The Reek, upon whose perch St Patrick had nestled for forty days and forty nights. The solitary mountain sits solemn and monkish, shadowing the village clustered at its base; its weary soul no longer fascinated by the sprawling valley of patchwork fields, stone-bordered lanes, and human folly taking place on Main Mall below.

The first day of spring, 1986, found Thomas McGuire standing on Ballinacroagh's main street, shuddering in his boots from the bleak morning drizzle. The burly bar owner had just opened the cellar doors to Paddy McGuire's, the moth-ridden public house he had inherited over twenty years ago from his father. Paddy's untimely death in a tractor accident had made a then nineteen-year-old Thomas the youngest pub owner Ballinacroagh, if not the whole of County Mayo, had ever known. Such early dominion over the town's favourite watering hole had, unfortunately, brought out the worst in the young man's already volatile temperament. Thomas's ill nature was the product of an undetermined mixture of *sard* (cold) and *garm* (hot), which nothing – not even Marjan's famously equalising recipe for tart pomegranate soup – could remedy. Not only was this lethal combination of humours the catalyst of countless irrationalities, but it also left him poorly equipped to deal with the sensuous wafts of cardamom, cinnamon and rose water that, this very morning, were blowing his way.

The smell first hit Thomas McGuire as he was directing the underpaid Guinness man down into the pub's freezing cellar. Its spicy, sinful intonations reeked of an unknown evil; a godforsaken foreignness that set off alarm bells in Thomas's large, potato head, and froze him to his spot. It was not until the Guinness man, Conor Jennings, also paused to catch a sniff of the air, that Thomas realised the strange scent was very real indeed.

'Jaysus, Mary and Joseph. If that doesn't smell like heaven I don't know what does, then.' Conor Jennings leaned against the keg trolley and snorted through his pug nose. A forty-year-old bachelor who still lived with his thrifty mother, Conor had just come from a disappointing breakfast of watered-down tea (bag used repeatedly) and a rasher sandwich on buttered, day-old bread. As he stood there sniffing, his ample stomach gave a long, mutinous growl.

Thomas scowled.

'You'll be seeing heaven sooner than you think if you don't get yer fat arse back in there and finish the stock! Go on with you then, and stop wasting my time. Or would you rather I give Seamus O'Grady a call? I'm sure he'd like to hear how one of his route men is doing.'

It was a particularly harsh slap, even for

Thomas McGuire, and Conor's face flushed a deep pink as he hauled another keg from his van. Grumbling under his breath, he disappeared down the cellar steps, leaving the pub owner alone to investigate the source of the scent. Thomas's awakened nose led him next door, to the rundown and long empty shop that used to be the old Delmonico pastry shop, Papa's Pastries. The Delmonicos had moved into town from Naples shortly after the Second World War, and had operated the same doughy bakery on Main Mall for over three decades. But ever since Luigi Delmonico's death five years ago, the bakery had been an empty shell, deserted and collecting dust. Or rather it *used* to be empty. Because, bleary-eyed as he was, Thomas could not deny the curious glint of light that was shining through the shop's newspapered windows.

The light grew brighter as he crept closer to the old pastry place, the dense, exotic aroma causing his stocky knees to quiver like a shy schoolboy's. Thomas squinted through a small tear in the newspaper, half-expecting to confront the devil himself, but saw instead the glitter of something golden; a bright obscenity that occupied his entire field of vision.

The surly drink baron growled and spat on the cracked pavement below the old bakery's door. It was pure witchcraft, that's what. No doubt about it. And he was going to find out exactly who was behind it all.

Chapter One

Dolmeh

Ingredients:

30–40 canned vine leaves
2 onions, chopped
250g ground meat, lamb or beef
olive oil
1/3 cup fresh summer savory
½ cup fresh dill
1/3 cup fresh tarragon
¼ cup fresh mint
½ cup fresh lime juice
2 cups cooked basmati rice

1 tsp salt
½ tsp ground black pepper

For Marjan Aminpour, the fragrance of cardamom and rose water, alongside basmati, tarragon and summer savory, were everyday kinds of smells; as common, she imagined, as the aromas of instant coffees and dripping roasts were to conventional Western kitchen corners.

Despite being born in a land of ancient deserts, where dry soil mingled with the crumbled remains of Persepolitan pillars, Marjan had a great talent for growing plants. She had learned from an early age how to tempt the most stubborn seedlings to take root, even before she could spell their plant names in Farsi. Guided by the gentle hands of Baba Pirooz, the old bearded gardener who tended the grounds of her childhood home, young Marjan cultivated furry stalks of marjoram and golden angelica in dark mounds of earth. The dirt drew its moisture from melted mountain snow, which trickled down from the nearby Alborz into Tehran's wealthier suburbs, before flowing into the Aminpour's large octagonal fountain. Bubbling at the centre of the walled garden, the pool was lined with turquoise and green Esfahani tiles.

While Marjan trained her eye to spot the first yellow buds of tarragon, or to catch a weed's surreptitious climb up the stalk of a dill plant, Baba Pirooz would recount the long line of celebrated gardeners who had been born on Persian soil. 'Avicenna,' Baba Pirooz began, clearing his throat, 'Avicenna was the most famous plant lover of them all. Did you know, Marjan Khanoum, that this wise physician was the first man ever to make rosewater? He squeezed the soft petals for their oils, then bottled the precious liquid for the world to enjoy. What a Persian, what a man!' the old gardener would exclaim, pausing only long enough in his lectures to ignite the strawberry tobacco he smoked in a knobby little pipe.

As an adult, Marjan carried the warm memories of Baba Pirooz and her childhood garden with her wherever she went. Not a day went by that she was not on the lookout for some mound of soil to plunge her fingers into. Using her bare knuckles, engraved with terracotta dust and mulch, she massaged her chosen herb or flower into the soil's folds, whispering loving encouragements along the way. And no matter how barren that slice of earth had been before, once Marjan gave it her special attention, there was no limit to all that could blossom within its charged chambers.

In the many places she had lived – and there had been quite a few in her twenty-seven years – Marjan had always planted a small herb garden, consisting of at least one seedling of basil, parsley, tarragon and summer savory. Even in the gloomy English flats she and her sisters had occupied for the last seven years since leaving Iran, Marjan had successfully grown a rainbow of cooking herbs in the blue ceramic flowerpots lining her kitchen windowsill. Always the consummate professional, no amount of rain clouds could tempt her to give up planting.

Marjan tried to keep her past perseverance in mind now as she stood in the old pastry shop's kitchen mixing a second batch of *dolmeh* stuffing. She wished she'd had more time to cultivate a healthy ensemble of fresh tarragon, mint and summer savory to add to the *dolmehs* that she and her younger sisters, Bahar and Layla, were making. Perhaps if she had planted something here in Ballinacroagh, she could have avoided the anxieties that were now creeping up her spine. Well, it was best not to have such regrets, Marjan reminded herself, especially when she couldn't do anything about them. There was still one more batch of the stuffed vine leaves to go – not to mention half a dozen other mouth-watering delicacies – and Time, that cantan-kerous old fool, was not on her side.

The Babylon Café was set to open in less than five hours. Five hours! In this new town that she could hardly pronounce, let alone spell. Ballinacroagh. Ba-li-na-crow. A whole town full of people who would come to taste her fares with questioning eyes and curious tongues. And, unlike her other stints in the kitchen, this time she would be responsible for everything.

Marjan's heart quickened as she browned the ground meat and onions together over the low, dancing flame. The satisfied pan hissed as she introduced dried versions of her precious herbs, which, if soaked overnight, worked almost as well as their fresher relatives. Working her entire torso, she mixed the herbs with the cooked rice, fresh lime juice, salt and pepper. She stirred with all her might despite the unrelenting ache in her shoulders, for such strong rotations were necessary to the *dolmehs'* harmony.

Rubbing her tired arms, Marjan glanced across the old bakery's kitchen at her sister Bahar, who was rolling up the first batch of *dolmehs*. With her wide and piercing eyes, Bahar always looked intense when she worked in the kitchen – as if her life depended on whichever vegetable or herb was being sacrificed on the chopping board before her. Surprisingly, out of the three Aminpour sisters, it was petite Bahar who possessed the greatest upper-arm strength. Fragile in most every other way, Bahar had shoulders and arms that were as powerful as those of a man twice her size, which came in handy whenever jars needed to be opened or there was mixing to be done.

Marjan picked up the wooden spoon and returned to the *dolmeh*. Her sister looked too busy now to help her beat the remaining stuffing, for not only was Bahar concentrating on rolling her own vine leaves but she was also keeping Layla's work in check. No matter how many times Marjan was reminded of the differences in her younger sisters' personalities, there was nothing like the simple act of rolling *dolmeh* to show her how poles apart Bahar and Layla really were.

Bahar, guided by a stern inner compass, smartly slapped each vine leaf (vein side up) on the chopping board. It was a consistent, methodical march that started with a no-nonsense scoop of stuffing with her left hand, followed by a skilled right-handed tuck of the vine leaf. Then, bringing the *dolmeh* to a clean surrender, she briskly rolled the vine leaf from the bottom up. Despite her rather gruff manner, Bahar's method for rolling *dolmeh* was always successful; she ensured that her little bundles of good fortune were secure on the road up, lest all that she had gathered should fall asunder.

Rolling was always where Layla faltered, for her method was more carefree and altogether too trusting. Although Marjan and Bahar demonstrated the right way endless times, Layla would still leave her *dolmehs* vulnerable to the elements. One could always tell which bundles were hers, for if neither of her older sisters was quick enough to catch the spill of stuffing, re-rolling the vine leaf while shaking her head, the moment of truth came an hour later with the opening of the oven door. Among the neat, aromatic green fingers expertly tucked by Marjan and Bahar would be the younger girl's unmistakable burst parcels of golden filling. And for some strange reason, they always smelled of Layla's signature scent – rose water and cinnamon.

It was a familiar enough smell, this faint perfume that accompanied Layla's every move, but odd for a recipe that did not contain either ingredient. The cinnamon-rose *dolmehs* never really surprised her sisters, though. Layla had a way of raising expectations beyond the ordinary.

When Thomas McGuire's spits and curses hit the pavement outside the old pastry shop, Bahar was in the middle of removing a tray of cooked *dolmehs* from the oven. After forty-five minutes they were as perfectly symmetrical as the greatest Persian carpets; the tray a clean loom upon which the stuffed vine-leaf fingers were lined in even clusters and patterns. Although the kitchen was at the back of the shop, Thomas's vulgar excretions carried clearly to Bahar's sensitive ears. Gasping with surprise, she reached for the hot tray of *dolmehs* with bare hands and paid dearly for her distraction with the start of smoking blisters.

'Quick! Get under the cold water! Layla – *aloe vera*! Bahar, stop squeezing your thumb like that!' Marjan yelled, pushing Bahar towards the sink. As the eldest of the three, Marjan was accustomed to directing her sisters in emergencies.

Bahar shuddered as the cold water ran over her scorched thumb. In the upstairs flat, a small one-bedroom residence that the Delmonicos had used as an office and storage area, Layla scrambled through open cardboard boxes looking for the green bottle of soothing gel.

'I can't find the aloe! Are you sure you packed it?' she yelled down to the kitchen.

'Yes!' Marjan hollered. 'Look in the small box that says "Miscellaneous"!'

'Don't worry. It's stopped already. See? I'll just

put an ice cube on it,' said Bahar, sticking out her horrified thumb so Marjan could see the rising welts.

Bahar tried to put on a brave face, but inside she felt a lot like that thumb of hers. Born, as her name indicated, on the first day of the Persian spring, she had the superstitious nature of people whose birthdays fall on the cusp of changing seasons. She was forever looking over her shoulders for fear that she had stepped on cracks or wandered under ladders. Bahar's inherent nervousness had escalated to a deeper malaise in recent years, the result of unspeakable events that had left indelible scars. Although her neurotic tendencies often irritated the more hardy teenager Layla, Marjan's heart just softened a bit more every time she saw her sister jump so.

'Are you sure you're all right? Listen, I'll finish the *dolmeh*. Just mix the rice for me, okay?' Marjan gave Bahar an ice cube wrapped in a torn piece of newspaper and placed the piping tray of *dolmehs* on a low, wooden island in the middle of the kitchen.

Made especially for a man of Napoleonic

measurements, this rectangular table had been the centrepiece of Luigi Delmonico's kingdom, where he rolled, powdered, slapped and whipped the exquisite paninis and chocolate-filled brioches he would later showcase in his beloved Papa's Pastries. It was also where Estelle, his bride of forty-five years, had found him dead – three hours after the bowl of meringue he was preparing had stiffened into a pink, cotton-candied tutu.

Of course, Estelle failed to mention this last point when she had shown the three sisters around the place five days ago; though, in reality, it probably would have made little difference. The girls' battered boxes were already shipped over and waiting to be picked up in Castlebar. Besides, the shop, complete with all the appliances and utensils of a working kitchen (albeit outdated and a bit rusty), was perfect for what Marjan had in mind. And it came at a bargain price.

'My niece told me that you are the best chef she has ever seen. Gloria, she's a very good girl, no?'

17

Mrs Delmonico had stood in the kitchen after the grand tour, the dying afternoon rays entering lazily through a narrow, stained-glass partition in the back door and illuminating the dust particles floating above her peppery hair. All surfaces, from counter tops to the stacks of pots and dishes, were cloaked in a good inch of the snowy stuff.

'Oh, Gloria was very good to us when we arrived in Lewisham. A great friend,' Marjan said. Behind her, Bahar and Layla both nodded in agreement. 'But, I think she was exaggerating a bit on my abilities. I was only a sous chef. She was the real talent at the restaurant.'

'Yes, Gloria knows how to cook *parmigiana* and *manicotti*, but who doesn't? Maybe to those English that is gourmet, but you should have seen my grandmother cook! Pfff! If she was still alive today she would be rich from her cooking, I tell you!'

Estelle Delmonico laughed and placed her chubby hands on her hips. The good-natured widow cocked her head and offered a smile to each of the three young women. Fate had it that, although blessed with the welcoming girth of child-bearing hips, she had never been able to give Luigi a baby of their own. It was one of her few regrets in an otherwise fortunate and colourful life. Thankfully, her barrenness had never turned to resentment; a blessing Estelle often accredited to her niece, on whom she was able to practise all the loving criticisms her own mother had lavished upon her. Gloria was a great source of release for Estelle Delmonico, and now she had sent her three darlings to look after as well.

'Okay, then? You will take the store, eh?'

Marjan turned to Bahar and Layla, both of whom appeared to be asleep standing up. Their drawn, exhausted faces had the look of *torshi*, pickled onions that have been pulled from their bed of vinegar and salt. Who could blame them, really? It had been a long four days since they left London, shipping off their hastily packed boxes and throwing a few personal belongings into two worn, tartan suitcases; the same suitcases that had seen them through the Iranian desert a long time ago. The plane ride from London to Knock had been painfully tedious; Immigration and Customs even worse. Answering the same questions about their religion and ethnic background over and over again. Then two days holed up in a backpackers' hostel in the nearby town of Castlebar, waiting for their boxes to arrive while they survived on white bread and some hard cheese that Marjan had bought from a corner grocery. Layla, of course, had complained all the way (such was the prerogative of her age), but Bahar had remained sullen, her big doe eyes wet with frightened tears.

But, thought Marjan, the worst certainly seemed behind them. Especially now that they were standing in this dusty little kitchen, with this generous Italian woman. It was time for a new start, time for them to take all the money they had in the world and finally make something of those years of hardship.

'You stay, yes?' Estelle Delmonico pulled a heavy, corroded key from a hidden pocket in her black dress. Toothy and archaic, it was the kind of key that would have released Pandora's own demons.

'Yes.' Marjan nodded, accepting the key. 'We'll stay. How would you like the rent paid? Monthly or weekly?'

'Agh, don't worry about that now. You give it to me whenever you have it, yes? I think what is more important is to get you a big bowl of my minestrone soup. That would put some energy in this pretty face, eh?' Mrs Delmonico walked over to Layla and lightly patted her left cheek.

Marjan, determined to keep up the momentum that had carried them from London, over the Irish Sea and into this land of crazed sheep and dizzying roads, shook her head, more to her sisters than to the jolly widow.

'Thank you, but I'm afraid we can't. There is so much to do. Bahar and Layla have to unpack, and I have to get to Dublin as soon as possible for ingredients. It would be much quicker than trying to find some of the food we need here, I suspect,' she said.

'Hah! You are right! My Luigi would sometimes get so red in the face about these village markets. Mini-markets, they call them! I could find more in my mama's back garden in Napoli than in most of these *mini-markets*.'

'Yes, Naples – Napoli, sounds beautiful. I hear the *erberias* there are filled with the most wonderful vegetables. I hope I'll be able to find everything we need for our menu in Dublin. We want to open the café by next Monday. The first day of spring,' said Marjan.

'Monday? Five days only? No, no. You will give yourselves more time, I think. Why the rushing? Wait a few more days,' said Mrs Delmonico, shaking her head in matronly disapproval.

'Monday is Bahar's birthday,' Layla piped up, suddenly awake.

'And it's *No Rooz*, the Iranian New Year. That's when Persians start their calendar year, the first day of spring,' Marjan explained. Originally a Zoroastrian holiday marked by thirteen days of feasting and merriment, *No Rooz*, or 'New Day' is now celebrated by all Iranians. It'll be a good omen to start things off fresh on such a day. And I think we'll make it, if we get started soon,' Marjan said pointedly.

'Oh, you young girls. So much ambition! I will leave you alone to do what you have to do. Maybe I come by on your New Year's, yes? I will tell you a little about the crazy people that live here. To prepare you. Okay?' Estelle Delmonico planted a departing kiss on each of their cheeks, holding their faces in that warm Italian way of hers that took them all by surprise.

Five busy days had passed since the little widow turned over the key to the old pastry shop, and the girls had worked a great deal of magic in that time. While Marjan took the tortoise CIE train across the endless, grassy-knolled country-side to Dublin, Bahar and Layla set about the arduous task of transforming Papa's Pastries into an Eastern-flavoured oasis. With its ashy white walls, peeling posters of gondoliers, a burnt-out neon Lavassa coffee sign, faded flags and maps of the boot-shaped country, the old shop had needed a lot of work.

Two large, wooden display counters occupied most of the terracotta-tiled floor. When Papa's Pastries first opened in 1946 a younger Estelle had covered the countertops and the shop's four metal tables with tartan tablecloths. The green and red check had turned a sickly yellow and orange in the intervening decades, and much of the binding weave crumbled into Bahar's hands as she lifted the musty cloths from the tables.

Estelle had fashioned the seating area as a place where customers would mingle, soaking the crusty edges of Luigi's lovingly baked chocolate and anise biscotti in their cappuccinos as they listened to Billie Holiday croon on an old Victrola. But, in the thirty-four years the Delmonicos' pastry shop was open, Estelle's tartan tables were hardly used at all, except as a place for tired housewives to dump their grocery bags and rumpled children. These exhausted, sallow-faced women would pay nervously for their crusty country loaves – and an occasional macadamia biscuit to shut drooling infantile mouths – before rushing out again into the rainy streets. After the cappuccino machine broke down in the winter of 1956, its pipes frozen by a freak ice storm raging outside, Luigi did not bother fixing it. Instead, he used the gargantuan installation as extra shelving for the model Ferrari cars he built in his spare time.

The cars were long gone now, but the cappuccino machine had stayed. Bahar and Layla spent nearly three hours disassembling its parts before unscrewing the whole contraption from its base.

Lifting the machine off the wall, the girls discovered the original colour of the centuries-old shop – an ugly greenish-brown that looked like cold turf. But that miserable colour was gone now, as was the whitewash of the other walls. Bahar and Layla had bathed the entire shop with the house paint Estelle Delmonico had given them, the day she showed them the space.

'Take it, take it. There are paintbrushes and rollers too. I bought it all just before my Luigi died, from that good-for-nothing John Healy. He owns the hardware shop near the church. Pfff! I said to him, "Mr Healy, I need some good, white paint. No cream or yellow." Luigi liked white. "Very clean," he said, "makes everything big." So that Healy man, he give me paint on sale. I bring here and open it and look!'

Mrs Delmonico prised the lids off of two paint tins in the corner of the upstairs flat. The paint, even in the dark room, pulsed out a vermilion that the three girls had seen in only one other place – within the incorruptible flesh of the fruits from the pomegranate tree in the garden of their childhood home.

'I take it back and said to him, "Mr Healy, there is a big mistake. This is not white. A beautiful colour, but not white." And do you know what he said to me, eh? "Mrs Delmonico, I can't give your money back. You opened the tins already." Can you believe this? I tell you, that man, he never had a wife. Has a big house with beautiful furniture, but all alone! Why? Because he is miserable! Agh, look, I am getting crazy all over again and it was five years ago! Maybe the paint is not so good any more, eh?'

But the paint was just fine. After a bit of a stir the colour regulated itself to an even brighter version than the spectacular vermilion Estelle had awakened. When the girls stripped the walls and gave them a taste of colour, the paint changed again, clotting into the dark crimson of Shiraz wine grapes.

On Saturday afternoon, after three days of coughing on sawdust and breathing paint fumes, Bahar and Layla both fell on to the solitary mattress in the upstairs flat. They slept through the whole night without stirring, and did not wake until Marjan's return from her shopping excursion early on Sunday morning. Groggy-eyed and with bitter breath, the two girls stumbled down the staircase and followed their eldest sister out of the kitchen door. They crossed the small back garden – a fenced-in patch of soggy, overgrown grass – and stepped on to a narrow, cobblestone alleyway that was shared by all the businesses on the right side of Main Mall. There, in the pre-dawn moonlight, stood a beat-up, lime green van with peace signs painted on its side panels.

'I found the van in the *Irish Times*. Paid some young kid five hundred Irish for it. Not the prettiest thing, I know, but it braved the rocky roads all right. And the brakes are good, too. I almost ran into a sheep – or at least I think it was a sheep – but stopped just in time. Come on, I bought as much as I could.' Marjan motioned to the van's back doors, and as soon as she opened them, the memories came spilling out.

A treasure-trove of spices that would have made the thieving Ali Baba jealous sat huddled in one corner of the van. The motherly embrace of *advieh* – a mixed all-spice of crushed rose petals, cardamom, cinnamon, and cumin – the warm womb of turmeric; and that spice worth greater in weight than gold – za'feran, saffron.

Like their home in Iran, their flat in Lewisham was always filled with these and other sumptuous grindings of barks and plant seeds. Though they had only left Lewisham a week ago, it seemed to be much longer. And no matter how intoxicating the smells were, this reawakening of the senses came with the price of memories none of them wanted to think about. At least not yet.

Bahar and Layla helped Marjan unload the boxes of spices, jars of vine leaves and bags of pistachios, almonds and dates she had found in an Algerian grocery on the outskirts of the capital city. Marjan had also purchased five kilos of feta, but she informed her sisters that this would be the last shop-bought cheese for a while, as they would start making their own to save time and money. Layla groaned at the thought of squeezing dripping cheesecloth, but Bahar didn't mind; she would make feta every day if it meant Marjan would not be leaving them again for another cross-country shopping trip.

The last of the van's inventory came in the

form of two long fold-out tables and twelve wooden chairs, which Marjan had found at a second-hand shop in the town of Mullingar. The long, communal-style tables would complete the cosy look she had in mind.

Marjan made one more trip in the green hippie van early that Sunday morning, driving to the storage facility outside Castlebar where the shipping company had deposited their eight boxes and four Persian rugs. Unrolled now in the shop's front room, the two larger Qashqui rugs told stories of primary-coloured villagers who poured endless cups of golden tea and danced in honour of their sun god. These two covered up most of the shop's cold tile floors, while two smaller rugs – woven slowly by blind old men – hung opposite one another so that their delicate, filigreed patterns could be fully appreciated. The vermilion walls complemented the new art work wonderfully, bringing out the roses that bordered the corners of one rug, while contrasting with the mint-green leaves of the other.

From the weary cardboard boxes came the shining tools of their new trade – what would truly set them apart from the rest of the businesses on Main Mall. Bahar unwrapped the items that she had collected over the years from Salvation Army sales and the odd suburban car boot sale around London. There were ceramic teapots in aubergine, mustard and midnight blue (good for one, sweeter still when shared between two drinkers); and forty small, thin glasses with curved handles, set in gold- and silver-plated holders etched with arabesque swirls. Bahar gingerly lined the tea glasses up on the counter where the cappuccino machine had been stationed. She tucked the teapots into the counter's glass-panelled belly, where they sat prettily next to twenty glass containers of loose-leaf teas, ranging from bergamot to hibiscus to oolong.

The larger counter, which sat closer to the shop's front door, had yet to be filled with Marjan's sweet creations. On the wall behind the counter ran a dark wooden shelf. Layla, the tallest of the three, was given the unsavoury task of scrubbing it, driving spatula and sponge through the stony clumps of baguettes and bread loaves that had petrified after the Italian baker's death. The shelf was now spotless and exhibiting better preserved artefacts: etched copper and brass trays, a framed woven calligraphy that read 'Tea' in Farsi, five old-style samovars (one belonging to the girls' grandmother, which Bahar had bundled up in her coat that day they left Iran for good), and a large print of a painting showing a traditional Iranian tea house (men only), complete with indoor fountain and hookah pipes.

The other brass samovars on display belonged to an older generation, precursors to the large, electric machine sitting on the counter next to the tea glasses. The diuretic samovar was plugged in and ready to be filled with water that it would boil and labour out into tea-filled pots. It was this very samovar, with its enticing golden gleam, that Thomas McGuire had just glimpsed through the cracks in the newspapered window.

The second tray of *dolmehs* were rolled and ready to submit to the will of the hot oven. Marjan pushed them into the heat and sighed.

'Well, that should last us the next few days. What do you think?' She fanned herself with an oven glove. The baklava they had baked earlier that morning was sitting on the kitchen island next to the first tray of *dolmehs*, but there was still so much left to do. And they only had four hours left before opening! She'd have to get started on the red lentil soup next.

Layla clunked down the stairs, pausing on the low landing as she leaned over the banister, swinging her legs. At fifteen, she was already fully aware of the effects these long, exquisite limbs had on men of all ages.

'I couldn't find the aloe anywhere. It wasn't in that box like you said.'

'It's all right. It stopped hurting.' Bahar held her thumb slanted, like a reluctant hitchhiker. 'So much for a good omen.'

'Bahar, please. No negativity right now. We need all the luck we can get our hands on. Look how far we've come already,' Marjan said, waving her wooden spoon around the warm, inviting kitchen.

Bahar and Layla set aside their own private thoughts to survey the fantastic bounty of tastes and colours around them. The ambrosial food and neat, cosy rooms were a real testament to their efforts; a great accomplishment for only a handful of days.

Yes, they had come very far. Very far indeed.

Chapter Two

Red Lentil Soup

Ingredients:

2 cups dry, red lentils
7 large onions, chopped
7 garlic cloves, crushed
1 tsp ground turmeric
4 tsp ground cumin
olive oil
7 cups chicken broth
3 cups water
salt
2 tsp nigella seeds*

* ground black pepper may be substituted

From her bedroom window, in a flat above The Reek Relics shop, Dervla Quigley could see the universe. Or its equivalent, which for her were the comings and goings of all who ventured up and down Main Mall.

A proud Ballinacroagh native through and through, Dervla had lived with her spinster sister Marie ever since her husband of forty-one years passed away. Although most in town knew the circumstance of Jim Quigley's ignominious death (a horse breeder from County Kildare, his grand demise found him squashed under the flanks of a spotted filly), no one dared speak about it. As Ballinacroagh's primary gossip, Dervla kept mouths shut with a combination of canine hearing and a vicious tongue that knew no boundaries.

At most times of the day – except during six o'clock Mass – Dervla could be found spying out of her bedroom window. Bolstering her hunched torso with large pillows, she stared with beady, rhubarb-grey eyes out into the damp street below, determined not to miss a minute of provincial drama. It was an admirable feat of endurance, this constant watch over all Ballinacroagh, especially considering the old gossip's unfortunate medical condition. At the height of her autumn years, and without warning, Dervla Quigley had been stricken with a terrifying incontinence, an embarrassing bladder problem that left her housebound and dependent on her long-suffering sister. Unable to control her own body, Dervla soon became obsessed with manipulating everyone else's. Gossip was not only her friend and solace, but a source of great power.

The week that the Aminpour sisters moved into the pastry shop would prove especially fruitful for Dervla Quigley. By Sunday, she had almost met her weekly quota of scandals: on Wednesday, at 1:17 a.m.: Benny Corcoran stumbled half-blind and drunk out of Paddy McGuire's, his hand on the arse of someone other than his saintly wife (Dervla blamed the broken street lamp over the pub for obscuring the floozy's face); on Friday at 2:47 p.m.: a convoy of ten decrepit caravans – tinkers with no shame to them, no shame at all – climbed up Main Mall towards the lower levels of the craggy mountain heap. *Tinkers.* Just the word made Dervla shudder. The old gossip's fury, of course, was a direct product of her ignorance. Despite her boundless curiosity, Dervla had never stopped to learn the tumultuous history of Ireland's travelling people. *Tinker* or 'Tinceard' in Gaelic, referred to the tin pots and cooking pans that, until only a few years ago, were mended and peddled by the freckly, pale-eyed Celtic nomads. Before plying their tin trade, these travellers had been storytellers, descendants of medieval Irish bards who earned their daily bread by belting out high-pitched ditties:

> *She went to live with a gentleman; one day came a tinker to solder her pan.*
> *He slyly got her behind the door, and gave her kisses over and o'er.*
> *Fa la la lero liddle lie day, fal la la lero li gee whoa!*

This clan of caravan dwellers, having survived centuries of famine and the follies of wigged Englishmen, no longer travelled in horse-drawn trains. Instead, they opted for mobile homes topped with shiny roofs of chrome, peach and Tipperary gold.

No matter how colourful they may have seemed to the outsider, Dervla told herself, *she* had little patience for the train of itinerants who took hold of road and field alike. Maybe she couldn't change Ireland's ridiculous by-laws, which allowed travellers to squat in any open field, but it didn't stop the old gossip from trying. Dirty, disgusting things, those tinkers, Dervla muttered. Dirty, disgusting things. She picked up the telephone and dialled the town council office. Someone had to tell Padraig Carey about those filthy beasts. If she wasn't around to look after things, just imagine what sort of scum could come cruising down her beloved Main Mall!

What came in the form of a bright green van, Sunday morning, 4 a.m. sharp. Dervla awoke to acrid exhaust fumes billowing into her open bedroom window. Annoyance turned to gratitude when she spotted the peculiar vehicle, for Dervla knew a juicy bit of news when she saw one. The van ambled around the corner into the back alley, its bright orange peace sign reflecting in the moonlight. She might be sixty-two, Dervla thought to herself, but she was well aware of what went on in the back of those hippie vans: lewd animal acts and drug use, that's what. No two ways about it.

Dervla sat frozen with anticipation, waiting for the shadowy driver (some sort of heathen hippie no doubt) to park and saunter into view, but nobody came. She waited an hour, then two, hobbling out of her bedroom only for an urgent toilet run. No one was out on the street at that time of morning; it was too late for pub crawls and too early for the delivery vans, so any suspicious footsteps could be heard easily. Dervla waited and waited, but nobody came.

The foggy light of Sunday morning brought Dervla little relief. There was the usual pedestrian bustle of Sunday bests parading towards the church; the same penitent drunks peeling themselves out of roadside ditches with warbled promises to do better next time. No mysterious hippy, though; no details of back-alley dealings, no chugging exhaust fumes. Hours of sitting and watching and all she had to report back to the

39

hungry beaks of Ballinacroagh's ten o'clock parish-ioners was a sinful Benny Corcoran and a bunch of dirty tinkers. It was simply not good enough.

Monday would prove to be much more rewarding. Not only did Dervla spot a light beaming through the cracks in the newspapered windows of the old Delmonico pastry shop, but her sharpened ears detected murmuring voices coming from the shop. She couldn't understand what was being said, but it didn't sound like English, that's for sure. Italian, more than likely. No doubt a version of Latin the Pope himself wouldn't have approved of. Had Estelle Delmonico lost her marbles altogether and decided to start up that sad excuse for a bakery again? Hadn't she learned her lesson the first time around?

Dervla sniffed the air outside her bedroom window.

Yes, a nasty reek of foreignness was definitely in the air. It was different to the smell she remem-bered coming from Papa's Pastries all those years ago. She recognised the same unyielding yeasty scent of rising bread and perky almond inton-ations, but there was also a vast and unexpected array of under- and overtones she could not name. The wicked, tingling sensation taunted Dervla's sense of decency, laughing at her as if it knew her deep, dark secrets; as though it had heard all about her dead husband's wanton ways.

When the crusty gossip witnessed Thomas McGuire's own fierce reaction to the new scent, she knew that she was on to something all right. She watched with glee as Thomas stormed up Main Mall (to the town council, no doubt) in his Land Rover, rubbing her wrinkly hands over her thickly veined thighs in a moment of unrestrained happiness. She was sitting over a gold-mine of news, enough to last for weeks to come!

Dervla Quigley would not have to wait long for further entertainment. Soon after Thomas charged off towards the town council building, the bakery's front door opened and out walked Layla.

It seems that Marjan, in all her meticulous attention to the extraordinary details on her grocery list, had failed to buy sufficient bags of onions, that humble servant of so many magical dishes. Her initial stock was already used up in the *dolmeh* and the pot of red lentil soup simmering away on the stove top, and she would need more to complete her opening-day menu. Panicked and unusually flustered, Marjan pushed Layla out of the shop door with instructions to buy as many white onions as she could carry in her long, slender arms.

Red lentil soup, although quite seductive in scent, is as simple to make as its name suggests. Marjan preferred to boil her lentils first, before frying the chopped onions, garlic and spices with some good, strong olive oil. Covering the ready broth, lentils and onions, she would then allow the luscious soup to simmer for half an hour, as the spices embedded themselves into the compliant onion skins.

In the recipe book filed away in her head, Marjan always made sure to place a particular emphasis on the soup's spices. Cumin added the aroma of afternoon love-making to the mixture, but it was another spice that had the greatest tantric effect on the innocent soup drinker: *siah daneh* – 'love in the midst' – or nigella seed. This modest little pod, when crushed open by pestle and mortar, or when steamed in such dishes as this lentil soup, excites a spicy energy that hibernates in the human spleen. Unleashed, it burns for ever with the unbound desire of an unrequited lover. So powerful is nigella in its heat, that the spice should not be taken in by pregnant women, for fear of early labour.

Indigenous to the Middle and Near Easts of the girls' past lives, nigella is rarely used in Western recipes; its ability to soothe heartburn and abolish fatigue quite overlooked. Modernity, it seems, prefers over-the-counter pills to the advice of ancient seers. Marjan, aware that the spice would not be readily available in Ireland, had packed several envelopes of seedlings in the boxes they had shipped over from London. Layla would never fully realise how fortuitous a move this shipping of seeds had been, for she was already following the destiny its perfume had assigned her, undulating as it was from Marjan's simmering pot all the way out to the sleepy street.

Benny Corcoran, owner of Corcoran's Bakery, was the first townsperson Layla encountered as she made her way down to Fadden's Mini-Mart. Rather than buying a van for delivery runs, Benny transported the loaves and rolls he packed for Fadden's in a large, red wheelbarrow. He had just finished his second trip to the grocery shop, sweat running down the creases in his freckled face and on to his wheelbarrow of bread, when he saw Layla. Almost at once, Benny was stung by the cloud of nigella that had blended with the young girl's own rose water and cinnamon bouquet. The poor man didn't know what hit him. One minute he was wandering around in his own lonely vacuum, the next he was in an Eden of tempting fruits, standing before an Eve whose long dark hair and fragrance soothed his very heart.

It would be easy to attribute Layla's effect on the opposite sex (and the occasional Sapphically inclined female) to her youth or sweet, natural perfume, but the real reason behind her attraction was far more complex. Of course, there was no denying her beauty, the consistency of her angled, porcelain features, to that tilt in her almond eyes, which shone like half-moons across her celestial face. Unlike her two older sisters, who sported wayward brown ringlets, Layla's hair was long and jet black. Tied up or let down, moussed or gelled, nothing could excite her stubbornly straight locks, which were a definite throwback to some latent Oriental chromosomes roaming deep inside her.

Had he still been alive, their father would have wasted no time in making a point of this Eastern descent. Javid Aminpour often boasted a lineage to Genghis Khan, beating his chest while yodelling Mongolian war songs, in imitation of an ancestry he was determined to stake a claim to. He died two months before Layla's fifth birthday, so she could barely recall her father's theatrics, but Bahar's many bedtime stories over the years had given Layla ownership over her own set of memories.

Layla never knew her own mother, for she died shortly after pushing her out into the harsh world. After a nine-year drought, it seemed that this last child had released in Shirin Aminpour an inner tourniquet that kept on flowing until there was nothing more to give. The weary doctors in Tehran General Hospital had no explanation for the merciless bleeding and just shrugged with defeat when they told Javid the news. They failed to mention that, as the last drops of blood seeped into the hospital's sea-green bed sheets, a tiny bud had popped out of his wife's womb. When the flower seed fell into the pool of blood it blossomed into the face of a full-grown rose. The fearful doctors had kept this to themselves, partly to avoid a malpractice suit, and partly because the rose water and cinnamon scent that accompanied the flower's miraculous unfolding reminded them of a time when military guards did not hover behind every surgery door. Such it is that people who are denied hope become greedy hoarders when granted even the smallest of drops.

But the doctors' selfish motives had made little difference in Layla's fate. Even from those first minutes on the outside world she was charming all who crossed her path. In Layla's hopeful aura, men like Benny Corcoran were free to relive the ambitions of their idle youths; dreams that were once entertained behind closed doors, as they rubbed away under sweaty teenage quilts. Those were the moments of pure self-indulgence, before the repercussions of manhood were thrust upon them in the form of soul-breaking jobs and nagging wives.

Sensing Benny's adoring eyes on her, Layla quickened her pace down Main Mall. A gaggle of primary schoolchildren milling about outside the news agency was too busy sucking gobstoppers between crooked teeth to notice her. On the opposite side of the street a beauty salon, Athey's Shear Delight, was just opening up its flamingo-pink window blinds. Still too early for customers, the three hairdressers were enjoying their morning tea inside as they flipped through old magazines. When Layla walked by on the street, the beauticians dropped their *Irish Women's Weekly* and *Celtic Hair* and stared with open mouths out of the window.

'Now who do you suppose that is, then? Would you look at the length of skirt on her!' Joan Donnelly, hair colourist and sister to the proprietor, slammed her teacup down and marched over to the window, widening the gap between two blinds with her fingers. Joan was a small, nervous woman. Although blessed with a talent for both hi- and low-lites, she had found no cure for the barrage of dandruff that fell daily from her own bowl-cut fringe; the flakes sat like a conscience on her pointy little shoulders. 'She looks right foreign to me. Spanish or Italian, wouldn't you say?'

'Haven't ya heard, so? Sure, I was meaning to tell ya!' Nineteen-year-old Evie Watson's sparrow voice piped up. 'That Delmonico woman, she's got the old pastry place up and running again. With some sort of foreign hippies, no less. To listen to Dervla Quigley tell it she's ready to put Corcoran's out of business.'

In spite of her bulimic frame, or perhaps because of it, Evie was always hungry for approval and did her best to gather titbits of Ballinacroagh information that might prove useful. Evie's eagerness, though, was quite different from Dervla Quigley's lust for gossip. Her chatter was grounded on good intentions and hopes that it would boost her position from salon apprentice to full-time stylist like she had always dreamed.

'If you ask me Estelle Delmonico has better things to do than break her back in that dust heap again,' said Fiona Athey, chief stylist and owner of the salon that bore her name.

Fifty pounds and another lifetime ago, Fiona had been on her way to great glories, re-enacting the entire opus of Irish fairytales before delighted audiences in the theatrical capital of Ireland, Galway City. But an illicit romance with Gerhard, a German puppeteer, had rendered her bed bound with a pregnancy that would produce the bane of her existence, her seventeen-year-old daughter Emer. After having her child, Fiona suffered a double-blow of indignity when she discovered Gerhard under the theatre rafters, in a compromising position with her very own understudy. The upstart bottle blonde – a primary reason why Fiona stuck to cutting hair and left colouring to her sister Joan – had taken advantage of Fiona's incapacitation to move in on her man and her starring role. Heartbroken, and vowing never to tread the boards again, Fiona had returned to her hometown of Ballinacroagh with baby Emer in tow, taking over her sickly father's barber's shop and eventually turning it into a nifty little business. Athey's Shear Delight was popular with the town's children and women folk, but most men steered clear of its peroxide-filled rooms – mainly to spare themselves the embarrassment of donning one of Fiona's flowery smocks. Pass Athey's Shear Delight on any given afternoon and you will find it a hotbed of oestrogen, where gossip mingles with the acetate fumes of nail polish and hairspray.

Fiona, who had endured tittering giggles and reproachful shakes of heads when she had first arrived back in town, usually refrained from voicing her opinions. She detested the constant gnawing condemnations that went on minute by minute inside her small, pink salon, but understood the necessity of such gossip for the health of her business. Because of her neutrality, when the odd moment arose that Fiona Athey actually did make her thoughts known, anyone within earshot would pause and pay her particular deference.

'I'd say Estelle's done the smart thing and rented the place out,' Fiona reasoned. 'That might be our new neighbour, so. Let's hope it's not another salon, that's all.'

'Sure, I was walkin' past the other day and saw the lights on through the small bit of window there. Something was cooking. I can't put my finger on it, but it wasn't anything like the Eye-talian food in that spaghetti place in Westport. It was something different altogether,' Evie keenly offered.

'Humph! Well, I don't care who they are or what they do, so long as that there hussy doesn't go distracting my boys from their Leaving Cert studies. They'll be going to seminary school whether they like it or not,' Joan retorted, pursing her lips and releasing the vertical blinds with a snap.

Fiona and Evie both nodded, well acquainted as they were with the drama of Joan Donnelly's identical twin boys, Peter and Michael. Convinced that her precious boys were intended for a higher power, Joan had pushed nightly catechisms into their mushy brains since an early age. Her ecclesiastical ambitions, however, had done little to curb the twins' appetite for weekend car-jackings, brothels and drunken cow-tipping parties. The boys were a constant source of worry for poor, neurotic Joan, and the real reason behind her falling scalp tissue. Lucky for Joan, she was not watching when her devilish sons nearly knocked Layla off her feet in front of Fadden's Mini-Mart.

'How's it going?' Peter winked at Layla as his brother let out a low whistle.

Layla, having just side-stepped Benny Corcoran's admiration, was not prepared for the wily twins' attentions. With an enchanting combination of teenage timidity and self-assurance, she nodded briefly in their direction before ducking into the mini-mart.

'Jaysus. Did you see her?'

'See her? Michael, I think we've just witnessed a miracle.'

The Donnelly twins, with their salacious grins and gawking eyes, were not affected by Layla's bloom in the same way as nostalgic older men. They were, after all, only eighteen, with the prospects of a whole world of debauchery and mischief before them (hang what their mother had in mind). The sight of Layla's long legs, tanned even under her thin stockings, produced the basic, primitive lust expected of boys their age. On any other day, the twins would have followed Layla into the shop. But this was Monday. The boys never stepped into Danny Fadden's mini-mart more than once on Mondays.

As a matter of tradition, and to spite their mother for making them sit through two Sunday Masses, Peter and Michael Donnelly habitually paid a visit to Fadden's Mini-Mart on Monday mornings before school. In a ruse that had started their first year of secondary school, Michael would keep Mr Fadden busy at the counter with some obscure mythology question, to which only the grocer, a devoted fan of Irish lore, would know the answer. Meanwhile, Peter would swipe two bottles of Beamish from the beer shelf, stuffing them into the pockets of his large duffel coat. The twins gleefully chugged their beers before school, passing them between the thick-necked boys who congregated in the woods beyond the football field. This ritualistic passing of back-washed ale was merely a frothy afterthought for the twins though, for it wasn't the beer or the thrill of stealing it, but the rather cruel game that they played on poor Danny Fadden that tickled them the most.

Every time Peter swiped two bottles of beer (always from the back of the shelf), he left a piece of green felt in their place, along with an IOU note signed 'Finnegan'. It didn't take long for Danny (a man who starred in his own daydreams as a love-struck Diarmuid eloping with a witchy Grainne) to put two and two together to make five. The green felt, the missing stout, the name Finnegan. It all pointed to one thing: the mini-mart had its very own leprechaun. Danny Fadden counted himself supremely lucky to be blessed with the touch of the little people and he awaited the leprechaun's Monday-morning visits with barely contained excitement. Of course, everyone in Ballinacroagh joked of 'Fadden's Fairy' and would often ask the shopkeeper, when stopping in for some milk or potatoes, how his little friend was getting along. Danny's wife Deirdre, on the other hand, did not find her husband's leprechaun fixation at all funny, and after nearly five years of his lunacy, she left Danny on the eve of their thirtieth wedding anniversary.

The shy grocer was softly tip-toeing up to the beer aisle when Layla walked into the store. Knowing full well the precarious temperament of leprechauns, with their complete dislike for anything human, Danny was always careful not to disturb his little friend's hiding place. He steered clear of the beer shelves from noontime Sunday to eight o'clock Monday morning, lest he should stumble upon his unsuspecting visitor and frighten him away altogether. This meant, of course, that he never made the connection between the notes and the Donnelly twins' Monday-morning visits. While Layla scoured the produce stands for onions, Danny was hunched over in the beer aisle, deciphering the meaning behind the little person's latest note: *I like barley, I like rye, I like stout in my pie. IOU Finnegan.* Neither of them saw Malachy McGuire standing patiently at the till.

The younger of Thomas McGuire's two sons, eighteen-year-old Malachy had somehow managed to sidestep the male McGuire DNA of turnip torsos and butchered complexions. Nor had he taken much from his mother's side, who along with Malachy's three plump sisters would have given a modern-day Rubens much to concentrate on.

Peaking at six foot one and slender, with the hands of a pianist, Malachy sported a mop of unruly black hair and sapphire eyes that sparkled like midnight suns. His luminous youth was something to marvel at indeed. He was nothing like his older brother Tom, who at twenty-one was an almost carbon copy of their father, though without the latter's ambition and talent for subversion. Tom Junior spent most of his time scurrying between amateur hurling matches and playing henchman for his father. Malachy, on the other hand, much preferred the complementary hobbies of football and astronomy, balancing the terrestrial with the heavenly, and excelling in both equally. Unknown to Malachy, the cosmos that he pored over so many nights from his bedroom window were in perfect alignment that Monday morning.

Like Peter and Michael Donnelly, Malachy was also on his way to school when he decided to stop into Fadden's for his morning Lucozade. But unlike the devious twins, Malachy McGuire's soul was as old as the constellations themselves.

To him, Layla's promising aroma was not a reminder of a long-lost boyhood or the instigator of teenage lust. No, for Malachy, the sight of Layla's exotic profile filling up a bag of white onions was a sign, a resounding *yes* to the age-old questions of the divine.

Yes, there was a God. Yes, there was life beyond the sleepy valleys of Ballinacroagh. Yes, there *were* undiscovered universes waiting out there for him. And one of them was standing right before him, in all her astounding milky ways.

Malachy felt suddenly weak and dizzy. As his vision fuzzed over and his legs gave way to the floor, he grabbed on to the nearest stationary object – a grocery shelf. Unfortunately for the star-gazing romantic, the shelf happened to hold a pyramid display of feminine hygiene products, and before Malachy knew it he was in a heap on the floor, covered – to his mortification – in specially priced, two-for-one boxes of super-sized tampons.

The clatter awoke Layla to her surroundings, and as she turned to the front of the shop, a burning sensation instantly took hold of her body. There, down the aisle before her, was the most beautiful boy she had ever seen. Layla tried to breathe but found instead the start of debilitating hiccups – catches of love-bitten air that would not end until she had taken a good swill of Marjan's famous *dugh* drink.

'Are you all right there, lad? Didn't hurt yerself now, did you?' Danny Fadden asked, rounding the corner of the beer aisle, his fish-bowl eyes blinking behind thick glasses.

Poor Malachy. For the first time in his life his natural grace had forsaken him. Surrounded by such private tokens of femininity, all he could do was bow his red, tender face and make a run for it. He didn't dare look back at Layla as he pounded through the grocery's door; didn't acknowledge the twins' mocking calls of 'I think ye forgot yer tail, McGuire', or even notice that he was running in the opposite direction from school, so lost was he in Layla's lovely perfume.

While her youngest sister was hiccuping romance in the mini-mart, Marjan was busy in the kitchen chopping her last onion, impatient for Layla to return with reinforcements. Frying the chopped onion with some olive oil, she flipped the pieces about until they were crunchy, but not blackened, then set the fried charms aside for later, to be sprinkled on bowls of soup ordered by expectant customers. Marjan considered this sizzled garnish to be the best part of her red lentil soup, for, after all, the humblest of moments can often be the most rewarding.

Layla would not appreciate the significance of this simple lesson until she had paid for her bag of white onions, smiled at Danny Fadden's dazed look, ignored the loitering Donnelly twins' low whistles, and made her way quickly back to the warmth of her sisters' kitchen, hiccuping all the way. Only then did she realise that she was still holding an onion in her palm, the last one she had picked up before seeing Malachy McGuire's wondrous face. When she unclenched her tight fist, she found that just like her heart, the little white vegetable was sautéed to a crisp.

Chapter Three

Baklava

Ingredients:

> 4 cups brown sugar
> 1 cup water
> ½ cup rose water
> 500g shelled pistachios, chopped
> 500g blanched almonds, chopped
> 2 tbsp cardamom
> 1 tsp ground cinnamon
> 15 frozen filo pastry sheets
> ½ cup unsalted butter, melted

The peach offices of Ballinacroagh's police station sit at one end of the town square, across from St Barnabas's Roman Catholic Church and immediately adjacent to the decaying Palladian building that houses the Town Council.

The Garda station, with its pasty, popcorn stucco façade, is nothing to boast about; nor does the crumbling plaster crest above the door, engraved with the words 'An Garda Síochána', intimidate anyone who crosses its creaking, musty threshold. 'An Garda Síochána', or 'Guardians of the Peace' for those unschooled in the Gaelic tongue, is the official title of the blue-vested, pot-bellied police officers comfortably stationed all over the Irish countryside. To the uninitiated, *Garda* may seem like a badge of glory, a name that alludes to winged, mythical protectors, the kind that hover above their human counterparts with ready crossbows in case trouble strikes. But such grand titles can often be misleading, as evidenced by the police station's two most regular (and reluctant) inhabitants.

Sergeant Sean Grogan sat in the processing room, feet up on his desk with eyes half-closed as he listened to the day's weather pattern on a hand-held radio. Flaccid in both body and soul, Grogan could usually be found listening to Mid-West FM; news of union disputes, foot and mouth epidemics and war-torn African countries always made him thankful for the monotony of his chosen occupation.

'Is that tea on its way, Kevin?' Sean Grogan asked, briefly popping open one eye to his second in command, Guard Kevin Slattery.

Every morning Kevin Slattery would ignite the hundred-year-old stove – a turf-powered range kept in a side room – before filling the dented tin kettle with cold water and arranging Grogan's favourite shortbread biscuits on a tea plate. On this particular Monday morning, though, Kevin had arrived late for work, having been detained by his pregnant wife's premature contractions.

'I was meaning to get to that now, Sean,' Kevin replied, lighting the range. He didn't know who was more demanding of attention – his water-retentive wife or his lazy superior officer. Calling it a draw, Kevin returned five minutes later with a grey circle of turf-ash on the tip of his round nose. 'The range's goin'. It won't be long now, so.'

Grogan grunted testily. He needed his morning tea and shortbread boost in order to concentrate fully on the International News.

To bide the time until the water boiled, Kevin Slattery crouched before a two-shelf bookcase set against one corner of the processing room and removed eight dusty ledgers from its shelves. Although most Garda stations in County Mayo were furnished with at least one humming new typewriter, Ballinacroagh still used the crumbling, ten-pound ledgers of yesteryear to record the town's illegal activities. Kevin Slattery had the wearisome job of handwriting the police reports, meticulously printing in the ledger columns each crime, with its corresponding date, time and alleged perpetrator.

Opening the most current ledger, Kevin read the last entry on the fourteenth of February, the day The Cat, Ballinacroagh's resident drunk and all-round malcontent, had delivered a two-fingered salute to the Saint of Sweethearts. The wizened alcoholic (no one in town *really* knew how old The Cat was) had decided to bring his Valentine's Day party to the rectory's roof, climbing up there with the uncanny ease of the scraggy animal for which he was named. The Cat spent a good three hours on the rectory's roof, lamenting lost loves and wailing into an unmarked bottle of misery, until Grogan and Slattery finally managed to bring him down with a cattle-prod.

The young officer shook his head at the memory and closed the ledger, sending up a poof of dust that made his eyes water. The kettle whistled sharply in the side room just then, over-riding the news crackling on the radio. Annoyed, Grogan leaned forward to turn the receiver's volume up, and happened to catch a sight of Thomas McGuire's Land Rover gunning into the Town Council's car park next door.

Both guards scrambled to the window and watched as Thomas thundered up to the council office. The hefty bar owner pounded on the closed door for a full two minutes, driving his fist senselessly into the wood panels and giving himself a right old nasty splinter, which worsened his mood altogether. It was only eight in the morning, too early for the lazy sods on the board to show up for their stab at municipal work. Still, the wee hour didn't stop Thomas from kicking the blue council doors in unadulterated rage, before retreating to his car to await councilman Padraig Carey's arrival.

'Doesn't look like he'll be filing any complaints at the town hall just yet,' observed mild-mannered Kevin Slattery. He would not have admitted it for the world, but the sight and sound of Thomas's violence frightened him something awful.

Sean Grogan sighed. 'Better get to the tea now, Kevin. It's going to be a long day yet. I'd put my money on it,' he said, out of habit, for Grogan was a man who regularly lost his week's wages to the horses. He nodded knowingly and turned the weather report up on the crackling radio.

. . .*Well now, folks, this just in from lovely Kathleen at our weather desk – be prepared 'cause it looks like the rain's coming and it's here to stay. Winds will be gale force eight, with*

a chance of strong gusts to storm force ten.
Don't forget yer umbrellas and do yer shopping
before lunchtime! This is Mid-West FM.
Mayo, Ireland and the world are listenin'!

Thomas turned the radio on in his Land Rover
with his splintery hand, hoping to drown out the
beats pounding in his head. That gobshite
Padraig better open the council office soon, he
thought angrily, or there was no telling what he'd
do. If he didn't get some answers for what he
had seen in the old pastry shop, God help him,
he'd tear the place apart with his own two hands.
He was fecked if he was going to let that Eye-
talian witch rob him of his dream a second time
around, that was for sure.

For Thomas McGuire, the dream had started
on 31 December 1961, the fateful birth night of
Irish television. The country's foray into technology that night brought him face to face with
the debonair moves of the Working Boys Band,
swinging live from Dublin's Gresham Hotel. As
his entire family sat gob-smacked before the fuzzy
receiver, fifteen-year-old Thomas stood behind

the line of straight-backed chairs set in the front parlour and felt his toes move with a life of their own. Before he knew what was happening, his pointy, two-toned shoes were swinging in uncontrollable dips and turns, following the televised rhythms of the Motown-inspired Irish sextet into a whole new world. Those feet of his mash-potatoed out of the parlour, did the twist up the stairs, and set a syncopated beat knocking about in Thomas's usually vacuous brain; a beat that did not stop thumping, not even when he was asleep.

Aware of the stigma that his growing obsession with popular dance steps would incur on the Gaelic football field at his all-boys' secondary school, Thomas hid his passion from everyone, and only indulged under the invigorating stream of a scalding shower head, shimmying as the shampoo bubbled down the drain.

Sometimes, while his snotty brothers slept in the bed next to him, he would fish out a flashlight to pore over the latest *Teen Beat* magazine he had 'borrowed' from under his sister Margaret's pillow. Pictures of apple-cheeked American teenagers on *Dick Clark's American Bandstand* and bowl-headed Brits bopping away to Top Forty hits from The Yardbirds and Herman's Hermits filled his gut with yearning. If only he was older, young Thomas would whisper to himself. He'd be off like a shot to London or New York. To make a name for himself. Thomas McGuire could be the next Elvis Presley or Paul McCartney, he knew he could.

Alas, it was not to be. With his father's untimely demise came the responsibility of an empire, or the start of one, which for young Thomas turned out to be Paddy McGuire's pub. He put his dreams of dancing fame aside for the more staid occupation of drink lord and town bully. Between 1966 and 1976, with the help of a much-touted marriage to Cecilia Devereux, the county mayor's two-hundred-and-twelve-pound nymphomaniacal daughter, Thomas McGuire would secure for himself a tidy monopoly on the town's precious leisure money. He relegated his six wayward siblings to the daily maintenance of his growing businesses, while he oversaw the whole machine with the eyes of a hungry beast. And it had served him well, this diligence of waking hours; his insistence on upgrading the Wilton Inn's upholstery (from an early-century leather to a Paisley velour) and pub menus (adding a bottle of sticky port wine to his growing list of stouts and ales). In a time when the average yearly wage hardly topped 8,000 punts, Thomas McGuire had managed to become a very rich man. With his six thriving establishments and nearly a third of the town's residents working under his fungied thumb, Thomas might even have taken a respite from it all. He might finally have set aside some time to tend to his ever-expanding wife and his growing litter of children. Yes, had Thomas not decided (in a rare moment of generosity), to treat his three hardworking brothers to a trip to the Spanish island of Majorca in the summer of 1980, he probably would have stopped for a stale breath or two. But destiny, it seems, had other plans. For it was on that trip that Thomas finally became free to relive his adolescent dream.

The idea hit him as he was standing on the patio of *Discoteca De Amor*, listening to the opening strains of Thelma Houston's 'Don't Leave Me This Way' pump out into the sultry

Spanish sky above him. Prompted by the liber-
ating ecstasy of synthesizers, the comforting
approval of slippery polyester, and a pretty brown
girl in enormous platform shoes jutting into his
groin to the rhythm of a funky beat, Thomas's
feet suddenly began dancing again. Swaying with
abandon to the loud disco music, the bar owner
felt like a newer, better version of himself. And
it didn't take long for him to decide that what
he needed more than anything, what he desired
above all else, was his very own discothèque.

Back in Ballinacroagh, a rejuvenated Thomas
set about pursuing his goal with the greatest
fervour. He sported bushy sideburns, grew his
curly hair out to his shoulders, and squeezed his
sausage legs into a pair of denim bell-bottoms.
At Kenny's Record Shop, he combed through
thousands of disco records, produced in such
exotic American locales as Bushwick, Brooklyn,
Downtown Detroit and Jamaica, Queens, and in
December 1980, he took in a total of twenty-
two screenings of *Saturday Night Fever* in
Castlebar's one-screen cinema. By the new year,
Thomas McGuire was ready to implement the

second step of his nightclub plan: finding the perfect dancing space.

It was no contest, really. There was only one spot Thomas would consider for his disco – Papa's Pastries next door. Chance had it that the wall separating the pastry shop from Paddy McGuire's was nothing but a shaky layer of plaster and rotting wood, an anomaly among the brick and stone of other shops. A three-man crew would need a day, two at most, to clear the way for the rip-roaring nightclub he had already christened 'Polyester Paddy's'. It was the perfect venue. All that mattered now was working out how he could get his hands on it.

Thomas McGuire wouldn't have to wonder for long; his disco prayers were soon answered with Luigi Delmonico's meringue-coated death in the spring of 1981. The sudden coronary waltzed Luigi out of this world and into the next. It also left the door open for Thomas McGuire to move in.

At least, that was the plan.

Knowing it would not sit well with the town's more religious factions if he rushed into demolition the day after the chubby pastry chef's wake, Thomas waited a whole month before knocking on Estelle Delmonico's door. Tradition must be adhered to, Thomas reasoned, if only for appearances' sake. The green-shuttered, four-room Delmonico cottage was situated on a remote and perilously steep mountain road that proved far too narrow for Thomas's mammoth Land Rover. Forced to park his prized vehicle at the bottom of the hill, the big man puffed his way along the rocky mile and a half to the cottage on foot, coughing on vapours of cow dung and pig fat that hung in the air. The hike felt to Thomas like penances paid in advance; his hairless inner-thighs burned with every step, his self-preoccupations blinding him to the beauty of the surrounding verdant valleys.

The lanes winding uphill towards the cottage are those quaint, postcard snapshots one has come to expect of the Irish countryside. Lined with rusted fences and stone borders, the leafy farm roads are liberally embraced by thousands of drooping, wet tree branches and stinging blades of nettle. But it is the clearing that suddenly springs upon the walker as he turns to the cottage that showcases the ultimate fairytale, the Druid's dream. For there is the ocean. The Atlantic feeds into the southern end of Clew Bay like a doting parent. On a clear day the view through the cottage's windows, bordered with sills of African violets, is simply magnificent. Wedged into the side of neighbouring Croagh Patrick, one can even see the greying blocks of a stone altar, where most climbing pilgrimages end and the redemption of souls begins.

Thomas reached the whitewashed cottage and paused to wipe his sweaty meat brow. Yes, he had done what decency required. He had waited long enough and now the pastry space would be his. All he needed to do was offer the old widow a tidy sum – probably more than she had ever seen come through that greasy, wog excuse for a bread shop – and Polyester Paddy's would become a reality.

Thomas tried to restrain his excitement as he knocked on the low cottage door. A minute later a short, plump woman in her mid-sixties opened up, her ample, apron-covered bosom jutting out

towards him in a way that brought back childhood memories of secretive peeking. For indeed,
there used to be a time when, as a young boy,
Thomas had been drawn to the decadent colours
twinkling through the pastry shop's windows.
Schoolboy Thomas had loved to watch Estelle
Delmonico administer sweet toppings to lemony
yellow meringue pies and frozen scoops of orange
gelato, smiling as she went along. He remembered
quite vividly how her then younger breasts
heaved passionately as she placed a single, pearl-
glazed maraschino cherry on top of each dessert,
from Danishes to chocolate éclairs. But that was
a long time ago, Thomas reminded himself. He
didn't know any better back then.

'Yes?' Estelle's puzzled greeting shook Thomas
back to reality. She cocked her head quizzically
– for she had difficulty remembering faces – but
Thomas interpreted the gesture as a shrewd
bargaining tactic from the Old Country. Well,
two could play at that game.

'Don't think we've met. I'm Thomas
McGuire,' he said, puffing out his broad chest.
The bully did not extend his hand or even

acknowledge the old lady with a nod, a basic Ballinacroagh extension of courtesy. He just stood there, looming over the Italian widow in unmistakable hubris, waiting for her to recognise his assumed superiority.

'Of course. How silly of me, eh? You know, I would not even know my own mama's face, may she rest in peace, if she was right in front of me. It's my eyes. They don't remember faces like they do recipes.' A surprisingly girlish giggle escaped from Estelle's mouth. Pools of sweat glistened on her downy upper lip and began to trickle down the cracks above her lipstick line. She rescued them with her darting tongue, slurping the water in sweet delight.

Thomas stared down into the widow's playful face and felt an unexpected shiver of fright. Was she not right in the head, then? Her husband was not yet cold in the ground and here she was licking her lips and laughing like it was Christmas morning. He had always heard she was a bit strange, but crazy?

What Thomas McGuire did not know, as he stood cultivating his jumped conclusions, was that Estelle Delmonico had sweated nothing but a highly potent mixture of pure sugar and water ever since she was a day old. Unlike the musk of normal feminine perspiration, her glands exuded no smell – but the taste! Her late husband Luigi, himself anything but ordinary, had caught on immediately to the magic of those sugary drops. Sweet Estelle was the greatest muse an ambitious pastry chef from Naples could ever wish for, and theirs was a match made in plum-sugared heaven.

'Would you like to come in? I'm making delicious baklava. Can you smell the happiness? The recipe is a special Persian dessert sent to me from my niece in London.' Estelle wiped her floury hands on her apron and stepped aside to welcome him in.

Thomas squinted into the dark house, expecting to see strange shadows and lacy doilies. He wasn't prepared for the strange smell that punched him in the gut. Stunned by the erotic mixture of cardamom and toasted almonds, he reeled two steps back down on to the gravel. Unknown to Thomas McGuire, this very aroma had once induced a lusty Achaemenian king to declare sixty-nine nights of love-making in his kingdom of honeysuckle fortresses. Concubines were ordered to comb their dark locks with powdered cardamom, as harem slaves drizzled their white belly buttons with a mixture of warm honey and almonds. But, rather than having a similar amorous effect on Thomas, the scent tied his bowels into a disturbed knot.

'No, no. I'm here on a business matter,' Thomas said, raising his hands in revulsion. There was something very wrong about a smell so strong. 'Sorry to hear about yer husband's death. See the shop's been closed since. Would'ya be leaving for yer niece's soon, then?'

'Gloria? No. She's young, free, in London. No, I don't go anywhere. Anyway, what would my Luigi do without me, eh?'

'Luigi? Yer husband?' Thomas was already crafting his speech before the County Council. This old bird was ready for the loony bin, for sure. She certainly was not fit to keep her hold over such prime Ballinacroagh real estate.

'Si, si, my husband. Luigi,' said the widow.

She stepped beyond the door's threshold and pointed past Thomas, towards the gravel path. There, at the beginning of the pathway, a large rose bush sat clinging to the ocean wind. Unlike the prim, Anglicised bushes spattered outside various Ballinacroagh houses, this plant burst with deep, primal magenta blossoms. Thick thorns curved around the flowers' petals like a good chaperone guarding a virginal yet very hormonal schoolgirl. Estelle Delmonico didn't seem to notice the thorns as she patted the flowers.

'Luigi. My Luigi. You see the ribbon?' She pointed to a thin white sash tied tightly around the bush's trunk.

Shivers ran up Thomas's spine as he realised that the sash he was looking at was no ordinary string. It was an apron string. A pastry chef's apron, to be exact. Now there was no denying it: the woman was mad.

'My Luigi is sleeping here. No, Luigi, I never leave you,' Estelle whispered. Leaning down towards the gritty soil, she kissed her hand and gently patted the base of the rose bush, where she had secretly sprinkled the late baker's ashes.

'Good. Right. Nice to meet you there, Luigi. And the shop? Is Luigi going back there as well?'

'No. That shop killed my Luigi. No more work for him. Now he rests,' she sighed, patting the mound again.

'Well so, that's that then! Just let me know what yer asking for the shop and I'll take it off yer hands right away. Just name yer price,' he said.

'No, I'm sorry, Mr McGuire. The shop is not for sale. No sale, but I rent it to you at a good price.'

'Well now, Mrs Delmonico. Renting is no good for me. It's a sale I'm after. Wouldn't you rather be free of the whole lot? Just spend yer days looking after, er, Luigi there?' He nodded uncomfortably towards the rose bush.

'No, no. Luigi says to me not to sell. I have to listen to him. He's so good with business. Me, no. I love the cooking, the baking, the bread,' Estelle turned towards the cottage. 'I'm sorry, Mr McGuire. No sale. But, I give you some baklava before you go, yes? It's a new recipe. You can be the first to taste.'

Estelle disappeared into the dark cottage. Situated as she was on the lonely crag heap, the little widow had few visitors and no one to taste her baklava besides a few confused hillock sheep, so she took the pub owner's visit to be positively providential.

'Look what I have for you, Mr McGuire. It's a lucky day for your sweet tooth.'

Estelle had returned to the doorway with a colourful plate piled high with baklava. She was humming an improvised aria under her sugared breath; a snippet from the second act of *Don Giovanni*, when the arrogant, sinful nobleman plunges into the open arms of hell. Little did Estelle know that the passionate chorus, *'such is the fate of a wrongdoer'*, combined with the overpowering seduction of the rose-water-soaked baklava pastry, would send Ballinacroagh's own misanthrope hurtling down her gravelly pathway and into the thorny hands of Luigi's rose bush.

'Oh, Mr McGuire! Do not move! You will get bad cuts from my Luigi's thorns if you do!' Estelle exclaimed, hurrying to where Thomas lay prostrate, atop a hundred and one sharp rose thorns. She was about to help Thomas off the rose bush, the hopeful plate of baklava still in hand, when the big man held up his beefy paw and roared.

'No! Stay away! Don't you come near me with those feckin' things!' Thomas lunged forward on the thorny stakes and managed to land on his feet. Backing down the rest of the path, he held up his two fists in front of his red face, an amateur pugilist shamefully defeated in the first round. 'And if ya know what's good fer ya, you'll sell that shite bakery to me! You'll be sorry if you don't!' he threatened weakly, before turning and running down the cottage lane.

Stunned, Estelle Delmonico watched the hulking man scurry away, his broad back pierced by curling rose spikes that resembled Beelzebub's own cowardly tail. And all the while, the operatic chorus chimed in her ear, *such is the fate of a wrongdoer'*, *'such is the fate of a wrongdoer'*.

That was five years ago. Thomas cursed under his breath and punched his good fist into the Land Rover's steering wheel. Five feckin' years.

He should have kept on at Estelle Delmonico like he planned instead of letting things go. But even he hadn't been able to forecast the series of travesties that had sent him lurching through the first part of the new decade.

The trouble had started with Kieran, that gobshite brother of his, who had abandoned his managerial duties at the Ale House to run away with some dope-smoking actress. The last Thomas heard, the two lovers had formed a performance troupe called The McGuire Family Circus, and were travelling the countryside in caravans, re-enacting the 'Feast of All Saints'. Put the whole family to shame, that Kieran. And then, of course, fortune dealt another blow with the flood of 1982. Torrential rains washed through half the businesses on Main Mall as if it was laundry day. Nearly took the Wilton Inn off the map, the flood did. The gushing water burst into the carvery room and floated silver trays of roasted meats on to the hilly street. For weeks people were picking soaked pieces of parsnip and rotten ham from the soles of their shoes. Getting the old inn back to working order had left Thomas with little time to devote to his disco cause.

Bleedin' Nature and all her feckin' rain. Thomas shook the morning drizzle from his thick hair. Ah, who was he kidding? The truth was he had become lazy, let things go. Taken it for granted that the pastry space would always be there for him when he was ready. It had never crossed his mind that the place could have a new life without his say-so.

Jaysus! Thomas growled and punched the steering wheel again. He should have known the old bat was holding out on selling the place for a better reason than her husband's dying wishes. She was planning to get back into business for herself all along. Well, that Estelle Delmonico was in for a surprise, Thomas told himself. A big surprise.

The synthesized vibrations of disco beats were suddenly pounding again inside Thomas McGuire's potato head. He was going to heed them this time around. No doubt about it.

Chapter Four

Dugh Yogurt Drink

Ingredients:

> 2 cups plain yogurt
> 3 cups mineral or spring water
> 3 tbsp fresh mint, chopped
> 1 tsp salt
> ½ tsp ground pepper
> mint leaves for garnish

Padraig Carey never had much luck with timing. If he had known that Thomas McGuire was waiting in the Town Council car park to unleash his wrath upon him, he would have stayed for another nine holes at Westport Pitch and Putt. Instead, he left in the middle of a great round, driven by guilt for having spent another workday morning putting the greens. Padraig drove his car into the Town Council car park and turned the ignition off, pausing before opening his car door to pat his golf bag in the backseat. Another day of mindless slogging before he could tee off again, he wistfully thought to himself.

A thin and unusually hirsute man, Padraig was in the unenviable position of being intimidated by the McGuire name in both domestic and public sectors. Having married Thomas McGuire's Amazonian sister Margaret (who, as the smartest of the McGuire clan had the difficult job of balancing all of Thomas's books), Padraig was completely cornered in his home life. He acquiesced to his wife's every decision, whether it was who controlled their finances (she did), when to have a rough and tumble in the bedroom (once a month) or what to have for dinner (salty bacon and boiled cabbage). In his public life Padraig seemed to be set up comfortably as head of

Ballinacroagh's two-manned council post. His lofty position as council speaker required little of him: the occasional management of road to farm land ratio and cutting ribbons at foreign-owned factory openings. But in reality Padraig had little peace in his job. His bully of a brother-in-law was always meddling in every aspect of Ballinacroagh's daily administration. Hardly a week went by without the councilman getting a complaint from Thomas, be it as trivial as the height of the hedges around the Town Council building or as dangerous as that time he had wanted to throw Estelle Delmonico into St Mary's Mental Institution. Still, Padraig thought to himself, as long as he could get himself on to the putting green most mornings, he could stand just about anything his job entailed. Even if it meant pandering to Thomas McGuire's every whim.

Oblivious to the bar owner's hulking approach, Padraig reached out across the backseat and absently traced the brass buckle on the strap of his golf bag.

'Padraig Carey.'

Thomas's booming voice made the short councilman jump in his seat.

'Hello there, Tom. Yer up and about early as usual, I see.' Padraig gulped. He hurried out of his car, angling his thin body to block the golf bag in the backseat from Thomas's view.

'Can't say the same for you, now can I? I want some answers, Padraig Carey! Just because you got my sister up the pole years ago doesn't mean I won't have you out on your feckin' arse before you can blink twice!'

'Sorry now, Tom.' Padraig could almost feel himself shrink before the steaming bully.

'Sorry now Tom? Sorry now Tom?! You've got some nerve, Padraig Carey! Why wasn't I told about the old witch's place? Why do you think I keep you in this shite post, if you're no good to me then?' Thomas's aubergine face contorted grotesquely. Standing on his toes, he towered over poor, inconsequential Padraig like a mighty skyscraper to a feeble pigeon.

'Now, now, Tom. Calm yerself. What do you mean? The old Delmonico place, is it?'

'Yes, the Delmonico place, you *eejit*! I've been

waiting five years fer the bit of expansion any man in my position has the right to. Now she's gone to openin' that piss-hole of a bakery again without any prior warning from yer bleedin' end! I have a good mind to tear the place down myself!'

'Estelle Delmonico? Another bakery? She couldn't be thinking about that now – not at her age.'

'How the feck would you know? You with your golf clubs up the arse while I slave away looking after this town! Where would this place be without me and my business, eh?' Thomas punched the air, grazing Padraig's shoulder. He climbed into his car like an angry gorilla and rolled down his window. 'I want you to find out what that old bag is up to. And meanwhile, tell Margaret and all she knows that if they want to stay on Thomas McGuire's better side they'd better stick to Corcoran's fer their daily bread.'

'Are you sure it's a pastry shop she's got running again, then?'

'Whatever it is I want it empty and closed within the week.'

Thomas revved the Land Rover and tore out

of the car park, leaving Padraig numbed and unanchored. The feeble councilman placed one hand on the hood of his car for support as his blood pumped furiously through his small, hairy body.

Estelle Delmonico carefully manœuvred her croaky Honda into the cobblestone alleyway behind the café. The little widow had got up earlier than usual that morning, the gale-ridden moans of neighbouring Croagh Patrick echoing her own as she pushed her brittle legs out of her feathery bed.

Despite Estelle's hearty laugh and steady eyes, she suffered from a degeneration of cartilage that caused her great misery. It had started with a seasonal prickling of wrists and fingertips that first year she and Luigi had arrived in County Mayo, and had slowly but surely expanded like a piece of pulled dough until it wrapped her in a cannoli of excruciating pain. Years of helping Luigi knead and punch endless loaves of bread exacerbated her affliction, and by the year preceding her husband's death, Estelle's arthritis had reduced her to sitting on a stool behind the shop counter while Luigi ran around tending to customers and ovens alike.

Of course, Estelle had tried the prescribed doses of steroid but found that it did nothing but give her unusually unmanageable underarm hair. She had even travelled to a Chinese acupuncturist who, in the height of the free-loving seventies had set up shop in Dublin's Henry Street. Although impressed by the Chinaman's fortitude – Li Fung Tao practised his morning tai chi in undisturbed serenity while fruit and veg hawkers spat their shrill wares all around him – his needles did nothing but make her feel like a piece of anchovy strung in an *Alici* marinade of oregano and chilli flakes.

Estelle had even tried her own concoction of rosemary and lavender, which she plucked from the little herb garden at the back of her cottage. Boiling the leaves down until only their dark oils remained, she would then mix in a good amount of Umbrian olive oil sent by her niece Gloria from London. The oil left her Mediterranean skin taut like snappy brindleberries, a fact that spurred

envy among the old townswomen and prompted
Dervla Quigley to spread rumours that Estelle
Delmonico had made a deal with the fairies, for
sure. Estelle didn't mind the suspicious stares,
even enjoyed them to be honest, wishing there
was some truth to it all. Because no matter how
aromatic and moisturising, the rosemary and
lavender massage was not magical enough to put
an end to the arthritis.

The Italian widow's aches were acting up as
usual on this day of spring reckoning, but she was
not going to let them stop her from whipping up
her famous osso bucco for her sweet new tenants.
She even made a side of her own mother's *gremolata*, toasting the woody pine nuts until they
turned dark brown. This veal masterpiece used
to be Luigi's favourite dish, and Estelle saved it
for special occasions when the frangipani of her
sunny homeland was especially missed.

'Hello?' Estelle knocked on the old bakery's
back door with her right fist and peered into its
blue, yellow and green stained-glass window.
From inside the kitchen her round face looked
like a medieval Venetian harlequin come to life.

Bahar, sitting closest to the back door, jumped at the unexpected knock. Her large brown eyes popped with anxiety and she tightened her grip on the sharp knife she was using. It had been a long time since a knock had not set off a flutter of fear in Bahar's small, birdcage chest or made her duck for cover. Ten seconds, counted out in thudding heartbeats, passed before she realised the knock was benign, but by then her complexion had grown ashen with the colour of unwanted oatmeal.

Darkest among her sisters, Bahar considered her brown skin tone as yet another sign that she was the least desirable Aminpour sister. As the middle child, Bahar was inevitably stuck between Marjan's intuitive compassion and Layla's willowy optimism. And, like many children who find themselves book-ended by extraordinary siblings, the gnawing desire to stand out, to take centre stage, becomes an all-consuming, if subconscious disease. Drama is vital to this sickness's survival and many middle children are thrown from one emotion to another, within minutes going from extreme anger to acute sadness to euphoric gaiety.

Marjan measured Bahar's unpredictable temperament according to the ancient and treasured Zoroastrian practice of gastronomic balancing, which pitted light against dark, good against evil, hot against cold. Certain hot, or *garm*, personalities tend to be quicker to temper, exude more energy and prompt all others around them to action. This energy often runs itself ragged, so to counter exhaustion, one must consume cold, or *sard*, foods such as freshwater fish, yogurt, coriander, watermelon and lentils. Most spices and meats should be avoided for they only stoke the fires inside. (Tea, although hot in temperature, is quite a neutralising element.) On the other hand, for the person who suffers from too cold a temperament, marked by extreme bouts of melancholia and a general disinterest in the future, hot, or *garm*, dishes are recommended. Foods such as veal, mung beans, cloves and figs do well to raise spirits and excite ambitions.

To diagnose Bahar as a *garmi* (on account of her extreme anxiety and hot temper) would have been simple enough, had she not also suffered from a lowness of spirit that often led to migraine headaches. Whether in a *garm* or *sard* mood, Bahar could always depend on her older sister to guide her back to a relative calm. Marjan had for a long time kept a close eye on Bahar and knew exactly when to feed her sautéed fish with garlic and Seville oranges to settle her hot flashes, or when a good apple *khoresh*, a stew made from tart apples, chicken and split peas, would be a better choice to pull Bahar out of her doldrums.

'Marjan? Who's that?' Bahar got up from the round table where she had been chopping mint sprigs, still clenching the knife.

'It's all right. It's only Mrs Delmonico,' Marjan reassured her sister. 'Did you eat anything this morning?' Without Marjan forcing her to take a bite, Bahar would not look after herself, often skipping meals altogether.

'No. Too much to do,' Bahar said tiredly, relaxing her tensed jaw. She placed the knife on the table and opened the back door. At once she was greeted by a friendly smile and the zesty smells of lemon thyme and fresh tomato sauce.

'Hello, Mrs Delmonico. Come in please. Let me help you,' Bahar leaned over and took the red enamel casserole dish Estelle was balancing on her left arm like a precocious baby.

Marjan left the pot of soup she was stirring at the stove and, taking Estelle's aching arm, gently led her to a kitchen chair.

'Mrs Delmonico, you look so tired,' she said. 'You are welcome here, of course.'

'I bring you my best cooking. Osso bucco with pine nut *gremolata*. It's good luck, you know. In Napoli we eat it on special times. So I bring it for your New Year's and birthday.' Estelle sat down at the round table, relieved.

'You shouldn't have,' said Marjan.

'Please, Mrs Delmonico. Would you like some tea?' Bahar was already running into the front room to pour a cup of hot water from the boiling golden samovar. Having worked for a year as a nurse in a Lewisham rest home, she immediately recognised the signs of osteoarthritis.

Estelle coughed, and unwound her twisted spine. 'Thank you, darling,' she said, wincing. 'And call me Estelle. Mrs Delmonico was my mama-in-law and you know, she was a very hard woman to like. Believe me.'

Bahar returned and placed a steaming cup of bergamot tea in front of the old woman.

'Thank you. Agh – this Irish weather is going to kill me!' Estelle threw her hands up with all the Italian dramatic flair she could muster. Leaning into the vapour of the steaming tea before her, she inhaled the bitter orange oils of the bergamot flower. 'Mmmmm, just like Napoli!'

'Yes, drink. And you have to have some of my red lentil soup. It will warm you up.' Marjan smiled at the sweet woman as she ladled out the fragrant soup and placed a bowl next to her teacup.

The combination of cumin, turmeric and nigella seed produced a healthy blush in Estelle Delmonico's face. Transporting her back nearly fifty years, the smell conjured up her first night of wedded bliss in Morocco, where, under a magical crescent moon, and with the smells of the spices rising from the bazaar below their open hotel window, the tumbling, bronzed bodies of twenty-year-old honeymooners Luigi and Estelle made love with all the vigour of their Latin blood.

'Mmmmm, wonderful, wonderful. So much food here, my goodness!' Estelle said, emerging from her romantic daydream.

At only nine in the morning the kitchen was already pregnant to its capacity, every crevice and countertop overtaken by Marjan's gourmet creations. Marinating vegetables (*torshis* of mango, aubergine and the regular seven-spice variety) packed to the briny brims of five-gallon see-through canisters, sat on the kitchen island. Large blue and terracotta bowls were filled with salads (angelica lentil, tomato, cucumber and mint, and Persian fried chicken), *dolmeh* and dips (cheese and walnut, yogurt and cucumber, baba ganoush, and spicy hummus) which, along with feta, Stilton and Cheddar cheeses, were covered and stacked in the enormous glass-door refrigerator. Opposite the refrigerator stood the colossal brick bread oven. Baking away in its domed belly was the last of the *sangak* bread, three feet long and counting, rising in golden crests and graced with scatterings of poppy and nigella seed. The rest of the bread (paper-thin *lavash*, crusty *barbari*, slabs of *sangak* as well as the usual white sliced loaf) was already covered with comforting cheesecloth to keep the freshness in. And simmering on the stove, under Marjan's loving orders, was a small pan of white onion soup (not to be mistaken for the French variety, for this version boasts dried fenugreek leaves and pomegranate paste), the last pan of red lentil soup, and a larger pan of *abgusht*. An extravaganza of lamb, split peas and potatoes, *abgusht* always reminded Marjan of early spring nights in Iran, when the cherry blossoms still shivered with late frosts and the piping samovars helped wash down the saffron and dried lime aftertaste with strong, black Darjeeling tea.

'If you think this is something you should see the front. We've been working since midnight,' said Marjan, smiling with the realisation that the hardest part of the day was nearly over. Everything was finally coming around, taking shape, in this place with such a funny name.

Bahar continued chopping mint on the round table, every now and again stealing a glance at Estelle as she slurped the last of her soup and leaned back, satisfied and refreshed.

'Oh, so delicious. I am a new woman. So, it is your birthday today, no? How old?'

'Twenty-four.' Bahar's shy smile was returned by a large set of teeth sparkling with various fillings of gold.

'Ah, so young!' Hands over head again. 'And what are you making there with the mint?'

'It's for Layla. I'm chopping this for her *dugh*.' Bahar's knife expertly sliced across the mint leaves, striking emerald mines. Helping Marjan in the kitchen had given her years of experience in peeling and slicing. If Bahar hadn't taken up nursing in London, she would have made an excellent sous chef, even gone to work alongside her sister in one of those trendy English restaurants. But then, that would have required her to spend hours over a hot stove, the burning saucepans staring up at her with gaping mouths; crucibles of a past that threatened to become present. No, Bahar was certain she could never do that. Even now she only went to the stove in emergencies. Only when Marjan had too little time and not enough hands for stirring all that she had cooked up.

'Doo—oo—gghhh?' Estelle emphasised the word's guttural ending, letting it tickle her throat. 'What is that?'

'*Dugh* is a yogurt and mint drink. We usually have it with *chelow kabob* – that's rice and barbequed meats. But Layla's been suffering from hiccups for an hour now and it doesn't look like they'll stop. This *dugh* will put an end to them,' said Marjan, as she grabbed a container of yogurt from the refrigerator.

Estelle watched as Marjan combined the yogurt, mint, salt, pepper and water in a large jug, stirring vigorously until the colour became a uniform creamy mint. She added some crushed ice to the jug and threw in a garnish of mint to remind Layla of the calming quality found in its green leaves.

Layla was indeed still in the throes of a hiccup fit but she was nowhere near suffering. The young girl was lying upstairs on the mattress the three sisters shared, splayed out like a star fruit with soliloquies of love-struck Shakespearian heroines running through her muddled brain. The image of Malachy's sapphire eyes sent tremors through her body; the hot node below her belly tingled and sent waves of pleasure down to her toes.

So this was how love was supposed to feel, Layla thought; like the ecstatic cries of a pomegranate as it realises the knife's thrust, the caesarian labour of juicy seeds cut from her inner womb. Like the gleeful laugh of oil as it corrupts the watery flour, the hot grease bending the batter to its will and creating a greater sweetness from the process – *zulbia*, the sugary fried fritters she loved so. Falling in love was amazing. Why hadn't anyone ever told her so?

Layla hiccuped again. Those sapphire eyes. Maybe she would see them again tomorrow, at her new school. For once Layla would not mind standing before a classroom full of staring faces.

'Layla! Your *dugh* is ready. Come down! Mrs Delmonico is here for a visit!'

'I'm coming!' Layla answered. Marjan's voice sounded tired and Layla felt a twinge of guilt for not helping her sisters more with the cooking.

Downstairs, Estelle Delmonico was drinking her second cup of bergamot tea.

'So, my Gloria tells me that you girls escaped the revolution. Yes?'

Marjan stopped stirring and cast a quick glance towards Bahar. Except for a dark shadow over her sister's soulful eyes, there was no sign that the word *revolution* had caused Bahar any agitation.

'Actually, we left Iran a little bit earlier. Just before,' Marjan said tentatively, still watching Bahar.

The foggy control towers of Heathrow Airport flashed momentarily into Marjan's mind. 1 February 1979, a date they would later learn had also welcomed a previously exiled ayatollah, one with a penchant for mystic poetry, into power in Tehran. Ushered into the clear-paned interrogation cubicles of the airport's immigration offices, the girls were completely unprepared for the barrage of accusatory questions and embarrassing searches of pockets and undergarments. Marjan recalled how little Layla had been forced to step out of her tatty panties, to reveal a wad of pre-revolutionary-exchanged sterling hidden where her underwear's elastic should have been; financial stability in untouchable hearths.

Marjan knew the kind widow was waiting expectantly for their story of escape, but found that she could not tell that tale. Not yet. At least not in front of her sensitive sister.

'We were lucky to get visas to the UK, lucky to get good jobs with the economy so bad . . . Layla was only seven, so she doesn't remember much.'

Despite her madcap moments, Estelle had an acute sense of boundaries, and decided to leave the subject alone.

'Yes, very young, seven. And where is that pretty girl, eh? She is not sick?'

'No, just a teenager. Layla, come on!' Marjan yelled towards the staircase again, unaware that Layla had been standing the whole time at the top of the landing. No one could see her from there, but she had heard. And it wasn't true. She remembered it all.

She remembered the sirens. The blaring horns, mounted atop military jeeps that appeared without notice to signal the nightly curfew, circling in and out of the soft-hued residential streets lined with marigolds, of households stocked with both *dugh* and Coca Cola. Soon after came the flapping. Funny how she remembers hearing it before ever actually *seeing* it; the funeral tint of that female tent that was lately becoming so commonly worn, even in the more affluent northern suburbs. *Chador, chador.* Three square metres of scratchy wool strategically wrapped and clenched in chattering teeth, revealing nothing above blinking pupils, nothing below dripping nostrils. *Chador, chador.*

Posters of these multiplying fabric ravens were popping up on university walls and shop windows daily, headlined with thinly cloaked threats. Bahar, who was sixteen at the time of the upheaval and very much under its influence, had used those very threats to induce Marjan and Layla to wear full-length veils. She would return home flushed with excitement after attending one of the many student revolts in Tehran's central and southern streets, filled with stories of bullet-ridden banners and a stern-browed ayatollah that made so many chadors swoon with delirium.

The chants, the demands for death, were

heard everywhere. *Death to the traitor Shah! Death to all things from the opiate West!* An end to the America that had brought Layla the Tom and Jerry cartoons and peanut M&Ms she loved so much. That had been enough to make her cry (secretly, of course), late at night in bed.

Bahar was sixteen, just a little older than she was now. Layla shook her head to dispel those dark thoughts. Maybe Marjan was right to change the subject, to try and put it all behind them. Layla hiccuped again, the sound releasing her from her hiding place. She walked down the stairs and smiled.

'Finally! Your *dugh*'s on the counter there. Drink it before it settles. And say hello to Mrs Delmonico,' Marjan barked, her nerves getting the better of her.

'Estelle. Call me Estelle.'

Chapter Five

Abgusht

Ingredients:

2 kilos boned leg of lamb, save bone
5 large onions, chopped
1 tsp turmeric
10 cups water
1 cup yellow split peas
1 tsp paprika
4 tsp salt
1 tsp ground black pepper
5 large potatoes, peeled and quartered
7 tomatoes, sliced

2 tbsp tomato paste
1 dried lime
2 strands saffron dissolved in
7 tablespoons hot water
2 tsp advieh*

Maybe it was all Thomas McGuire's doing. Not trusting Padraig Carey to the effective dissemination of his message of hate, Ballinacroagh's chief publican had promptly set up camp inside McGuire's Ale House after leaving the Town Council car park on Monday morning. From his favoured stool at the high end of the oak bar, Thomas deftly expounded, like a seasoned politico of the Roman forum, on the dangers of foreign smells.

Perhaps Dervla Quigley had a finger in it as well, hissing the news up and down Main Mall until all of Ballinacroagh knew exactly what to avoid. 'Forget the infested ways of the tinkers,' Dervla would have whispered darkly to anyone

* optional: equal amounts crushed rose petals, cardamom, cinnamon and cumin, mixed

standing beneath her window. 'It's these foreign hippies we've got to hold fast against.'

Or, it could have simply come down to the uncontrollable caprices of lady luck; Bahar's blistery thumb and the persistent Atlantic rains signs of imminent trouble ahead.

Whatever the culprit, the opening of the Babylon Café that first day of spring was not half as grand as Marjan had hoped. To her utmost disappointment, not a single customer had stepped inside the inviting café the whole of Monday.

'Maybe we need to put up a big OPEN sign. What do you think?' Marjan said on Tuesday morning. She stood perplexed before the café windows, with folded arms and knitted eyebrows.

'A sign? Open your eyes, Marjan. We had the curtains opened and all the lights on yesterday and no one even stopped to look through the windows. A sign!' Bahar sniffed, shaking her head.

'I just don't understand it. Not even one customer! Maybe it's the rain.' Marjan pressed her forehead against the cold glass windowpane.

The rainstorm had started on Monday around noon, blasting down in stinging sheets, rattling hinges and windowpanes and wiping Main Mall of any pedestrians. Most shops had soon shut down for the day, their tired proprietors heaving sighs against the wind as they struggled to lock their shopfronts. Battling gusts with overturned umbrellas, they quickly scattered home on foot, or for the luckier ones, in freezing, water-clogged cars. Even Dervla Quigley, who hardly counted the daily village drizzle as a reason to leave her window, had retreated behind the pleats of her chintz curtains at the height of the storm.

'Well, it doesn't look like the rain'll stop anytime soon. Look at it! I didn't think any place could be wetter than London,' Bahar commented, gazing outside. The street gushed with an unappetising soup of broken glass, stray turf blocks, cigarette stumps and the salty tears of a darkened sky that had yet to end its purge.

'I bet we'll get at least fifty people in today. Right, Marjan?' Layla looked up from her breakfast of *lavash* and feta. She was already running late for her first day of school and was scarfing down her food as fast as she could.

'Of course, *joon-e man*. We'll have the whole town in here soon,' she replied, trying to sound upbeat.

'It's a good thing you made Mrs Delmonico take some food home with her yesterday. We'd never get through all the pots of soup and *abgusht* you made,' Bahar said disapprovingly.

'Okay, wish me luck!' Layla rose abruptly from her half-eaten breakfast. She was decked out in her newly starched uniform of light blue sweater, crisp white blouse and brown tweed skirt. Grabbing an umbrella, she slung her schoolbag on her shoulders, smiled radiantly at her two sisters and swung open the café door.

The dense mist that usually sat upon Croagh Patrick's shoulders had descended on the village, insidiously inhabiting all crevices and street corners. Layla eagerly joined the train of school-children braving the cold rain and fog, pushing through a shrouded Main Mall up towards St Joseph's Secondary. She paused for a moment to wave excitedly at her two sisters, before disappearing in the heavy veil of mist. Bahar, worried for Layla's well-being, waved back anxiously, but

Marjan looked on with delight, happy to see Layla so energised. In a decade of regularly televised hijackings and terrorist bombings carried out by masked Middle-Easterners, new schools for Layla tended to be breeding grounds for endless taunting sessions; accusations of 'terrorist' and 'hijacker' were thrown around the school playgrounds like break-time diversions. Their youngest sister would usually be too terrified to sleep the night before she started at a new school. But Layla had surprised her sisters this morning, getting up early with bright eyes to pack her own lunch of basil, tomato and yogurt–cucumber dip wrapped in *lavash* and to iron her school uniform. There was no nervousness in her gestures, no fear on her beautiful face as she nearly skipped up a drenched Main Mall.

Layla's unexpected cheerfulness was a good sign, Marjan decided. Any optimism was welcome, especially in light of yesterday's failed opening.

A saviour, and the Babylon Café's first customer, came that very Tuesday afternoon, in the merry shape of Father Fergal Mahoney.

Father Mahoney was on his way down to Marie Brennan and her sister Dervla's dimly lit parlour for the first meeting of the 1986 Patrician Day Dance committee. For the past thirty-nine years, the good-natured priest had served as coordinator of the Dance that celebrated the annual pilgrimage to the peak of Croagh Patrick. Every summer a stream of pilgrims climbed the mountain's stony shoulders – some with bare feet – as penitence for choosing sinful paths during the rest of the year. To commemorate this turn for atonement, Ballinacroagh celebrated the first Sunday climb in July, Patrician Day, by hitching up coarse canvas tents, stringing up Japanese lanterns, and brandishing life-sized, cut-out posters of a rather soused St Patrick. Fold-out tables were loaded with Thomas McGuire's latest ale and enough bacon and cabbage from his carvery at the Wilton Inn to give everyone in town heartburn, with a three-pound charge, of course.

As coordinator of the Dance, Father Mahoney had a lot on his plate: not only was he in charge of choosing a band for the Dance (always a success but for that unfortunate year a group of three Dublin nuns shocked the crowd with their a cappella renditions of '99 Red Balloons' and 'Relax'), but he was also designated Master of Ceremonies for the event. It was a delicious role for the extrovert priest, who often peppered his Masses and homilies with humour. As MC, Father Mahoney happily indulged in a good half-hour of jokes that, for one time each year, were unfettered by his religious duties.

Preoccupied with new punch lines, the funny priest did not notice the Babylon Café's welcoming glow until he was standing right in front of its sparkling windows. Having prepared himself for the committee's usual fare of afternoon tea, crumbly digestive biscuits and gossip, the priest was stopped dead in his tracks by the savoury aroma of lamb *abgusht*. Dumbfounded, he peered in at the warm blush of the café's walls with his mouth open, not even minding the cold raindrops that pierced his round face and priestly overcoat.

Marjan was just making her way out to the

café's front room with a tray of washed teacups when she spotted Father Mahoney's hungry face outside the window.

'Hello! Please come in! We're open for lunch,' Marjan enthused, thrusting the shop door open. Were priests allowed to eat outside of their homes? Marjan wasn't so sure. But now was not the time to hesitate.

'Lunch? Ah, so this is what Estelle Delmonico's been up to. I heard a thing or two about it from the ladies after Mass. Are you a relative of Mrs Delmonico's, then?' Feeling a bit woozy from the saffron that hit him when Marjan opened the door, Father Mahoney had forgotten the introduction he customarily dished out with a joke or two on the collared profession.

'No. We just met last week, actually. I'm Marjan Aminpour. My sisters and I are renting this place from Mrs – ah – from Estelle.' She pointed to the sign hanging over her head and smiled. It was a simple wooden square that Bahar had made with the leftover paint, writing out the café's name in red cursive flourishes.

'Ah, yes. The Babylon Café. Very clever. The

Hanging Gardens of Babylon. Birthplace of Nebuchadnezzar II and all that he created.'

'Not far from where we come from.'

'Is that so? And where, may I ask, is that?'

'Iran. We left over seven years ago, though. For London.'

'London. Fabulous town. Lots of fantastic theatre on the West End there. I'm not keen on the English sense of humour, though. *Monty Python* and all that Holy Grail stuff. I much prefer the Americans for a bit of a laugh. Richard Pryor and Bill Cosby. Fantastic, they are.'

'Yes, I suppose so,' laughed Marjan, surprised by the incongruity of a priest with a sense of humour. He reminded Marjan of a ripe quince fruit, pale skinned and tart flavoured. Unexpected.

'I'm Father Mahoney. It's my parish you'll be coming under. Right up the Mall there.'

'Oh, but we're not Catholic.'

'Right so. I won't tell if you won't.' He laughed, his little blue eyes twinkling beneath folds of fat and skin. 'Ah, sure, I'm a bit of a tease. You'll learn that about me sooner than later, I'm afraid.

Mmmmm . . . but that smells fantastic. What is it?' He sniffed, his round nostrils moving with a life of their own.

'It's called *abgusht*. Lamb and potato stew. Are you sure you can't come in – for a cup of tea at least? You'll be our first customer.'

Father Mahoney glanced at his watch: fifteen minutes to spare before Dervla Quigley rang the parish looking for him. Besides, it would only be a cup of tea. How long could that take?

'Your first customer, you say? Well, I can guarantee I won't be your last! You'll be the first café we've ever had in Ballinacroagh, as far as I can remember. Sure, the Wilton Inn's carvery doesn't even come close. No lovely smells like this lamb and potato stew,' he said, stepping inside. 'Hmmm, Iran, did you say? Have you heard the one about the priest, the rabbi and the mullah?'

'Just who does she think she is? I hear they're Indian or Pakistani or something of the like,' Dervla Quigley said churlishly. The crabby gossip had taken up her usual roost at her bedroom window and had just witnessed Father Mahoney's encounter with Marjan across the street.

'I think it was Iranian. Assumpta Corcoran herself was telling me so just now.' Marie Brennan leaned over her sister's curved back, gawking. 'That one there was at the market looking for tarragon of all things. Tarragon! Now what do you suppose that is?'

The two old women watched as Father Mahoney took off his coat and settled into one of the front tables with the look of a man possessed.

'Whatever they are it can't be civilised. And what do you suppose that Father Mahoney is thinking now, sitting there like some Romanian beggar and just before teatime? He knows very well we're expecting him. If he's even one minute late – I'm counting it's seven minutes to three on my watch – I'll be telling him a thing or two.'

'It's a café! Babylon Café! Says so right there on the sign!'

'I can see it with my own eyes, Marie,' Dervla snapped at her younger sister. 'Babylon! Sinful, that is.'

'It's in the Bible, as I recall,' Marie muttered, hurt by Dervla's mean tone.

'So's Sodom and Gomorrah. Humph! Will you look at him sitting there! That Father Mahoney better have a good excuse. Is that a meal now he's having? Marie!'

'Looks like it, Dervla,' Marie answered weakly, as she edged out of the room. Dervla sure knew how to suck her dry. Years of tending to her bitter sister's every need, whether it was helping her on to her toilet seat or into the black pleated skirt Dervla favoured for Sunday Mass, had left Marie Brennan a ghost of a person. Sometimes, God help her, Marie wished she'd come home to find Dervla at her window, staring at nothing but the pearly gates of St Peter himself. Every time she imagined this, though, she made a beeline to St Barnabas to see Father Mahoney. The kind priest always made time for the lonely spinster's frequent, guilt-ridden confessions.

'Marie!'

'Yes, Dervla?'

*   *   *

Marjan left a fascinated Father Mahoney to take in all the fineries of the café's front room and returned to the warming pot of *abgusht* to taste its progress. She lifted the lid and breathed in the slowly simmering lamb stew, which she had cooked with a large piece of *limuomani*, or dried lime. Just one of these limes is enough to add an intense flavour to any savoury dish, its tart essence rising to the occasion.

As Father Mahoney gaped at the radiant vermilion walls and the curious belly of something that looked like it belonged in a fairytale – the samovar bubbling with contentment – Marjan placed a bowl of broth on an oval, silver serving plate that was etched with a village scene of children dancing around a donkey. Next to the bowl she arranged a plate heaped with *gusht kubideh* (mashed meat and veg), warmed *lavash* bread and mixed-spice *torshi* (sliced onions and radishes). Marjan would have loved to include some fresh tarragon, but it was one of the few key ingredients she had forgotten to bring back from Dublin, so she settled for fresh sprigs of mint and basil and made a mental note to get some seedlings on her next trip to the city. She was going to turn that craggy patch of a back garden into a blooming herb garden yet.

Marjan steadied the heavy platter and pushed through the swinging doors. Father Mahoney stood next to the northern wall, running his fingers over the hanging tapestry.

'Extraordinary, absolutely extraordinary. Handmade, I take it?'

'Yes, from Iran,' Marjan replied. 'You know, each region in Iran has its own specific rug pattern. Tribal families would weave their histories into their rugs, passing down their secrets to the next generation. So, you could say that in a way, they were magic carpets.'

'Enchanting!' exclaimed the priest.

Marjan smiled, placing the platter on Father Mahoney's table. She noticed that his cup of jasmine tea was already drained dry. 'Here's the *abgusht* I promised. I hope you enjoy it.'

'I'm sure I will. You are too kind. My goodness! What smells, what smells indeed. This ab-abba-goosht is not a Portuguese dish, by any chance, is it? I used to be quite the connoisseur

of Portuguese dishes in my day, that's why I ask.'
Father Mahoney sat back down and looked into
the platter and instantly forgot about the
committee meeting he was about to be late for.

'No, it's Persian, through and through. It's
hearty, but contains some very delicate ingredients. Would you like another cup of tea? Or a
pot, perhaps?'

'Oh, well, I can't say no now, can I?' He peered
at the various *abgusht* components, at a complete
loss for where to start. Father Mahoney picked
up his spoon but paused over the broth as if afraid
he was going to hurt it.

'The broth is clear enough. You can take it
throughout the meal, but the real treat is the
meat paste there. The thin bread is called *lavash*.
Use it to scoop some of the meat, then add onions
and herbs and whatever else you like there as you
go along. It is a very nourishing dish, especially
during the winter months,' Marjan explained,
pointing to the food as she spoke.

She took the priest's empty cup to the samovar
for a refill. Instructing the priest on the finer
points of eating *abgusht* had somehow stirred

Marjan's memories of home. She pushed the lever down on the samovar and watched the tawny liquid fill the glass and gold-plated teacup. If she was in Iran now this tea would be accompanied by either angelica-powdered pomegranate seeds, crackling pumpkin nuts or sticky saffron and carrot halva. On the night of the winter solstice everyone in her family would gather on the living-room rug to share such treats and tell stories. If it was particularly cold, they would snuggle around the *korsi*, a low table covered in a quilt, and wrapped a second time in a pretty embroidered cloth. Underneath the table would be a small electrical heater that warmed their hearts and laps as they sat, recounting memories and their hopes for the year ahead.

One year her cousin Mitra had kicked the heater, nearly burning off her big toe in a fit of passionate storytelling. Another time, her great-aunt Homa had made everyone scour the snowy garden and front yard until dawn, convinced that her prized ruby bracelet had been lost, only to realise in the morning light that the piece of jewellery had surreptitiously crept into the folds of the blanket she had been sitting on. Why were all these memories coming back to her now of all times? Marjan wondered. Now that she was the furthest she had ever been from her place of birth? Why this homesickness today?

The tea overflowed the cup and gushed over the edges of the saucer Marjan was holding. With a noisy clatter, she released the samovar's lever and grabbed a towel, soaking up the hot puddle beneath her feet. The commotion, however, did not wake Father Mahoney from his own reverie. He was softly brewing over his *abgusht*, his round cheeks rosy and full of life. Marjan finished cleaning the spilt tea and leaned against the counter, not wanting to disturb the priest. She understood exactly what was happening to Father Mahoney.

If Layla inspired lust in younger men and youthful dreams in their older counterparts, then Marjan worked her magic over both men and women in a more practical, yet equally intriguing manner. Through her recipes, Marjan was able to encourage people towards accomplishments that they had previously thought impossible; one taste of her food and most would not only start *dreaming*, but actually contemplate *doing*. It was no different for Father Mahoney. As the priest chewed his last bit of meat-filled *lavash*, he felt a little lump in his stomach. It was a seed that would not bloom for at least another month, forever changing the course of his life, but for now it only rustled against the *abgusht* and gave him an unsettled feeling. Father Mahoney did not know what had happened to him exactly, but he knew that he was a very different man from a half-hour ago.

Father Mahoney stood up. He reached for his coat hanging next to the door, his arm shaking slightly.

'Oh, are you leaving already?' Marjan smiled at the euphoria in the priest's hazy eyes.

'Yes, I'm afraid I've got to run. I'm sure I had an appointment somewhere, but for the life of me I just can't seem to remember what it was. How silly of me.' Father Mahoney's confusion was sweet, steeped as it was in a greater force. He needed to lie down somewhere, anywhere. There was a lot to think about. He was not sure what it all was, but he knew that he needed to think about it.

'I hope you enjoyed your *abgusht* and tea,' said Marjan.

'Enjoyed it? I have never, in all my years travelling, tasted anything as divine – excuse me, Father.' The pudgy priest looked up to the ceiling and quickly crossed himself. 'Never. You, my dear, have a true talent, a calling. I have no doubt that this enchanting little place will be filled with customers in no time. Enchanting!' He shook his head and placed a few notes on the table.

'Oh, no, it's on the house, Father. You are our first customer, after all.' Marjan shook her head.

'Nonsense. That's precisely why I insist on paying. I wouldn't have that fine distinction if it was a freebie, now would I? And I'll be back, you can count on it. Well, goodbye. And thank you, young lady!' With that he left the Babylon Café, heading in the direction of the parish without a second thought to the Patrician Day Dance committee.

Marjan stuck her head outside the café door,

chuckling softly to herself as she watched Father Mahoney toddle up the rainy street, too dazed even to bother opening his umbrella. Hearing a rustling behind her in the shop, she turned around. Bahar, rumpled and woozy from the remnants of a headache-induced nap, was crossing the room towards her.

'How's your headache?'

'I've had worse. It's fine. Who was that?' Bahar asked, blinking to readjust her blurry eyes.

'Our first customer,' Marjan replied.

'Well, let's hope he's not our last.'

'He won't be.' Marjan turned back to the wet street. The funny priest receded into the horizon, but she knew he would be back soon for more of her *abgusht*. Lunchtime had been a success, as far as Marjan was concerned. Even if Father Mahoney was to be their only customer for the day.

Chapter Six

Elephant Ears

Ingredients:

1 egg
½ cup milk
¼ cup sugar
¼ cup rose water
½ tsp ground cardamom
3¾ cups all-purpose flour
6 cups vegetable oil

Garnish:
1 cup icing sugar

2 tsp ground cinnamon

'Colm Cahill and those Donnelly twins, now. They're after one thing only. Best give them the cold shoulder, Layla. They think they're God's gift, those three.'

Emer Athey's blond curls bobbed as she pointed out a group of Fifth Year boys, the same hooligans that congregated around Peter and Michael Donnelly's fermented offerings before school. It was only mid-morning break, and Layla's second day of school, but already every boy in that group was set on winning the exotic new girl's attentions.

'And steer clear of the rest of the lot there.' Emer frowned at the beefy boys, before returning to her snack of Jaffa Cake biscuits.

Fiona Athey's fiery daughter had taken Layla under her wing immediately, giving her a thorough tour of St Joseph's expansive grounds. Before its latest incarnation as a co-educational secondary school, the medieval buildings had, throughout the ages, served as a monastery, an experimental love shack for a Gallic viscount, and a shelter for unwed mothers. Emer had also introduced her to Regina Jackson, a pert redhead who wore Argyle knee-socks pulled tight over her skinny legs. Although by no means unpopular, Emer and Regina were rarely involved in the St Joseph social scene, which consisted mainly of Friday-night piss-ups and Saturday-morning football matches. Saturday afternoons spent bowling in Castlebar and the occasional traditional music *seisiún* in Westport were more to their liking.

Layla was surprised by how simple it had been for her to make such quick friends in Ballinacroagh. Emer and Regina listened attentively to Layla's concentrated version of her life story (Tehran, Lewisham and now Ballinacroagh), and Layla, in turn, appreciated their advice on boys.

'What about Malachy? Is he like them as well?' Layla asked, praying hard under her thumping heart that he wasn't. Malachy with the Sapphire Eyes had not been in any of her new classes, so she had only learned his name that day from Regina.

'Malachy McGuire? Na – though there's a bit of a surprise he came out looking and sounding the way he does, going by who his dad is,' Emer replied.

Emer, Regina and Layla watched the boy in question from under a large oak tree. Malachy was crossing the rugby field in gallant strides, deep in his own amorous thoughts, when he caught the girls looking at him. Blushing profusely, he walked towards them and waved shyly.

'What do you mean? Who's his dad?' Layla asked, her eyes still glued to Malachy.

'Don't you know? Well, you will. Thomas McGuire, the original egomaniac. Thinks he owns the town, he does. The pub next to your café is his. And the rest of the drinking holes on the Mall. That's why I go to Westport for my beer. He won't be getting my money any time soon. My mum hates his guts and isn't afraid to say so,' Emer pronounced.

Regina snorted.

'Well, she's isn't, Regina! Not when she needs to. Don't you remember the summer we both turned five, or do I have to remind you?' Emer retorted hotly. While she and her mother often had screaming matches that rang out from the salon all the way up Main Mall, Emer loved Fiona very much and was always the first to defend her against gossips.

'What happened?' Layla asked.

'He tried to buy out the salon,' said Regina, munching on a bag of prawn-flavoured crisps.

'Let him try, that feckin' gobshite!' Emer's round face turned a bright shade of magenta. Besides a streak of Athey stubbornness, Emer had inherited little else from Fiona. It was from her philandering puppeteer father that she took her Germanic features and hearty Braunschwegan appetite – endless reminders to Fiona of tangled marionette strings and an ache that seventeen years had not dulled.

'Well, he did own half of the place,' Regina muttered. She too had a deep hatred for the uncrowned king of Ballinacroagh. Her alcoholic father had lost seventy-five per cent of his farm to Thomas McGuire, after running tabs the size of the river Shannon in all three of his pubs.

Regina's good Catholic upbringing prevented her from fully expressing her resentment, though. For this she looked to Emer. Regina would often push the louder girl's buttons as a way to release her own bottled-up anger.

'Own, my feckin' foot! More like wormed his way in when no one was looking. Anyway, that was all my granddad's fault. My mum owes Thomas McGuire nothing.' Emer pouted.

By August 1974, after nearly five years of snipping thinned hairlines and nodding through endless rounds of mind-bending gossip, Fiona had finally saved enough money to buy out Thomas McGuire's shareholdings – only to discover that the man had his own plans for the beauty parlour. In a moment of unmistakable egotism, Thomas had invested half of his money (even giving the bank the deed to the Ale House and news agency), into The 10 Minute Tan – a chain of tanning salons that, as the name implied, promised ten minutes to bronzed beauty. From Cong in the south to Belmullet in the north, Thomas McGuire – with the help of the Turbo Tanner 200, a new line of sun beds straight out of the corrugated sheds of a Limerick whole-saler – was determined to bring pasty pores and blue-veined thighs out of their woollen shells. Starting with Fiona Athey's beauty parlour as his flagship tanning salon, Thomas was going to make Mayo the St Tropez of Ireland.

Underhanded wrangling and legal manœuvres followed, with the pub owner visiting Fiona daily with threats that just made the former stage queen even more determined to see her business through to the last act. She hired a big-time lawyer from Galway (one of her many admirers from her theatre days) and embarked on a defence that gave Dervla Quigley enough news to munch on for months. A week before the two parties were to meet in the county courts, tragedy struck. As a preview to sunnier days to come, Thomas had set up a tanning bed in the back of one of his quieter pubs, the Ale House, and invited the whole town to have a test run of it. Filomina Fanning, the town's librarian and most devoted church-goer, was to be the first (and last) victim of the shoddily built Turbo Tanner 200. At 8:30 a.m. Filomina walked into the Ale House white, round and heaving from the extra 146 pounds she carried on her small frame. At 8:40 a.m. she was wheeled out on a stretcher headed for Mayo General Hospital, blistered and burnt by a tanning bed turned torture chamber. The Turbo Tanner 200 was really just a large microwave gone haywire and Thomas McGuire was the eejit who had bought into it all.

'He sold my mum his share of the salon after that. Even Thomas McGuire couldn't afford to have two court cases on his head. I'd tell your sisters about him if I were you, Layla. Word's out he's got his eye on—'

'He's had his eye on that Delmonico place for years,' Regina interrupted.

'Yes, thank you, Regina. Anyway, he'll come hassling, sooner or later. Layla?'

But Layla was not listening. She was lost in Malachy McGuire's blue eyes; already too entangled in her own enchantment to heed Emer's warning.

In its first week of business, the Babylon Café could count the number of its regulars on one hand. But within a month, its daily clientele had increased to nearly two dozen, with many more hesitant customers pausing before the café windows in wonder. The glint of the samovar and the smell of frying elephant ears were reasons enough for most to step inside. For a look, at least.

Gush-e fil, or elephant ears, like their fellow fritters, are fried until golden and dripping with all things forbidden. In shape each pastry resembles a giant bow, much like farfalle pasta, but in taste it belongs to the doughnut family of treats. *Gush-e fil* is normally made in celebratory moments when the satisfaction of its simplicity is unmatched by more complicated desserts. On that day in April, Marjan had decided to make elephant ears to celebrate the good fortune that had come their way since they had moved to Ballinacroagh, nearly a month to the day. Not only were lunchtimes filled with steady orders, but the cloud that had followed Bahar around the first couple of weeks was dispersing. Who knew, Marjan thought to herself, maybe this time things were really going to work out.

Marjan smiled with contentment as she beat three eggs in a large bowl. After adding the flour, she vigorously kneaded the dough, not even minding the tenderness that the constant pushing and pulling created in her lower left shoulder. Hidden there, just at the juncture of her arm and shoulder, was a raised, one-inch scar, so silver and slight that no one could have guessed the vulgar weapon that had created it. Through the circular windows of the kitchen's swinging doors, Marjan could see Bahar taking Mrs Boylan's order, as Father Mahoney nodded in approval. The friendly priest had kept his word, returning every day for lunch, and sometimes a second time for afternoon tea with several elderly ladies in tow. The only days he hadn't shown up were Sundays, which Marjan assumed were the busiest in his line of work. Today he had brought his housekeeper and had begged Marjan to give away her elephant ears recipe, so that Mrs Boylan could replicate the doughy treats whenever he had a midnight craving. More than happy to lend out her expertise, Marjan found a green index card and wrote in neat, round letters:

ELEPHANT EARS

Roll dough out on a clean surface with a floured pin until it is paper-thin. Using the rim of a wide-mouthed glass or cup, trace and cut out a circle. Pinch the centre of each circle with your thumb and forefinger to form a bow. Set aside. Repeat until all circles (approx. 30) are done.

'That priest of yours is really funny. Did you know that they're allowed to drink, these priests? No women, but alcohol is fine!' Bahar walked in waving Father Mahoney's order. Her usually skittish eyes were bright and – dared Marjan hope? – happy.

'They drink beer like water here. Last Saturday I saw an entire family, with young kids, leaving the bar next door. At eleven at night!' Marjan replied with awe. She read Father Mahoney's order:

1. pot of Darjeeling x 2
2. bread and cheese platter
3. 1 chicken salad
4. 1 *abgusht*

137

'Certainly likes the *abgusht*, doesn't he? It's the fifth time he's ordered it this week.' Bahar shook her head in amazement. She enjoyed *abgusht* like the best of them, but too much made her feel sluggish.

'Father Mahoney's raved about it to everyone. The shopkeeper at the mini-mart told me this morning that "his Finnegan" – I think that's his son – had heard all about us. He was wondering if we do take-away packages! If this keeps up we'll be out of debt in no time!' Marjan said cheerily.

Besides Father Mahoney and Mrs Boylan, the regular lunchtime crowd in the Babylon consisted of Evie Watson and Fiona Athey. It wasn't only Father Mahoney's praises that had drawn the two hairdressers inside, but three days of intense curiosity heightened by the smells of fried elephant ears and cinnamon-roasted walnuts. The perfume blew into the beauty salon on the ocean breeze, creeping through the door's crevices and floating above the bouffant hairdos and hairspray fumes. Evie and Fiona sat at one of the window-side tables now, each drinking her own bowl of red lentil soup as vague ruminations – prompted by Marjan's magic – swam in their heads: Evie could see neon pink letters spelling out her name over the salon's door, while Fiona imagined hers lighting up a theatre marquee once again.

Even the elderly ladies of the Patrician Day Dance committee had heard Father Mahoney's descriptions of the sweet, exotic pastries and teas to be had at the Babylon Café. Forgoing their usual meat and two veg lunches at the Wilton Inn, they now sat at the café's long communal table before platters of minty chicken salad and bowls of sweet onion soup.

Unlike her sister Marie, Dervla Quigley never took part in these girlie lunches. She considered Father Mahoney's absence from their first committee meeting as a personal affront to her already overwrought dignity, and officially moved her vigil to the Thomas McGuire camp. Upon Thomas's request, Dervla was to continue her watch over the café and report back to him daily on the exact nature of the Babylon's epicurean operations. Thomas wanted to know the types of food supplies that were being bought and delivered, the start of each day's lunchtime rush, and the average turnover of tables, hoping to pinpoint in such rudimentary details the mysterious alchemy behind so many diners' glowing smiles and rounded, satisfied bellies. Excited by her new patrol, Dervla bought a small spiral notebook and with her claw-like fingers wrote down the name of every soul who walked in and out of the café, even recording the times when Marjan opened the windows or Bahar crossed the street for the butcher's. In addition to ranting from her bedroom window, the old gossip dialled every parishioner in her tattered address book and repeated the same indignant spiel: 'There's no tellin' what's in that food. Unhygienic, I'd say. Down right dirty. Babylon Café! Sinful, that's what it is!'

Orders slowed down after lunch, giving Marjan the opportunity to finish the last batch of elephant ears. The morning tray was already sold out, gobbled up by schoolchildren who had given up their usual penny sweets runs for the flaky pastries. Soon, afternoon-tea junkies and the occasional passerby would once again wipe the silver platters clean of her baklava, fried *zulbia*, waffle-like window cookies and elephant ears, so she had to be ready.

Marjan plunged two pinched elephant ears into a deep pan of hot oil for thirty seconds, and then transferred them with a slotted spoon to a sheet of kitchen paper. Beads of excess oil dripped luxuriously off each pastry and were instantly swallowed by the thirsty paper towels. When the entire batch cooled, she sprinkled the glistening ears with a mixture of sugar and cinnamon that made her nose tickle. Ever since childhood, Marjan had adored these fried pastries. After all, she thought, a little oil every now and again never hurt anyone. Not unless you were standing too close to the pan, that is.

Malachy McGuire waited five weeks before he roused the courage to ask Layla for a date. The young man proposed a walk along the hilly roads leading to Clew Bay Beach, holding out his hand and locking Layla in his jewel-toned gaze. Sitting atop the crest of a high dune, the teenagers masked their timid hand-holding in the long sea grass as they watched the effervescent tide and felt the warm, powdery sand beneath their heated bodies.

Layla stole a shy peek at the boy sitting next to her. Was he going to make the first move, she wondered, or should she take the helm? And what if he did try something? What would she do then? She could feel droplets of sweat dampen her school uniform and trickle between her breasts, settling in her belly button. Her cinnamon–rose perfume was growing denser by the second, emanating from her flushed skin in heady waves. Hoping Malachy hadn't noticed her growing blush, Layla turned her face away from the boy and pointed up towards Croagh Patrick, which was staring down on them with grandfatherly approval.

'That's a beautiful mountain. Such a perfect triangle,' she squeaked.

'That old heap? It's nothing special. Nothing like the places you've been. What was your old home like?' Malachy inched closer.

'England?'

'No – Iran. Isn't that a very dangerous place?'

Layla's almond eyes were suddenly very far away. She slipped her hand out of Malachy's and planted it deep in the sandy mound next to her, as if to steady herself.

Now it was Malachy's turn to blush hotly. He certainly knew how to stick his foot in his big gob, didn't he? What was he thinking of, asking such personal questions? Maybe she didn't want to talk about Iran; maybe she was just humouring him by coming here; maybe he should apologise – midway through his consternation came the kiss. It was a quick one, on the lips, but it still counted.

'Oh,' Malachy whispered, his voice cracking with pleasure. He returned Layla's soft kiss, drawing her against his thumping chest as he inhaled her cinnamon–rose scent.

Malachy's warm arms were a cushion of comfort for Layla's confused emotions. What was wrong with her? she wondered. Was she ashamed of Iran, of being Iranian? Was that why she had cut Malachy off so abruptly? He only wanted to know about her childhood home; there was nothing complicated in that, was there? This boy with the beautiful sapphire eyes wasn't afraid of her foreignness, he wouldn't judge her for the violent country of her birth. But what should she tell him exactly? Where to start?

Prickles shot up her right arm. Her hand had fallen asleep. Lifting it off the sand, Layla noticed the impression her palm had made in the white powder. A perfect handprint. The deep fate lines engraved in her palm, the forked markers of destiny, rose in curving ridges of sand across the hollow. She lightly traced the lines with her finger, feeling a shiver of recognition run down her spine, other sets of handprints suddenly clouding her mind.

The night they left Tehran for ever was a September night like no other. It was still the twilight of summer, but the anorexic trees outside had already shed themselves of all delusions, scattering their leaves on the pavement below. From their kitchen window, on the fourteenth floor of the decaying apartment complex they lived in, a then seven-year-old Layla had watched the sun set behind the neighbourhood mosque; its brilliant turquoise dome changing into a mystical, deep lapis in the gathering dusk. There had been no wailing of bedtime prayers that night, no ardent devotions blaring from the mosque's high minaret. In fact, there had been no prayers at all since Friday. Even the usual gunfire had died down, with only a sporadic *rat-tat-tat* coming from the former South Street Bazaar. Most of the neighbourhood's revolutionaries were holed up in the empty Bazaar; they had been there ever since the Imperial Guards gunned down demonstrators in Jaleh Square. Only three days had passed since the students, marching peacefully against the Shah's regime, had been greeted by indiscriminate military bullets. Thousands had met their immediate death, falling on the pale stone ground of the open square.

Layla glanced down the street towards the Bazaar, before turning her attention to the flow of blood, still seeping, still weeping its way along their leafy boulevard. The bloody handprints were spattered all over the dirty pavement, bright and fresh, though the hands that had been raised to the cause were long gone. Several handprints were even slapped on house walls, the blood dripping from the bases of palms like new sets of fingers. The red rivulets seeped into the pavement cracks, greeting their compatriots on the ground with a shake, a wave of defiance that acknowledged the mutual source of their misery. Jaleh Square, only ten blocks away from their apartment.

Black Friday, they were calling the massacre, but all Layla could see was red. Red everywhere.

'Bahar, can I go to school tomorrow?' Layla asked, even though she already knew the answer. There would be no school tomorrow; there had been no school for many days. That was what *martial law* meant, Marjan had explained to her. That was what the Shah had declared, sending his Imperial Guards, the 'Immortals', to scour the streets, looking for radicals and the odd, confused Communist.

'Stop asking me stupid questions and get down from that chair! Do you want someone to shoot you?' Bahar pushed Layla off her perch. As she pulled the flowery curtain across the window, her headscarf slipped, revealing a crusty cut near her right ear. The skin around the wound was blotchy and jaundiced, matching the purple and yellow stains on Bahar's forehead and cheeks. Bruises. Layla couldn't help staring at them.

'Stay in the living room until Marjan comes home,' Bahar commanded. 'I hope to God she got our passports,' she said, more to herself than to Layla, as she returned to the hot stove.

'But I'm hungry,' Layla complained. She eyed the pan of pomegranate soup that Bahar was stirring.

'You're such a brat. Marjan could be caught by the Guards by now and all you can think about is your own greedy stomach. Move it!' Bahar whacked her wooden spoon against the pan.

Layla stifled her tears and padded out of the kitchen. She hadn't thought about Marjan being out on the bloody streets past curfew. What if Bahar was right and Marjan had been caught by the Imperial Guards? What if she never came back and Layla would have to live alone with Bahar for ever?

Saltwater blurred Layla's eyes and landed on her tongue, as she crept through the hallway towards her favourite hiding place, the pantry where Marjan stored her dry goods and spices. She opened the wicker door and slipped into the comforting darkness, touching the wooden shelves, the grains and powders asleep in their jars. Reaching behind a tall terracotta jug, Layla's little fingers clasped the familiar glass container of *sumac*. The ground-up product of the astringent *Rhus* berry, *sumac* was a brick-red spice that Marjan used sparingly on her kebab dishes. Layla would sneak into the pantry at least once a day, more when she was feeling particularly sad, to scoop some of the lemony spice into her puckered mouth. She was reaching for her second scoop when she heard Bahar scream.

It was a primitive jungle holler. A bloodcurdling howl that was suddenly cut short by a terrifying blow. To Layla's young ears, it sounded like the pounding of *kubideh* – the tender kebab meat Marjan flattened with a mallet, hitting the beef over and over until it sighed, finally defeated. The hammering grew louder and more frequent.

The shadowy spices jumped in their jars around her, mimicking Layla's own lurching, acidy stomach. She clenched the lump of *sumac* tightly in her fists, so tightly that the sour powder began to burn her palms. Suddenly, a high-octave cry broke from within the pantry's suffocating walls, shocking her tender senses, for she was the one screaming.

She never heard the pounding stop, her cries were so loud. She didn't hear the soft feminine sobs outside the pantry walls, or even sense Marjan seeking her out in the darkness. When her eldest sister finally rescued her from the over-turned jars of dry fava beans and quince-lime syrup, Layla's eyes and ears were welded shut in agony.

'Shhhh . . . Layla *joon*. *Joon-e man*. Shhh . . . don't cry.' Marjan stood in the kitchen holding Layla in her arms, kissing her face and *sumac*-tainted fists. With her wet lids anointed by her sister's kisses, Layla felt safe enough to finally open her eyes. The mangled body lying on the kitchen floor made her wish she had kept them closed.

Legs clothed in dark men's trousers lay spread apart on the linoleum. Bony, boyish ankles, matured by irregular tufts of black hair, met a pair of green army boots caked in mud. A dark, thick liquid seeped from beneath the thin calves, spreading so quickly that it momentarily lifted the man on its surge, before engulfing the body in its crimson flow. Layla's eyes followed the sharp crease ironed into the man's rigid trousers, the cheap gabardine kind worn by street vendors. Her gaze settled on his thin, splayed knees just as Marjan showered her tear-stained eyes with kisses once again.

Fourteen flights of crumbling stairs never went by so quickly, Layla remembered thinking with surprise. Any other day and her sisters would have scolded her for jumping two steps at a time, but Marjan and Bahar skipped three and four steps themselves on their way down to the street. The fallen leaves and bloody handprints were underfoot, but Layla kept her gaze on the night sky as she held tightly on to her sisters' clammy palms. Marjan's face was outlined by her black chador, ashen, yet determined, her other hand lugging a heavy suitcase. Bahar was to Layla's right, her full-length robe and veil covering everything but her bloodshot eyes, which blinked rapidly with fear. Neither said a word to Layla, not when they reached the end of their neighbourhood walls, not when they crossed the vacant railway lines, not even when they made it to Tehran's Bus Terminal, which was teeming with other suitcase-carrying, silent chador-framed faces, and climbed on board the bus heading for the East.

East, to the lawless town of Zahedan, a den of opiate dealers set on a scrap of transitory land, a trepidation of shifting sands. Iran's Dasht-e Lut desert, the province of tribal lords, with their lifeblood of camels, carpets and caravans. And the last stop before the Pakistan border.

The bus dropped them off at the edge of Zahedan, where several Baluchi tribal men were busy setting up their night's camp. Each of the camp's twenty tents was lined with hand-woven *kilims*, the brightly coloured carpets extending beyond the lips of oilcloths and canvas openings. A few of the men loaned them a tent, hitching it up as their womenfolk spooned *mast-o khiar*, their traditional yogurt and cucumber soup, into earthen bowls. The cooling liquid soothed Layla's dry throat and brought some welcome colour back to both Marjan and Bahar's faces.

Still, good as it was, the yogurt and cucumber soup did not loosen her sisters' tongues. Nothing was said about what had happened back there, in the middle of their apartment's kitchen floor, in the midst of a revolution, deep into a Tehran night.

'Jaysus.' Malachy whistled under his breath. 'Did your sisters ever tell you what happened that night? Who that man was in the kitchen?'

Layla shook her head, unable to speak for the lump in her throat. She did find out, eventually, but that story wasn't ripe for the telling. Maybe she shouldn't have shared so much with Malachy, but she needed to confide in someone after all these years of silence.

'Don't worry, Layla. You're safe here in Ireland. With me,' Malachy said tenderly. There were still many questions he wanted to ask, but sensing a peculiar sadness stirring within her, he instead put his arms protectively around Layla and kissed her again.

Though she felt the burning sensation of love more than ever, Layla's mood remained solemn. Her mouth puckered up again, the tissue in her cheeks remembering a sourer time; the taste of *sumac* suddenly everywhere.

Chapter Seven

Lavash Bread

Ingredients:

1 tbsp quick-rising yeast
½ cup warm water
¼ cup olive oil
1 cup milk
2 tbsp sugar
2 tsp salt
4 cups all-purpose flour
½ cup poppy and sesame seeds

Thomas wasn't terribly surprised when he finally heard that his youngest son was cavorting with one of those 'foreigners'. Dervla Quigley had seen him strutting down Main Mall in broad daylight, no less, hand in hand with that darkie girl.

Shameless, good-for-nothing gobshite, that Malachy. It was just like him to dip his toe into bog scum, Thomas thought to himself. Probably going back to his own bleedin' kind, for all he knew. Because, self-assured as he was, Thomas wasn't blind to the obvious: Malachy, with his unnatural mop of black curls and a tongue that named major constellations before ever sputtering a reluctant *Da-Da* or *Mam*, was not like the rest of his children. If Thomas could have attributed Malachy's tall frame and razor-sharp intelligence to his wife's genes, then maybe he could look at the boy without needing to punch something. But squat Cecilia, with her flat features, brittle blond hair and triple chins, was as different from Malachy as Thomas was. Like it or not, he had to admit that his suspicions about the summer of 1967 were correct.

Just around that time, Thomas had been busy expanding his empire with a second pub on Main Mall. While he was knee-deep in the new Ale House's punctured septic tank, a boatload of swarthy Andalucian fishermen had surreptitiously docked in Clew Bay Beach. The frisky Spaniards had come up from Galway, mistaking Clew Bay for the Aran Islands after a drunken night of poteen poker. Their two-ton fishing boat hit a sharp limestone shelf, driving a foot-wide hole into the *Hermosa*'s oak belly, and leaving the fishermen no choice but to camp out on the beach while they patched up their ruptured vessel. Other than a few food and *vino* runs, the Spanish sailors kept to themselves on the beach, so Thomas had no major complaints. It wasn't until a week after the seamen left for their sunny homeland that the bar owner began to notice an unusually sated smile on his wife's face. Only then did he detect the strange smell of crayfish that had crept into every corner of his house, and notice for the first time the strings of seaweed that floated curiously into tubs and basins whenever he turned on the water taps. And then a dark-haired Malachy arrived eight months later, premature and completely alien.

Feckin' foreigners, thought Thomas, laying their filthy paws on what was rightfully his. And now it was happening all over again. Not only was his so-called son blatantly disobeying orders by stepping foot in that stinking café, but he was also shagging one of those Arabs as well. All behind his back. Just like his cheating mother, that Malachy.

Determined to give the young man a fine bollixing, Thomas sent his eldest son, Tom Junior, to fetch his wayward brother. It was a charge that the sadistic bully-in-training carried out with the utmost glee, as he had little love in his small heart for Malachy. Marked since infancy by their differing constitutions, the McGuire boys never shared anything minutely resembling a brotherly bond. Malachy did not understand Tom Junior's penchant for pub piss-ups and violent martial arts films, and Tom Junior hated how the younger boy buried himself in his books and telescope, with that faraway smile like he knew something the rest of them didn't; as if the pub life was below him. He couldn't wait to see what their father had planned for the bloody bastard. Tom Junior chuckled cruelly to himself, as he pounded down Main Mall. He found Malachy in Fadden's Mini-Mart, engrossed in a conversation with the shop owner on the origins of fairies.

'You see, lad, each country has its own race of fairy folk. No two fairies are alike. Anywhere,' said Danny sagely, pushing his thick glasses up the bridge of his bulbous nose.

'Are there fairies in Iran?' Malachy asked, with a twinkle in his eyes.

'Oh, yes. The Peries of Persia. Lovely little things with wings. Mind you, you can't see them with the human eye, but they're there. Like to roam the forests looking for perfumed flowers.'

'Fairies! Should've known it'd be the sort of thing yer into,' Tom Junior cut in with a harsh laugh from just inside the mini-mart's door.

Malachy glared at his brother in silence, though he was surprised to hear Tom Junior address him. Weeks could go by without either of them saying a word to each other, and when necessity called for one of them to speak, it was usually Tom Junior coming at him with a biting insult.

'Move it, gobshite. Dad wants ya at the Ale House.'

'What for?'

'Just get yer arse down there now, ye poofter!' Tom Junior bellowed.

Malachy turned to Danny Fadden, who was cowering behind a stack of Bisto gravy packets on the counter. 'Sorry, Mr Fadden. I'll be back soon to hear more about those Persian fairies.'

'Take your time, lad,' Danny whispered meekly.

Tom trailed Malachy up to the Ale House, muttering insults with every step. A furious Thomas was sitting in a booth at the back of the bar waiting for them both.

'Here now, boy-o,' he sneered, rising from his seat. 'What's this I hear about you and that Arab whore?'

Tom Junior grinned uncontrollably behind Malachy's back. The McGuire money was as good as his now. No chance of any of the pubs going into Malachy's hands when their dad finally croaked.

'She's Iranian, not Arab. And don't you ever call her a whore or I'll—'

'Or you'll what? You better watch who yer talkin' to, boy! And I'll tell you something else, whore or not she's still the enemy. Her and her darkie sisters. They're stealin' what feeds that gob of yours nightly, and I better not see you anywhere near them.' Thomas's face was so close that Malachy could count the burst capillaries on his slack, beetroot-red cheeks. The boy stood his ground and narrowed his eyes, even as his father threatened him with his shaking fists.

'What's with the sudden interest in what I do? Didn't think you even knew I was alive,' Malachy pushed.

'Another word out of you and yer going to wish you were dead. Am I making meself clear?'

Thomas had certainly made himself clear, but his threats wouldn't stop Malachy from seeing Layla every day after school. After all, his defiance was just further evidence of the independent streak that had marked him from birth. Malachy knew the future held greater things in store for him than nights of coughing up tar and misery in one of his father's pubs. He was going to catch Orion from under an Arizona desert sky, and watch as Cassiopeia danced over Norwegian fjords. And he was going to do it all with Layla by his side.

It was as much of a proposal as an eighteen-year-old could make, and for her part, Layla agreed wholeheartedly to a lifetime of thrilling adventures with Malachy. Neither mentioned their future plans to Bahar and Marjan though, when, two weeks after their first date, Layla introduced him to her sisters. Dressed in a formal button-up shirt and school jacket, Malachy came by the café after closing time. Seated at the round kitchen table, the young man was alternately discouraged by Bahar's unresponsive eyes and heartened by Marjan's warm food.

'Layla tells us you're an astronomy buff. Is that what you want to study after school?' Marjan flashed Malachy an encouraging smile as she handed him a cup of oolong tea.

Malachy nodded. 'I'd like to take a year off and travel first,' he said. 'See the world.'

'Travel?' Bahar said, sharply. She squinted

disapprovingly at Malachy, her lips pressed in a hard line.

Marjan shot Bahar a reproachful look.

'Malachy loves your plants in the back garden, Marjan,' Layla offered, rescuing the awkward moment.

'It's a grand-looking garden,' Malachy said. 'Astronomy and gardening aren't that different, when you think about it. Mythically speaking.'

And with that inspired observation, Malachy charmed his way into Marjan's heart. A few minutes later he found himself standing at the kitchen island with Layla, peeling onion skins and sifting through piles of basmati rice for Marjan's *chelow*. The young man had never known there to be such joy in cooking, subjected as he was to the gristly pork sausages and limp carrots of his usual home meals. Marjan, the eternal gardener, was only too happy to answer his questions on the fickle nature of Irish top soil and the medicinal uses of sweet basil leaves. Together they spent the afternoon detailing the similarities between the heavens above and the earth below, marvelling at the diverse palette of creation. Bahar remained silent throughout the boy's visit, but it did not go unnoticed by anyone in the room that she got up to refill Malachy's teacup not once, but twice.

After Malachy left, with a good amount of *zulbia* packed in his school bag, Layla turned to Bahar and Marjan, unable to hide her excitement any longer.

'Well? Isn't he beautiful? Do you like him?'

'He's wonderful, Layla! Your first boyfriend! And those eyes, my goodness! He reminds me of a boy I knew in school. Before the revolution, of course. He had green eyes,' Marjan said, wistfully.

She stopped wiping the kitchen island and stared dreamily into space as she thought of Ali, the green-eyed boy of her youth. Such thoughts were usually limited to private moments when Marjan could sneak into the flat's tiny blue bathroom and lock the door behind her. Reaching into the upper shelf of a four-tiered medicine cabinet the Delmonicos had bought on their Moroccan honeymoon, Marjan would gingerly remove a small wooden jewellery box carved with beautiful desert roses. Inside she kept a few golden trinkets and the childhood identity bracelets given to them by their father. The box's rose satin lining was worn in spots and grains of sand had become embedded in the dark wood, reminders of their flight through the Dasht-e Lut desert.

Settling on the covered toilet seat, Marjan would pull a faded photo out from beneath the jewellery. The picture, now slightly yellowed and crinkled at the edges, was taken on a school field trip to Istanbul. Her senior class had caught a ferry on the Black Sea shore, arriving in Istanbul just as the sun was setting over the city's Grand Covered Bazaar. Ali had led her through the Grand Bazaar's labyrinthine aisles, past insistent *bazaari* hocking their wares, clusters of carpet stalls, and tents filled with copper serving trays and brassy samovars. At the centre of the Grand Bazaar sat the jewellers' booths, piled high with gems and stones that would eventually be brought home by eager husbands. It was in one of these bejewelled stalls, alongside a line of half-priced, multicoloured bangles on a low table, that

Marjan first saw the wooden jewellery box. Although humble in appearance, to her the jewellery case looked like it could hold all the treasures of the Magi. On the ferry heading back home to Iran, Ali surprised Marjan with the small box, and made her promise to keep a picture of him always tucked inside its satin pockets.

For ten years Marjan had kept that promise. Whenever she felt like breaking down, she would cling to the fading photograph of Ali, sitting there in his white polyester shirt and frayed bell-bottom jeans, with the Turkish sun in his eyes. He was smiling then, life pulsing through his beautiful body. But of course, Marjan reminded herself, that was before the revolution, before everything changed.

Unaware that her two sisters were witnessing her tender reminiscence, Marjan smiled sadly at the cleaning rag in her hand. Bahar's stern voice brought her out of herself and she blushed for her indulgence.

'Well, he's smart, I suppose. But that still doesn't mean you're ready for a boyfriend, Layla.

You're fifteen, for God's sake! Still a child!' Bahar slammed the kitchen table with opened palms. 'Besides, we haven't even been here two months. Certainly not enough time to start trusting people.' She pushed her chair away from the table and walked tiredly up the stairs. Her left hand gripped her temples, the right held tightly on to the banister. 'I'm going to lie down. It's in your hands now, Marjan.'

'Don't worry,' Marjan whispered, sensing that Bahar's pessimism had dimmed Layla's excitement. 'She'll come around. Did you see how she offered Malachy another helping of baklava when she thought we weren't looking?'

Layla nodded slowly, but Bahar's sadness was infectious; she could taste its metallic flavour in her mouth. Still, no matter how much Bahar's neurotic behaviour aggravated her, Layla understood why her sister was so anxious, so untrusting.

'Marjan?'

'Yes, *joon-e man?*'

'Whatever happened to that boy with the green eyes?'

'We just lost touch after Baba died, when we

166

moved to the south. These things happen sometimes.' There was no point in telling Layla the
truth now, Marjan thought. Best to spare her the
details.

Javid Aminpour died not long after that senior
class trip to Istanbul, more of a lonely heart than
from the attack doctors diagnosed. He was happy
at last, joining their mother where she lay in
Zahirodoleh cemetery, but for Marjan it was more
tragedy than she could bear. At seventeen, she
became sole guardian of fourteen-year-old Bahar
and baby Layla, who hadn't even turned five yet.
Their great-aunt Homa, cousin Mitra and the
rest of their closest relatives had heeded the
sinister winds of an oncoming revolution, and
escaped to a land of endless sunshine and fertile
valleys – California. With no family to take them
in, Marjan was forced to sell their childhood
home and move into a small apartment on the
southern edge of Tehran, where the pristine
Alborz mountains were obscured by the New
City, a rampant brothel settlement only a few
blocks away. Marjan took a job washing dishes

at the Hilton Hotel's famed Peacock Restaurant, and it was there that she picked up the tricks of the trade while cleaning up the chefs' messes. Two years would pass before she saw Ali again, this time in the laboratory rooms of Tehran University, where she was studying for her degree, cramming classes in between restaurant shifts.

Marjan had been in the lab for half an hour, legs stretched across the stool in front of her, hands cupping her chin. She was listening to the splat of the city rain outside and trying hard to ignore the rapid germination taking place on the slide under her microscope. There was nothing affirming about Molecular Parasitology, Marjan decided. She abhorred the slaughterous trails of cannibalistic cells, their lack of compassion, the endless specimen slides. Studying Botany had been her first choice, but Botany wasn't going to put food on the table, or uniforms on Bahar and Layla's backs.

Closing her left eye, Marjan squinted through the microscope once again. When she lifted her head she found Ali staring at her in disbelief. He was standing in the laboratory-room doorway with transfer papers in hand, his light brown hair shorn tightly at the sides. He had grown a beard, which bristled against Marjan's face as she buried herself in his chest.

Not long after their reunion in the university lab, Ali introduced Marjan to the revolutionary students who comprised his circle of friends. They were beginning to distribute their own underground newspaper, *The Voice*, printed in the basement of Ali's uncle's house with a rotary printing press from the era of Reza Shah, a time of complete stupidity and ignorance, Ali explained to her. And now his idiot son was squeezing the country dry and senseless. Claiming an improbable connection to the great Zoroastrian rulers of the Persian Empire, the short Shah crowned himself King of Kings, and robbed the last shreds of dignity from the Persian people. As most of his subjects rotted away in mud huts devoid of electricity and proper sewage, barely existing on pittance wages, the Shah filled his coffers with American-bought weaponry, African diamonds and Parisian furs, financing it all with the land's vital organ, oil. But they weren't going to let him get away with his pillage, Ali told her. Did she want to join him in his journey to freedom?

At first Marjan found Ali's radicalism frightening. She felt especially uncomfortable around the girls in his group, whose grey, unmade-up faces and black chadors were so different from the rest of the women on campus who preferred liberal coats of lipstick and swinging miniskirts. Marjan couldn't see how covering herself would better society, but she soon came to accept it as one of the many facets of the new Iran they were all dreaming of. Taking up the chador was too drastic a change for her, but she did stop wearing miniskirts and make-up, and covered her hair with a *roosarie*, a head scarf of dark colours. For his part, Ali made no comment on the addition to her wardrobe. He just smiled his beautiful smile. He never pressured her, but merely coaxed her with those eyes. Soon enough, Marjan was in the middle of it all, writing and printing revolutionary articles for *The Voice*, organising weekly meetings, painting banners and stuffing straw effigies of Uncle Sam in the newspaper's underground offices, all the time not realising the consequences, the inevitable price of her involvement. For unbeknownst to Marjan, her world was about to break open, bursting and bleeding like the rich yolk of quail eggs cracked over a hot skillet.

Late one spring morning in 1978, as she was arranging typesets on the ageing printing press, an axe broke through the basement door and immediately reduced it to splinters. Marjan later remembered feeling thankful that no bullets were fired, as Ali's desk was close to the door and he would certainly have been hit. How naïve of her really, to give such quick thanks, to have such belief. She made a desperate play for the telephone on her desk, but the handcuffs were quicker. The cold metal sliced into her soft flesh, its invincible clutch claiming the futility of goodbyes. There would be no calling home from where she was going.

The rough blindfold was yanked over her face, strangling her eyes. The final glimpse Marjan had, before the light was extinguished by the dark rag, was the back of Ali's shorn head. It was the last time she ever saw him.

Gohid Detention Centre. A maze of interconnecting injustices, where the walls were covered in shame. A temporary ground where revolutionaries were taken by the Shah's secret police, slated either for a quick death or for days of torture and mind-bending interrogations. If, God forbid, you ever find yourself inside Gohid's walls, Ali had once warned her, don't say a word. Don't tell them anything, Marjan.

A hand grabbed Marjan's neck and led her, still blindfolded, deep into the detention centre's subterranean levels. These floors, assigned to female revolutionaries, were hollow-sounding and smelled of kerosene and burning skin. A high-pitched wail echoed in the distance, then faded. Countless footsteps and metal hinges clanged, doors opened and slammed shut. Then, suddenly, the black blindfold was ripped away and the iron door of her cell was bolted behind her.

Marjan's pupils slowly adjusted to the harsh

light; a naked bulb dangled on a chain in the centre of the cell, shining on rough brown walls that curved in a semi-circle from the door. A strange, slobbering creature sat slumped in one corner on a straw mat. At first, Marjan thought her eyes were playing tricks on her, because the leering woman was an almost identical twin to her cousin Mitra. Or, rather, she could have been her cousin had Mitra spent the better part of her life hopping beds in flea-infested brothels.

Khanoum Zanganeh was a rather jovial prostitute whose body rose in bumps where fat had accumulated and then sunk into bony, hungry areas that were black and blue with bruises. She was dressed in a tattered black shirt and red miniskirt whose sequins she picked at for entertainment.

'Welcome to the Palace!' she chortled. She patted the stony ground next to her. 'Sit, sit!' When Marjan did not move, the prostitute narrowed her eyes and pursed her lips. 'Who do you work for? No, don't tell me – you're one of Toothless Taraneh's girls, aren't you?'

Marjan swallowed hard and slid down to the

floor, closing her eyes. Frenzied thoughts looped through her head as she pictured her sisters waiting for her back at the apartment. Who would make them dinner if she wasn't there? What would happen to Bahar and Layla if she didn't make it out of this terrifying place? How could she have been so stupid, getting involved with Ali and his friends? Curling her knees up to her chin, she laid her head in her arms and began sobbing deeply. Thankfully, Khanoum Zanganeh had stopped her alcoholic banter, leaving Marjan room to mourn her fate alone. She cried for most of the night, never looking up from her arms until the cell door was thrust open once again.

A yellow-skinned, big-boned woman dressed in military fatigues strode into the cell, her heavy boots pounding the damp concrete. She wound a woollen blindfold tightly around Marjan's eyes, her breath stinking of cheap fried meats and stewed okra. Two sets of muscular hands painfully clasped under her armpits and dragged her through the crumbling corridors, her feet skimming over cracked tiles, then tumbling down steep stairs to lower, denser levels. Soon a stool was shoved under her, and grating male voices knocked around her head and body.

What was your role in the newspaper? Who is this Ali you're working for? What were you planning to do with all this propaganda?

The booming voices echoed over and under her like an earthquake.

Your boyfriend Ali is in for a good, long bleeding session if you don't talk. Did you hear me? Your little editor is going to rot in here! Did we tell you about his accident? No? We didn't tell you how he tripped over his own shit and knocked his ugly eye out? All because of your disgusting deeds. We know what you did already!

The laughter of animals in heat, panting, and the smell of sweat surrounded her. Someone touched her breasts then, cupping them in his grubby palms, before tweaking her nipples so painfully that she was forced to break her silence with a gasp.

Tell me, which would you like more, your pimp's lips or that sausage of his you love to eat so regularly? We know what your real occupation is, Khanoum Journalist!

175

She remained silent amidst the roaring voices, remembering Ali's advice. Don't say anything, Marjan, she told herself. Don't say a word about Ali or *The Voice*, and for God's sake, don't tell them about Bahar and Layla, waiting back at the apartment, all alone. It was the same routine, every day, for an hour; a volley of violent groping and unanswered questions, after which the voices threw her back into her cell, unable to be satisfied. Not even starvation – a denial of her daily rations of water, *lavash* bread and rancid sheep's cheese – would induce Marjan to speak.

'Khanoum Aminpour, take this piece of *lavash* bread from me. Go on, don't be shy! I've the fat to stave the hunger, believe me.'

The stale piece of *lavash* bread crumbled in Khanoum Zanganeh's hand. When Marjan finally accepted the rationed food, the weathered prostitute settled back against the cell wall and told her how she had come to be arrested by the Shah's secret police.

'The bastards think I know something about the Committee. Me! What do I know about these political things? I'm just a whore with good teeth!'

Marjan had heard about the infamous Committee, a militant minority that had ballooned seemingly overnight, bringing with it a plethora of undernourished beards and a hunger for vengeance against the capricious Shah and his supporters. Fundamentally inclined, this rag-tag group of Islamic vigilantes answered only to the Turbaned One, the exiled ayatollah with all the answers, as they set about intimidating local neighbourhoods in the name of God. Although the Committee was the most powerful organisation to emerge in the last year, it still held loose associations to many revolutionary movements, especially those involving university students. Friends of Ali's, supporters of *The Voice*. The Committee.

'Don't worry,' Khanoum Zanganeh continued, cocking her henna-coloured head towards the cell door. 'You'll be out of here in no time. The secret police have no patience for women. It's the men they want.'

Somehow, Marjan knew then and there that

she'd never see Ali again. She had been mistaken about so much, got involved in a business she didn't really understand, didn't really want a part of. And for what? For love? Was that it? How could she have bartered safety for a taste of romance?

By the time she was released from Gohid four days later, thrown out of an unmarked van with a kick of disgust, Marjan had an excuse lined up for her disappearance. She would tell Bahar and Layla that an emergency had kept her from calling them, maybe a fire in The Peacock Restaurant's kitchens. She'd tell them that she had been injured – only a slight burn, nothing major – and had spent the last four days in the hospital, recovering. And then she'd take her sisters and run. They would go to America, to California. Do anything to get there. Sell everything and try for new lives, away from this revolution, this murdering. Just go.

But she was too late. By the time Marjan got home, the revolution had already begun.

Khanoum Aminpour, take this piece of lavash *bread from me.*

178

Eight years on, and the memory of the old prostitute's kind offering still set Marjan's stomach rumbling with unexplainable hunger. And, as much as she loved the smell of baking *lavash* bread, she couldn't deny the hint of dread she felt each time she rolled out the dough for a new batch.

Marjan bent over the wooden work island in the café's kitchen, the soft morning light illuminating her floury hands as they kneaded the tough dough before her. There was definitely something wrong with her technique today, she thought to herself. No matter how much she pushed and prodded the white mass of yeasty flour, it kept catching in chalky clumps beneath her fingers.

'Hello there? Anybody home?' The sing-song voice behind her gave Marjan a start. The unlocked back door creaked open slowly to reveal Fiona Athey, with an apologetic look on her face. She was holding a stack of fliers under her left arm. 'I hope I didn't wake you up, now? I'll come back another time, then. Sorry.' She turned to leave.

'No, stay,' Marjan replied. 'I've been up since

five. Making a new batch of bread. Why don't you come in for a cup of tea?'

'I couldn't.'

'Don't be silly. Please. I could use the break.'

'All right then. Just for one cup so, and then I'll let you go,' Fiona said, closing the back door behind her.

Wiping her floury hands with a chequered tea towel, Marjan placed the kneaded dough back in its bowl and covered it with a clean cheese-cloth. She was glad to be free of its memories, even for a little while. While Fiona settled into one of the window-side tables, Marjan measured three big tablespoons of Darjeeling leaves into a pretty yellow teapot. The samovar was already bubbling away happily when she pushed its lever down to release boiling water into the pot. Fiona Athey, who had befriended many an Eastern-European travelling troupe in her Galway theatre days, recognised the shiny electric water boiler instantly.

'That's a Russian-made samovar, isn't it?'

'Yes. How did you know?' Marjan was surprised.

'I haven't always lived in Ballinacroagh. I was an actress once. Met a lot of performers from all over the world in my day,' replied Fiona, smiling proudly.

'How exciting! And have you done anything lately?' Marjan said, filling a platter with elephant ears, *zulbia* and almond delights.

'I stopped right after my Emer was born. At the time I thought leaving the theatre was what I wanted, but now I realise my mistake. I threw away so many years, so much of what I loved for a man.' Fiona sighed and told Marjan all about Gerhard and the seduction that had left her out in the cold.

'Yes, it's a wonder what we do for men,' Marjan reflected.

'Have you ever been married, Marjan? I hope I'm not being too forward by asking.'

'Me? No, never married. I wouldn't have been able to cram it into my busy schedule.' Marjan cracked a wry smile and shrugged shyly.

'Ah, sure, men will always be there when you're ready. But look at what you've done! This café, your food – now that's something. This town doesn't know how lucky it is,' Fiona said. She reached over and patted Marjan's hand warmly.

'Thank you. That means a lot,' Marjan said, feeling a sudden rush of gratitude for the caring hairdresser. She should definitely make a point of coming out of the kitchen more often, she thought to herself. 'Now, are you going to tell me what those fliers are for?'

'Oh, these?' Fiona waved her hand nonchalantly over the stack of papers, but her squeaky voice gave away her excitement. 'Actually, I'm a bit terrified about it all. Seeing it's been so long since I've tried my hands in the theatre.'

'Are you putting on a play?'

Fiona nodded. 'Thought it'd be just the thing for Patrician Day.' She handed Marjan a light purple flier from the thick stack. 'It's for a bit of a laugh, really,' Fiona giggled nervously.

Marjan held the flier before her and studied the vibrant, fuchsia-coloured print:

Over The Hill Productions Presents:
FRUITS OF LABOUR

LAVASH BREAD

A play in two acts
by Father Fergal Mahoney
ANY INTERESTED PARTIES PLEASE
ATTEND AUDITIONS:
WEDNESDAY & THURSDAY, 3 P.M.
NEW GYMNASIUM, ST JOSEPH'S
SECONDARY SCHOOL,
BALLINACROAGH

'Father Mahoney has written a play!' Marjan exclaimed.

'I was surprised about it myself. He's no stranger to the stage, so it seems. Used to be comedian, would you believe! Told me so himself on the phone the other night,' Fiona relayed.

Father Fergal Mahoney had indeed been a seasoned stage ham before he entered the seminary. A rising comedic star, to be exact. As a young man he played the circuit of crumbling town council halls, festivals and fairs around his hometown of Listowel, perfecting his repertoire of impersonations and bawdy jokes. Fergal Mahoney's comedy routine had become so popular that by the age of twenty he was opening for the great Jimmy O'Dea in Dublin's famed Gaiety Theatre. On stage his rendition of the British Royal family's bathroom etiquette left the whole house rolling in the aisles, but it was back-stage that Fergal really learned the meaning of impropriety. After his performances, he not only mingled with third-tier celebrities and dodgy politicians, but also enjoyed intimate moments with a surprisingly flexible Portuguese showgirl named Pepita. All in all, it was a grand life for a farm boy from County Kerry. Little did Fergal know then that, within a year, he'd be knee-deep in sacramental studies and endless readings of The Pentateuch at a Tipperary seminary.

On one misty autumn night in 1945, after a session of piss and puns in The Brazen Head, the mother of all Dublin pubs, Fergal Mahoney was ambling across O'Connell Bridge on his way back to his swanky bachelor's pad when Fate inter-vened. Fergal was so busy replaying the jokes he had delivered that night on stage, the roaring laughter and thunderous applause that had followed, and Pepita's throaty love moans in his well-lit dressing room after the show, that he did not notice the rotten banana skin beneath his shiny shoes. Before he knew it, he had slipped on the skin and was sliding head-first over the bridge's great Georgian wall towards the infested waters of the river Liffey.

Time stopped for Fergal then. He heard nothing as his soft body tumbled into the Dublin night. For the longest five seconds of his life, Fergal was surrounded by complete silence. Just when he thought he was going to somersault all the way to the peaks of the great Himalayas, Fergal's body abruptly stopped its cartoonish defiance of gravity and plummeted towards the dark river below. In a last-ditch effort to save himself, Fergal shut his eyes and prayed hard and fast for divine intervention. He pleaded with God to save him; he promised Him that he would do anything, if only he could see his sweet Pepita's sparkly face once again. Fergal didn't expect his prayers to be answered, but he prayed anyway, hoping, like all last-minute converts, for a sign.

The young comedian did not die that night. Nor did he even splash into the dreaded muck of the river Liffey. Fergal's life was spared, his prayers answered when he landed on his whiskey-filled belly in the most reliable of river vessels – a hardy little tugboat. It took a good minute for Fergal to realise that he was alive and that his fall had been cushioned by the tugboat's mountainous cargo load – cartons of bubble-wrapped, silver-crossed, Guatemalan rosary beads.

Fergal Mahoney knew a SIGN when he saw one. He had been given a second chance by the big man Himself, and now he had a promise to fulfil. Bidding farewell to a tearful Pepita, Fergal left for Tipperary's best seminary the very next day.

Not until the moment he first tasted Marjan's *abgusht* had Father Mahoney allowed himself once again to entertain his comedic ambitions. But, after a month-long battle with his conscience, Father Mahoney was finally able to pin-point the strange exuberance that always coursed through his body after tasting Marjan's delicious lamb dish. Hastily finishing his lunch one afternoon, the priest rushed home to the parish and pulled out his old electric typewriter and began writing. He didn't stop for Mrs

Boylan's usual Thursday ham and chive colcannon and nearly missed the Henley twins' christening that Sunday, he was so immersed in his new project. When Father Mahoney finally stopped writing a week later, he had before him a two-act play dedicated to the pleasures of the mind and body.

'And I agreed to direct it for him!' Fiona gulped, her eyes fluttering with excitement.

'How wonderful for you both!' Marjan exclaimed. 'I'll take two fliers, please. One for the window here and one for the door, so there's no missing them. Are you making your way up the street with the rest?'

'Thought I would. Start early and all, before I open up the salon. Besides, it gives me a bit of headway before all those bleedin' gossip tongues start flaring.' Fiona gave Marjan's arm a friendly squeeze and wriggled her fingers as she left through the café's front door.

Gathering the dregs of their impromptu break-fast and tea, Marjan returned to the kitchen with a new spring in her step. She wouldn't have thought so, but it felt good to talk to Fiona. It had made her strong somehow to hold a positive conversation with a new acquaintance. She felt lighter, as if something pressing had been raised from her chest.

Marjan slowly lifted the cheesecloth off the bowl of *lavash* dough. The airy, white mass had risen in the time she had been away and felt almost weightless in her hands. She rolled the dough out once again, marvelling at how much easier it worked under her fingers this time around. Perhaps she too was like the *lavash* bread, thought Marjan: given some time and a warm, comforting environment, anything was possible.

Chapter Eight

Torshi

Ingredients:

2 large aubergines, cubed
500g small cucumbers, cubed
500g carrots, cubed
2 large white potatoes, cubed
8 garlic cloves, peeled
3 cups cauliflower florets
500g pearl onions, peeled
250g green beans
3½ litres white wine vinegar
4 cups chopped fresh herbs

(parsley, basil, tarragon, mint, coriander)
2 tbsp salt
2 tsp black pepper
½ tsp cayenne pepper
1 tbsp nigella seeds
Torshi all-spice mix (½ tsp turmeric,
1 tbsp ground cumin, 1 tsp ground saffron,
1 tbsp ground cardamom, 1 tsp ground
cinnamon)

makes 5–6 small jars

Unlike the standard pickled gherkins one finds on supermarket aisles in most Western countries, gentrified and cut into slices or wedges, vegetable *torshi* comes packed in a variety of sizes, shapes and colours. On Persian tables or upon the venerable spread of a *sofreh*, a hand-sewn cloth that requires limber, cross-legged positions from picnickers, *torshi* is nearly always the first platter served. The most common variety is a combination of fresh vegetables and herbs, pickled in good quality white wine vinegar, but the list expands to mango chutney, date pickle, aubergine *torshi* and fruit chutney, all marinated in allspice and a pinch or two of salt. Integral to most Persian meals, *torshi* not only complements dishes but its briny, vinegary crunch reminds the palate never to take any taste for granted.

Bahar was given the task of preparing the twenty jars of *torshi* that Marjan had promised the ladies of the Patrician Day Dance committee for their table of charity. Although a great fan of sour cauliflower florets herself, she wasn't keen on the lasting spray of vinegar that would take several showers to scrub off. Drying the clean vegetables thoroughly, she added them to a large bowl of salt, pepper, cayenne, nigella seeds and the *torshi* all-spice. After ladling the *torshi* into six canning jars, she tightened the lids, pumping her powerful forearms with a renewed gush of blood.

Bahar's muscles had always served her well, especially when she had worked as a nurse in Lewisham's Green Acres Home for the Newly Retired. Her sturdy arms had pushed many decaying, insubordinate Englishmen back into their bedpans whenever they insisted on showing her their withered willies. Despite her stern hand, though, Bahar's heart broke every time she witnessed her elderly patients' sad attempts at virility. It was this very withering away of life, she knew, that was behind the second and less-appetising definition of the word *torshi*.

Coming from a tradition where fifteen was the average age of marriage and twenty full-blown motherhood, twenty-five was the hallmark for spinsterhood. As a result, many an unmarried Iranian woman had been branded with the dreaded T-word. Of course, in the latter part of the twentieth century, the marriage age in Iran had risen considerably, but the use of *torshi* to describe a girl who had a certain use-by date, and who was left to dust away on the shelves of love, was still common in gossipy circles. As a teenager, Bahar would never have thought that by the age of twenty-four, she would not only be single again, but also quite happy to see the vast lonely road before her. The single life was actually quite satisfactory, in her opinion; maybe Layla had her little boyfriend and Marjan, well Marjan had her planting and cooking and the café and who knew, probably some white-faced Irishman with a good appetite on the horizon, but *she* was content to see her days out alone, in peace, God willing. She did not want a man in her life – never again.

Shaking her head, Bahar twisted shiny purple ribbons around the lips of the *torshi* jars, tying them into proud bows. No, she would not be ashamed of being labelled a *torshi*, she decided. Despite the assault of vinegar, *torshi* vegetables somehow managed to survive their pickling period. And that's what she wanted to be: a survivor, afraid of nothing.

Having packed and decorated the fat jars, Bahar lined them beneath the stairwell, where they would sleep and acquire their distinctive sizzle, the piquant edges of cayenne and nigella softened by the sour vinegar. The *torshis* would have sufficient time to marinate by the Patrician Day Dance in July.

'Mrs Delmonico's just come in. She wants a bowl of lentil soup, a hummus and grilled aubergine wrap and a pot of bergamot. Later she wants baklava and two pieces of *zulbia*,' said Layla, pushing into the warm kitchen. She slapped Estelle's order on the kitchen island. 'Can I go now, Marjan? Ms Athey's posting the audition results outside the school offices this afternoon.'

'Yes, but be back soon. We might get a rush later on like last Saturday,' Marjan replied.

'Thanks!' Layla shot out the back door.

'I suppose I'll have to go out front now,' Bahar said peevishly. 'You know she won't be back for at least another hour.'

'Go easy on her, Bahar. This play's really important to her. She auditioned for the lead role, you know. Fiona said she was really good.'

'Why am I not surprised?' Bahar said, more grouchily than she felt. The truth was that part of her was proud of Layla. Her younger sister seemed to have quite a talent for finding friends in this new town of theirs, something Bahar had never had much luck with anywhere. Making friends required disclosure, the sharing of secrets and emotions, none of which Bahar could ever see herself doing with perfect strangers. Back in her Green Acres days, her reticence had kept most of her nursing colleagues at bay; she was never invited to after-shift drinks in Doc Watson's pub, and her lunchtimes were spent not in the cafeteria exchanging notes on petulant patients, but rummaging for bargains in the thrift stores that lined nearby Aldersgate Street. Losing herself in the dust of pre-loved knick-knacks had comforted Bahar somehow; each bargain buy, be it a tapestry throw from Tuscany, or a battered but still lovable copper teapot, kept her mind off how lonely she felt.

With an order pad in hand, Bahar shuffled out to the cacophonous front room, resigned to another afternoon of waiting tables by herself. She rushed back into the kitchen moments later, her face filled with concern. 'You better get out there, Marjan. Mrs Delmonico doesn't look too well. Her skin's bright red and she's drenched in sweat.'

Marjan dropped the fried chicken salad she was preparing for the Donnelly twins and hurried through the kitchen doors. Even from across the room it was obvious that something was wrong with the old lady.

Ever since the day she brought her new tenants

her famed osso bucco, Estelle Delmonico had been one of the Babylon Café's most devoted fans. Although plenty of women her age sat near by with their daily doses of rose-water-infused treats, Estelle always took her tea alone. She would close her eyes and lick the sugared sweat from her upper lip, before sipping her favourite brew, bergamot tea, and biting into an elephant ear or two. Sometimes, the Italian widow would even hum a low aria to herself, one of the many songs her Luigi used to belt out of his robust lungs as he scraped curlicues from a chunk of dark chocolate at the kitchen island.

Marjan usually waited until Estelle had finished her first cup of tea before sitting down at her table for a chat. Lunchtime boom or not, she always spared a few minutes out of the kitchen chaos to say hello to the little old lady with the rickety frame and hearty appetite. She had never watched Estelle for prolonged periods of time, though. As Marjan stood observing Estelle at her lone table now, it dawned upon her that the widow's self-imposed seclusion was not entirely voluntary.

Estelle Delmonico's eyes gave her away. Every

thirty seconds or so they would dart over to the long communal table where the ladies of the Patrician Day Dance committee sat, before flicking back to the spoon on her table. She would then dab at her swollen nostrils with an embroidered silk handkerchief taken from her small, patent leather handbag. The committee ladies were too busy deciding on the Dance's decoration theme (should they stick to the usual tri-coloured salute or take on a Caribbean flavour with the colours of terracotta, pacific aqua and hydrangea pink?) to notice they were being watched. They did not detect Estelle's quiet pleas as Marjan did, recognising the signs of desperate loneliness.

Perhaps she could ask Marie Brennan to include the Italian woman in next week's committee meeting, thought Marjan. Surely, the ladies of the Patrician Day Dance committee could use an extra pair of hands with all the activities they had planned for Patrician Day. And, Marjan reasoned, once Estelle felt she was needed, she wouldn't feel so shy about taking the initiative to make new friends herself. Pleased with her idea, Marjan eagerly approached

Estelle's table, and was about to greet her kind landlady when something in the old woman's face made her pause. Estelle Delmonico's complexion was growing a dangerous shade of red by the second and sweat was streaming liberally down her cheeks now, too quickly to be wiped away. Startled, Marjan peered closer at Estelle's flushed face and realised that the sweat was, in actual fact, tears. Large, fat tears. She dashed forward just as the Italian widow fell towards the floor, letting go of the crushed rose she was holding to her heaving chest.

An oppressive melancholy set in that lasted the rest of the afternoon.

The Donnelly twins helped Marjan lift Estelle from her fainted slouch and carried her to the back of the green hippie van. Father Mahoney, who had stopped by for a lamb and cucumber sandwich to go, climbed in next to Estelle's limp body and held her soft hands, praying hard as the van careened towards Mayo General Hospital in Castlebar. Soon, the rest of the diners also abandoned the café, scattering as if driven away by bad weather, leaving their half-eaten baklavas and sweet syrup drinks behind in a congealed mess.

Bahar locked the café door and set about gathering the dismembered rose petals from underneath Estelle's table. She would be the first to admit that the old widow's collapse had shaken her to the core. It had reminded Bahar that not everything was as secure as Marjan would have them believe. Any accident could uproot them again, send whatever success this café had been experiencing into distant memory. What would all their regulars think now? Probably that their food was indigestible, unhealthy, cooked in a kitchen rampant with rats and other diseases. That perhaps it was something Estelle ate that made her fall into a death-like trance.

Marjan and Layla may have been too busy with their own fantasies to notice, Bahar told herself, but she wasn't blind to the stares thrown her way whenever she stepped out of the café doors. How could she ignore the obvious cuts of silence, the breaks in street conversations whenever she walked by a cluster of townspeople? Why, it had happened in the butcher's just the other day, as she was paying for the café's weekly order of lamb and ground meat for shish kebabs. Three crotchety gossips, standing near the Galtee Back Bacon Rashers display, had scanned her up and down with their myopic eyes when they thought she had her back turned. She should have returned their disapproving looks with a piercing stare of her own, thought Bahar. Put those old bags in their place. But all she had done was keep her head bowed as she hurried out of the butcher's shop, glad to have escaped the old women's merciless scrutiny.

Well, what else could she have expected from such a small-time town? And now who knew when all their regulars would feel comfortable enough to come back, or if they would at all. Bahar sighed as she swept a pile of food crumbs into a dust pan.

Really, as long as they were able to survive, to plod along in this sleepy town, she didn't care much about its size, its prejudices. So long as no one on the outside world, beyond the craggy boundaries of the western village, knew that they were there. That was all that mattered.

*   *   *

Estelle Delmonico awoke in her hospital bed, rehydrated and cool after the heat stroke and heartache that had caused her to faint. At least that was the doctor's explanation for the old lady's extraordinary colouring and bubbled breathing when Marjan and Father Mahoney admitted her to Mayo General. An hour later, after she had been thoroughly replenished with nutrients from a much-needed IV tube, the Italian woman shared the real reason behind her fainting spell.

'Please! Heat stroke! There is no heat outside for a stroke!' She paused for a moment, her eyes travelling to the hospital-room window and its view of green and brown hills that rolled under grey, fast-moving clouds. 'I tell you the truth. Today my Luigi and I, we are married fifty years. I was just not feeling happy, you understand?'

She stopped there, all of a sudden aware of Father Mahoney's presence, of Marjan's concerned nods, and reddened again. In all her forty-five years in Ballinacroagh, and especially since her husband's death five years ago, Estelle had never shown her vulnerability, her raw need for company, to any of its townspeople. Not even in her weekly confessions to Father Mahoney, where she would expound on the loving, yet distant relationship she had with her niece Gloria, would Estelle mention her isolation, her longing to connect to life forms besides the achingly beautiful rose bush outside her little cottage. And now, on the day when as a young bride she had expected to receive the golden platitudes of loving grandchildren gathered at her knees, she had taken one look at the table of involved, comforted committee women, all in the bosoms of elderly friendships, then looked at the vacancy of her own table, and breathed the last hold on her privacy – only to find herself fainting, of all things.

Luckily, Father Mahoney rescued the pained silence with his own mark of humility and comedic grace.

'Sure, Estelle, we'll be needing your fine expertise for play rehearsals. A modern *Bacchae* of sorts – all that love-making and wine-drinking – it's all Greek to me. It'll be up your alley, now, I'd say.'

It had made Marjan blush to hear the word

'love-making' from the old priest's smiling lips, but Estelle Delmonico just giggled out loud. Father Mahoney's generosity had broken the ice, giving the once lonely widow an invitation to the camaraderie and community she had longed for over four decades.

'Where is she, Marjan? It's nearly six o'clock! What if something happened to her on the way home?' Bahar looked like an asylum escapee, pacing up and down the empty café aisles as she wrung her hands. Five hours had passed since Layla left to check the audition results, an excursion that, in Bahar's opinion, should have taken her an hour at the most to complete.

'I already told you, Bahar. I called Fiona. She saw her last outside the school offices with Malachy. They both got the lead roles in the play. She's probably out celebrating with her friends,' Marjan replied quietly, trying to sound calm.

'Malachy! Who is this Malachy, really? Yes, I know he's polite and smart, but do we know anything about his family, about what kind of people his parents are? What if they're crazy murderers?'

'Bahar, please.' Marjan shook her head. Her sister could be so dramatic sometimes. Any moment now she might crumple up in a ball of hysterical tears, right there in the middle of the café floor. At least she had stopped cleaning. Marjan had known something had gone awry as soon as she arrived home from the hospital. She found Bahar inside the kitchen with a copper coil and a bottle of bleach in hand, deep in a frenzied cleaning match with the oven door. Bahar resorted to such crazed cleaning only when she was too upset to complain; she would scour the floors and countertops until she had spent most of her nervous energy.

'Okay, fine, maybe not murderers, but we still don't know much about Malachy and she's out with him everyday. She should be helping me wait tables instead of doing God knows what with that Irish boy. And you, Marjan – you're not helping!' Bahar pointed her finger at her sister accusingly.

'Me! What did I do?'

'Letting her go off without a curfew. It's almost ten past six now!'

'All right,' Marjan acquiesced, not wanting to argue. 'I'll check the school. She's probably still there. Just stay calm, okay?'

Marjan hopped into the van and gunned anxiously out of the alleyway for the second time that day, working hard to silence the murky, fearful thoughts that rumbled through her mind. She might have acted composed with Bahar, but she too was extremely concerned. Layla had been gone for over five hours now, without as much as a phone call to let them know where she was. Of course, Marjan reasoned, Ballinacroagh was by no means the most dangerous town they ever lived in; Layla could be testing out her adolescent boundaries in far worse places. But still, one could never be completely sure.

St Joseph Secondary sat on a low hill about a quarter of a mile from the high end of Main Mall, so Marjan pulled into its gravelly driveway within minutes of leaving the café. She felt her level of panic rise abruptly as her eyes scanned the school's empty, rain-drenched front lawn. The main building's front doors were stopped open, but its towering, Gothic windows were dark. The only sound she could hear was the clangour of St Barnabas's rusty church bell tolling in the distance. It was Saturday after all, Marjan reminded herself, trying to regain her composure. She parked the van outside the front doors and hurried into the building's shadowy corridors.

Heavy, wooden classroom doors lined either side of the hall, contrasting with walls painted in pistachio green. Every ten metres or so, muted light fixtures attached to dividing archways cast eerie pools on the speckled moss tiles beneath her feet. The offices must be along this way, she told herself, as she rushed down a long passageway. Layla might still be in there with Malachy and her friends, clustered around the audition notice, too excited to see the night falling quickly outside. Marjan was rounding a hallway corner when she bumped into the dark veils.

They came upon her so swiftly that she shrieked in horror. She grabbed on to a nearby trophy case for support, her knees suddenly buckling under her.

The veils, habits to be precise, belonged to two elderly nuns. Sisters Agatha and Bea were on their way back to the convent, having just finished a meeting of the Popular Canticle Club held in the school's new gymnasium.

Marjan recovered from her shock and found her voice.

'Ah, excuse me. Is the school closed?'

Sister Agatha, a woman who had renounced a life of Jazz-era partying for Christ, smiled at her kindly.

'You're the girl who's taken over Estelle Delmonico's place, aren't you?' She poked Sister Bea with her elbow. 'This is the one Father Mahoney was telling us about! FATHER MAHONEY!' she yelled into the shorter nun's ear. 'She's hard of hearing, Sister Bea is,' Sister Agatha explained.

Sister Bea looked confused and stared at Marjan with vague, opaque eyes.

'Oh. Yes. I'm actually looking for my younger sister. Layla Aminpour? She's in Third Year?' Marjan's heart slowed down its frantic beating.

'Well, I can't say I know any of the students

nowadays. Sister Bea and I haven't taught for quite a few years, you see.' Sister Agatha leaned into Sister Bea's right ear. 'Not taught here for a LONG TIME! HAVE WE, SISTER?'

Sister Agatha's croaky voice finally registered with the deaf nun. Sister Bea smiled broadly and nodded, showing her pearly dentures.

'You won't have much luck today, I'm afraid, it being Saturday and all. Though it's a great thing Sister Bea and I finally have the chance to meet you. I was wondering now, can you tell me where to find some of that lovely saffron stuff Father Mahoney has been telling us about?'

Because of the priest's many praises, both nuns were well aware of Marjan's potent *abgusht*. Even half-deaf Sister Bea had heard about the stew's divine ingredients, the recipe reverberating against the convent walls long after their last prayers were whispered. After answering the two nuns' string of cooking questions as best she could, Marjan quickly retreated to the van. With her heart still hammering, she climbed into the driver's seat and jammed the key into the ignition, but stopped before she turned it to start. A strange clamminess had chilled her skin, causing her teeth to chatter uncontrollably. As comic as the nuns were, those navy habits were just too close to the choking chador for her liking. Had she not been in peaceful Ballinacroagh, Marjan would surely have taken them as a sign of impending doom.

A stroke of amber, the last sigh of a darkening horizon, guided Bahar on her own search for her errant sister as she hastened up Main Mall. She had never been this far up the street on foot before. Her shopping errands kept her in close proximity to the café; the butcher's and the mini-mart were only a couple of minutes away from the Babylon's front door. Nevertheless, Bahar had decided to brave the unknown, sure that she would go mad if she waited in the café any longer. If Layla was out with friends (and Bahar hoped to God she was), she might be slurping milk-shakes in the burger and chip place on Main Mall, or perhaps trying her luck with a more illicit brew in one of the town's many pubs. Bahar was determined to find her, wherever she was.

And when she did, she was going to give that sister of hers a mighty earful.

Layla wasn't in the Blue Thunder burger bar, nor was she in Paddy McGuire's pub next door. Thankfully, Bahar surmised this without having to step foot in either place; both establishments had large, street-front windows from which patrons could be seen downing pints and scoffing greasy curry chips. Perhaps she should try asking some of the shopkeepers along the Mall if they had seen a dark-haired girl with too much time on her hands, thought Bahar. She stopped abruptly in front of the first shop that looked open, Corcoran's Bakery. Good place as any to start enquiring, Bahar decided, nodding silently to herself. Pushing through its yellow door, she stepped innocently inside, entirely unprepared for the chilly reception she was about to receive from Assumpta Corcoran.

A lot had changed in the Corcoran household since the day Layla had crossed paths with Benny Corcoran and his bread-filled wheelbarrow, nearly seven weeks ago to the day. Layla's youthful promise had thrown the reluctant baker into a kaleidoscope of what ifs and could've beens, prompting him to examine his choices in life.

Benny's loveless marriage and his particularly close friendship with Mr Jack Daniels had turned his once athletic body into a pitiful lump of fat and freckles, the glorious head of red hair he once had as a young man reduced now to a handful of unruly strands. Once inspired, though, Benny threw himself into a full exercise regime worthy of the harshest boot camps. He installed a pull-up bar over the bakery's back door, from which he pumped up and down at three in the morning, and began to experiment with comb-overs and hair volumisers, purchased from Athey's Shear Delight (but only after swearing Fiona Athey to secrecy). Benny even dug out his wide-lapelled leather jacket from the bakery's cobwebbed attic, along with the Gaelic football trophies he had won as a proud teenager; awards he had forgotten in all these years of kneading the unsavory rolls of both his profession and the body of his cold wife, Assumpta.

Though named in honour of the ascension of the Virgin Mary, Assumpta Corcoran considered her own soul eternally damned. Her weekly church confessions were filled with the guilt of bodily functions, of her husband's carnal demands and of the wifely responsibilities that she could never live up (or down) to. After each confession, Assumpta would rush home to cleanse herself with a scalding bath and a harsh loofah, hoping to scrub away her own confused soul in the process. When Assumpta noticed that Benny's gut was no longer straining against the last hole of his belt buckle, and that his florid complexion had toned down to a pleasantly muted pink, she knew that all her praying had come to nothing – her husband had finally given into his dirty ways and taken a mistress, just as so many in town had believed he had for years. Frigid as she was, Assumpta had always assumed that the sanctity of her marriage was safe despite the gossip. But a new Benny who refused his drink and pored over diet cookbooks was by no means playing by the rules. Benny Corcoran was changing and it wasn't for her benefit, that was for sure. But who was the floozy who had caught her husband's degenerate eye? The pieces of the puzzle did not fall into place for Assumpta until that very moment, when a flushed and worried-looking Bahar stepped timidly into the bake shop.

'Hi, I'm Bahar Aminpour. My sisters and I own the café down the street.'

Assumpta's eyes narrowed. She had passed by the new lunch place several times since it had opened its doors, hoping to catch a sight of the foreigners who were running it. But, other than the young girl with the black hair who walked past the bakery on her way to school, Assumpta had never spotted any of the other darkie women Dervla Quigley yammered on about. Now she could see that the old gossip's suspicions were well-founded. The brown-skinned woman in front of her was the embodiment of John's warning in Revelations: the Harlot of Babylon had just made herself known. God be with them all.

'What can I do for you?' Assumpta's voice was icy.

'I'm looking for my younger sister Layla. She's fifteen, long dark hair, about this tall?' Bahar's hand measured a half-foot above her own head, before dropping listlessly to her side.

'No. Haven't seen anybody like *that* around here,' Assumpta replied, making the word *that* sound almost filthy.

'Oh – thanks anyway.' Bahar turned sheepishly to leave, feeling another terrible headache coming along.

Just then, Benny huffed and puffed into the shop from the back kitchen. He had finished an agonising lap around the town centre and was sporting velour head and wristbands that were soaked in his middle-aged sweat. The baker immediately recognised Bahar as one of the three angels from the café, whom he had spotted on his daily bread runs up and down Main Mall.

'Why, hello there. How can I help you today?'

Benny's eyes glazed over, clear confirmation for Assumpta that she was staring at her husband's mistress.

'It's all right. Sorry to bother you.' Bahar nodded a shy goodbye and quickly slipped out of the bakery. Overcome by a sudden exhaustion, she pressed her right hand to her thumping temple and continued rather wobbly up the street.

Benny watched her walk off, then turned to his wife. He was taken aback by the look of smug satisfaction spread across Assumpta's normally disappointed face.

'What did ye say to her now, to have her running out the door like a wild banshee?'

'Don't you go telling me what's right or wrong, Benny Corcoran. I know what your jogging and vegetarian diets are all about. Put me to shame, you have! The whole town's talkin'! And don't think I'm going to stick around to see you gallivanting with some foreign hussy!'

Assumpta was close to tears as she grabbed her coat and ran to the door.

'Assumpta!' Benny yelped. 'Where are ye going?'

'To Mass! To pray for our souls, dirty thing! And you better be at the pub when I get back!'

Marjan's lime green van idled in the school car park, her thoughts floating across the gloomy windscreen before her. The nuns' dark habits had resurrected unexpected ghosts, memories she had hoped would lie dead and buried. Maybe some spirits are just not meant for the afterlife, she told herself, their season of haunting lasting for ever.

The phantoms had come flapping out of their ghoulish graves when she wasn't looking, the same spring day in 1978, when she was released from Gohid Detention Centre. The first person Marjan saw when she stumbled into their apartment after her secret incarceration was little Layla. Fattened with buttery dishes, her apple head wrapped in a matronly headscarf, Layla was sitting on the living-room carpet holding a photo of a turbaned idol of the revolution in her plump fingers. Snatching the photograph into her own shaking hands, Marjan was about to tear it into a thousand pieces – as many as it would take to erase the furrowed face that was being painted on all neighbourhood walls – when she saw the ghosts.

The kitchen was swarming with them. Black chadors and gremlin faces, their gapped teeth slurping at oily broths and overcooked *chelows*.

Marjan almost fell over when she realised that one of them was her sister.

At sixteen, and in less than four days, Bahar had become a militant member of the Women's Party.

The darling sister of the male-only Committee, the Women's Party was a local organisation led by their neighbour, a large, pointy-faced woman named Khanoum Jaferi. Born to a snake-charmer father and a gypsy mother whose hobbies ranged from tea-leaf readings to mid-afternoon trysts with pubescent shepherd boys, Khanoum Jaferi had grown up to abhor all such excesses. She had taken to the veil and chador at the age of twenty and slowly moved up the ranks of pious women's groups by attending monthly summits on the proper length of chadors and techniques for avoiding pleasure during dutiful matrimonial copulation.

In no time at all, the cunning Khanoum Jaferi had pushed her way to the forefront of the revolutionary movement by establishing her own corps of female fundamentalists – the Women's Party. Weekly meetings of the Women's Party were held in Khanoum Jaferi's lavishly carpeted apartment. There, devoted members spent hours extolling the virtues of The Turbaned One, the mullah who promised to rid the country of all evil decadence and establish an Islamic society. Over scalding cups of unsweetened black tea and goat's tongue stew, Khanoum Jaferi preached passionately on the need to purge their beloved Persia of Western influence – the Shah, that sweetheart of America, included. She had been waiting thirty years for the Islamic Revolution to cleanse their society, she told the chador-clad women, and she wasn't going to stop until she saw her dream realised.

Khanoum Jaferi, Marjan later learned, had come to the apartment with pots of rice and split pea soup when news spread that she hadn't returned home from The Peacock Restaurant. Never one to miss a recruitment opportunity, the militant matron also came equipped with paint and white banners, setting Bahar to work on writing anti-American slogans while she reheated her tasteless pots of food.

If it wasn't for Khanoum Jaferi and the Women's

Party, Layla and I would have starved, Bahar had said, disregarding Marjan's warnings about the group of reactionary chadors proliferating in their kitchen. *Independence, Freedom, Islamic Republic! Marg bar Amrika, Death to America,* she exclaimed, before launching into Koranic passages so long and complicated that Marjan was stunned into silence by Bahar's aptitude for rote memorisation. The most frightening thing of all, though, was not Bahar's newfound zeal for the revolution, nor the weekly Women's Party meetings she insisted that the three of them attend, but the unquestioning loyalty she now had for Khanoum Jaferi's only son, the man who was going to be her husband.

Hossein Jaferi. A salamander of a man, not yet informed on the responsibilities of belonging to the human race. Severely punctured by mishandled forceps at birth, Hossein wore his slashed skin like a badge of honour, proud to have survived the first of life's many obstacles. The metal contraption had marred Hossein's baby face with such deep indentations that his mother, Khanoum Jaferi, had fallen off the high labour bed and broken her hip in two places from the shock of it all. As a young man, Hossein had been arrested by the secret police for burning an effigy of the diminutive Shah, but six years in jail had done little to stem his restlessness, and upon his release, the first place he visited was his local mosque. Inside its cool, mosaic-covered walls, Hossein received divinations encouraging him to movement, to establish himself as a leader of believing men. And so, prompted by God and his zealous mother, he joined a local grassroots initiative – the Committee. A perfect platform from which the sadistic, thirty-one-year-old Hossein Jaferi could launch his career in the open territory that was the revolution.

Marjan nearly fainted when she heard the name. The Committee. But her objections carried little weight; Bahar had made up her mind and a whole community of underground chadors would back her decision.

On the sleepless night before Bahar and Hossein were to be married, Marjan passed away the dark hours with her hands deep in sticky dough, trying to think of a way to stop her sister from ruining her life. It was Marjan's job to bake the delicacies for the wedding feast, the baklava, the mulberry–almond paste, and the walnut, chickpea and rice cookies. As she rolled out the pastry for the baklava (enough to feed the entire militant party of two hundred), Marjan tried to reason with her gnawing stomach, with that voice that was telling her to take her two sisters and run. This Hossein and all that came with him – the Molotov cocktail parties he organised, the martyred uncle he worshipped, his domineering mother who seemed to have Bahar under an unbreakable spell – were wrong. All wrong. And there was nothing Marjan could do to alter her sister's fate.

The day after her ill-fated wedding, Bahar moved in with her new husband's family. Her move relieved her sisters from having to attend meetings of the Women's Party every week, but it also left behind such a void, such an empty space in Marjan's heart. And although she only lived a few streets away, Marjan did not see Bahar until nearly four months after her wedding day.

*   *   *

Assumpta Corcoran's cold gaze seemed to have imprinted itself on Bahar's temples. The tingling overtures of a headache accompanied her as she stepped inside McGuire's Ale House, hoping to find Layla sitting in one of its ratty booths.

Now, Thomas McGuire wasn't the kind of man to let an attractive woman go unnoticed in his establishment. Although he reserved his true affections for the likes of Donna Summers, Gloria Gaynor, and Thelma Houston, and only exposed his chunky private quarters to the embraces of his lusty wife, Thomas was certainly not blind to the swagger of feminine hips. When Bahar walked into the pub the bar owner was busy going over the weekly shift roster with his bartender, but he paused in mid-speech to gawk at the young woman who had disturbed the stale fog of cigarette smoke and soft flatulence.

That's no ordinary woman, Thomas realised with a sudden shudder. *She's one of those tarts from the café!* He jerked his eyes off Bahar, and curling his thick lips in a soft snarl, gave his bartender a knowing nod. *Bleedin' Arabs.*

Bahar approached the bar like a lamb to the slaughter.

'Sorry, hello?' she said, raising her hand like a schoolgirl. The bartender, a pudgy man with heavy ginger sideburns, mirrored his boss's sneer. He turned his back on Bahar and pretended to make conversation with an inebriated old-timer slumped over in his own drool.

'I was just wondering if anyone had seen my . . .'

Everyone at the bar, from Thomas McGuire to old lady Lennon cradling her gin and tonic at the corner table, had turned their backs against her. Silence. Several seconds passed, during which Chaka Khan's velvety voice could be heard purring from a large jukebox in the corner. Someone coughed as a lazy cloud of tobacco smoke drifted in front of Bahar's eyes. She looked down at the diamond-patterned carpet at her feet, which was gritty with the previous night's revelry of powdered potato crisps, cigarette butts and peanut casings. Chaka Khan hit an unnaturally high note and the jukebox lifted the record off, returning it to a fanned stack of shiny black

LPs, and went silent. And still, no one turned to look at her.

Angry embarrassment washed over Bahar's cheeks and sent her stomach into a spin. Something was very wrong here, not only in this dirty pub, but in the bakery next door as well. Something that went beyond the sad, little curiosities of the old women in the butcher's. Whatever she thought of that kind of small-mindedness, it was nothing compared to the bald hatred before her. It was an exclusion as foul as she had experienced in those scary early years in London, when the whole city was under alert of terrorist threats, and anyone who looked slightly foreign was watched with suspicion.

Turning on her heels, which crunched on the littered floor, Bahar pushed through the pub door, anxious to escape the dread that was rising in her chest. Just as the door slammed behind her, a sinister voice called out: 'Go back to yer stinking camels!'

Raspy smokers' laughs enveloped the rest of the smarting insult.

* * *

'Over there. Right next to that cumulus that looks like a rabbit – that's Jupiter. It's always there, even during daylight hours. You should see it at night, though, with a telescope.' Malachy's long arm pointed towards the sky over Clew Bay.

'You can see it from your bedroom?' Layla snuggled closer to him on a surprisingly warm patch of sea grass.

'Yeah, but I like to bring my gear out here when I can. Even if it gets up my dad's wrong side.'

'Your dad?' Layla had forgotten about Emer's warning. She wondered if the rumours were true about Malachy's father wanting the café space, but sensing it would be a sore subject, let it go. Instead, she rested her head on his reclining chest and gazed dreamily up at the sky. 'So are all the constellations named after Greek gods and goddesses?'

Malachy, relieved to have side-stepped the subject of his domineering father, smiled and nodded.

'Yup. Though the Babylonians discovered them before the Greeks. They had a whole system worked out.' He wiped his hand across the heavens, stopping on a slice of sky that blinked brighter than the surrounding pale clouds. 'Next to that patch of sky there is Venus. You can't see it, but trust me, it's there.'

Layla gulped and nodded. Venus. Goddess of Love. Yes, it was definitely there.

Somehow, somewhere between the planetary blessings, the gentle lulling of the Atlantic tide and the canopy of their linking fingers against the sky, they had fallen asleep. The next thing Layla knew, she was staring into the giggling black hole of a toothless six-year-old mouth.

'D'yis tink their dead?'

'Naw, they're pr'bly jest shaggin'.'

Laughter and spittle landed on Layla and Malachy's opening eyelids. An urchin gang of three boys and a girl, ranging in age from six to twelve, had surrounded them. The children were dressed in grey and navy tracksuits, their matted hair and freckled faces streaked with dirt. Globs of mucous lined the corners of their eyes, and their mouths were edged with melted chocolate.

'Go on! Get!'

Malachy shooed them towards a distant cluster of caravans parked at the base of a sandy hill. A makeshift clothesline hung between two of the mobile homes and several plastic fold-out chairs encircled a campfire. Three women, wearing tight, stone-washed jeans stretched over emaciated thighs, were shivering over the fire as they passed a long cigarette between them. Layla was surprised she hadn't seen the camp earlier. But, then again, her attention had been wholly consumed by Malachy. She trembled just thinking about the boy at her side.

The tinker children laughed loudly and scampered off. The oldest boy jabbed his two fingers up in the air, a time-honoured insult, before disappearing behind the shoulder of a giant, shadowy dune. As if snapped out of a trance, Layla noticed that everything was suddenly dark around them. Even the stars were beginning to show their twinkling smiles in the night sky above.

Bahar sat at the kitchen table with her head in her hands, crying, and for the first time in a long while, praying. It was all her fault they were stuck in some mean little village at the end of the world, with nothing but cooking burns and the stink of fried onions to look forward to. It was all her fault, and she had no way of remedying it.

'Bahar?' Layla whispered. She was standing just inside the kitchen doorway, afraid to move an inch.

Lifting her wet face from her palms, Bahar stared at Layla in silence. Opalescent shafts from the outside light converged around Layla's head like a halo. Blinded momentarily by the bright glow, Bahar was forced to blink hard several times before she could make out Layla's face, but once assured that her sister was alive and well, her anger was swift.

'Where have you been? I've been going crazy waiting here!' she yelled, staggering up from her chair.

'I was with Malachy. At the beach,' Layla replied casually.

'It's seven o'clock, Layla!'

'I know. Sorry.'

Shocked by Layla's carelessness, Bahar stared at her with wide eyes, her mouth falling open. Her sister obviously had no concern for what she had just been through, Bahar thought with increasing anger, searching frantically up and down the street, having to belittle herself in front of such ignorant people. She was with Malachy, simple as that. How dare she? As if she deserved such freedom, as if she had earned the right to go on dates at her age. Had Layla forgotten everything she had been through? Bahar searched for words that would put the fear of men into Layla, but what finally came out of her mouth was: 'You'll end up like I did – is that what you want? I forbid you to see this boy again!'

'Bahar!'

'No! I mean it, Layla! We didn't come all the way here so that you could end up in bed with some stupid Irish boy!' Bahar's voice was shrill.

'You just want me to be as bitter as you are!' Layla fired back. 'I deserve some happiness, you know! Don't forget it's because of you we had to come here in the first place!'

Layla ran up the stairs and slammed the flat door, leaving Bahar choking on her angry, misplaced fear.

Chapter Nine

Chelow

Ingredients:

    3 cups uncooked, long-grain basmati rice
    6 cups water
    2 tbsp salt
    ½ cup olive oil

Marjan picked Estelle Delmonico up from the hospital the following morning. Although the doctors at Mayo General had wanted her to stay on for one more day, in case another fainting spell came along, the feisty Italian

woman had insisted on being released as soon
as possible.

'I am okay, not to worry so much. And you
know, I can't eat one more day of this horrible
hospital chicken. No flavour, my goodness!'
Estelle protested. Not even in the dark days of
the World War, when her family had been forced
to ration their weekly supply of linguine and clam
sauce, had she ever tasted food as bland and unin-
spiring.

Remembering Estelle's complaint, Marjan had
packed some freshly made elephant ears and a
large serving of herb *kuku* in a brown paper bag
before leaving for the hospital. One whiff of the
fried treats and the taste of boiled hospital meals
would be long forgotten, she thought to herself.

Marjan couldn't help but notice how frail the
little widow looked in her thin hospital robe.
Even so, Estelle had rejected the nurse's offer of
a wheelchair, and would have walked out of
Mayo General all by herself had it not been for
her arthritis. Estelle's joints were inflamed as a
result of her spell, the stretched tendons in her
fragile hips and knees aching with every step, so

Marjan had to hold the old lady steady by her elbow and shoulder for their walk out to the hospital car park. Luckily, the sturdy green van was narrow enough to handle the sharp mountain road to Estelle's white cottage. Marjan helped her slowly down from the passenger's seat and together they tackled the steep gravel path leading up to the bright red door.

'That's a beautiful rose bush,' Marjan admired.

'Thank you, darling. Yes, that's my Luigi,' Estelle said, pleased.

'How lucky for you to have him so near,' Marjan replied, understanding the significance of the roses immediately.

'He is always close to me.'

Estelle handed Marjan a knobby, rusted key on a large metal ring. The door opened to reveal the dim, warm front parlour, a neat little room boasting cushiony cream furniture, lace curtains and vases filled with gardenias. Both women paused at the threshold as the sea breeze fluttered the leaves of the rose bush behind them, Luigi's own personal welcome. Marjan led Estelle across the cosy parlour's polished flagstone floors.

'Which way to your bedroom, Estelle?'

'Just down this hall, darling. Make a left.'

They turned into a brightly wallpapered hallway lined with framed portraits. There was a young Estelle on her wedding day, her hair in a pert chignon covered by an elaborate lace veil; another sepia-toned photograph with Estelle in her bride's dress, this time standing next to a squat, jolly-faced young man with a thick moustache that curled at its ends. Luigi.

'Ah, so many memories!' Estelle exclaimed. She traced her feeble fingers over the prints, moving along the happy years; the Delmonicos on their honeymoon in Morocco, posing outside Papa's Pastries on its first day of business, even one of her niece Gloria, in her chequered chef's uniform and tall paper hat.

They passed a sunny, daffodil kitchen on the right, crammed with a wooden table painted purple and chairs and cabinets stencilled with periwinkle blue daisies. Once in the bedroom, Marjan helped Estelle into a cotton nightgown and tucked her into her big mahogany and duck-down bed.

'Wait here. I've got something for you in the van,' Marjan said. She returned promptly with the brown paper bag of treats.

'Elephant ears!' Estelle clapped her hand like a happy child.

Marjan opened the sugary packages on Estelle's handmade quilt and immediately eased the old woman's icicle joints with the lush smells of sweet pastries and a still warm egg and herb pancake. She looked so healthy and calm after eating that Marjan took the opportunity to ask the widow for some precious advice.

'Let the two of them work it out by themselves,' Estelle began wisely, after Marjan finished telling her about her sisters' fight. 'They are big girls now, Marjan.'

'I know, but sometimes I can't help feeling responsible for everything they do. I am the eldest, after all,' Marjan replied, twisting the paper bag absently in her hands.

'Big sister, yes. Mother, no. I was never lucky to have children, but I have Gloria and let me tell you, girls are not easy. This Malachy. You say this boy is good?' Estelle looked sceptical; she knew Thomas McGuire too well to expect much from his offspring.

'He's wonderful. A very good boy.'

'Well, then that is okay, yes? I met my Luigi when I was fifteen. I don't say Layla is going to be married now, but if he is a good boy, then that is okay. His father, he is Thomas McGuire?'

'I was meaning to ask you about him,' Marjan said. She had heard all about the self-important man who had given Bahar such a hard time in the Ale House the day before. Marjan relayed the information from Emer Athey that Layla had finally remembered to pass down.

'Apparently Malachy's father wants us out of business,' she said.

'I tell you something about Thomas McGuire and the rest of those silly people,' Estelle said. 'They are all scared. You should see them when my Luigi and I moved here. Two, three customers a day for so long! You know what my Luigi did then? He take a table and put it out the window and everything on it was free! Free biscotti, free amaretto delights, free cannoli! Even free espresso! These people love free!'

Estelle sat forward on her bed and gestured excitedly with her warmed hands. 'I say don't worry. You smile at them all, at that McGuire, at all the women in church who look like they eat a bad egg. You teach them about being good.'

Buoyed by Estelle's wisdom, Marjan decided not to worry, but instead to smile and keep her doors open. The café was thriving with its daily patronage of regulars, and she could always rely on Father Mahoney and Fiona Athey to show up, if no one else did. As for the rest of the town, Marjan thought to herself, well, they would eventually succumb to the smell of her fried elephant ears and herb-filled *kuku*. Maybe she couldn't get everyone in Ballinacroagh to come into the Babylon, but Marjan knew there would still be enough customers to keep Bahar, Layla and her busy from morning until closing time. It was all she had ever wanted for the three of them and now it was coming true.

One thing was certain, though. They had not come all this way to sink to the likes of Thomas McGuire. Or anyone else, for that matter.

*   *   *

Chelow, or steamed rice, is vital to Persian cuisine as it lays the foundation upon which other main dishes are built. Not only does *chelow* offer excellent companionship to stews, barbecued lamb, Cornish game hens, beef or fish, but the rice can be combined with an assortment of goodies such as pistachios, lentils, dried cherries and lima beans to make a complete meal in itself. The simplest and most popular recipe, though, is white *chelow*. The rice – each grain a separate pearl of wisdom – needs to be cooked slowly for an hour before the famed *tadig* can be made.

Marjan busied herself with making the *tadig*, the crunchy bottom layer of the *chelow* that fries into a large rice cake dripping with goodness. She used a deep soup pot to heat the olive oil until it was popping with anticipation, before spreading down an inch-thick layer of rice. The *tadig* would need to be covered and gently cooked on low for thirty minutes before it would form into the savoury cracker whose crunch attracts diners to the table like nothing else.

The simple touch, the gentle touch, Marjan nodded solemnly to herself, as she lowered the heat under the pot of rice. That was the way to approach any situation, whether in cooking or in life. She was glad she had listened to Estelle Delmonico's advice.

The Babylon Café was doing so well three months after opening that Marjan had hired Jerry Mulligan – one of the boys who worked in Healy's Hardware – to moonlight as a delivery boy. Wiry, nineteen-year-old Jerry valiantly pushed his bicycle up the hilly roads with brown bags of *lavash* and *dolmeh* stacked in the basket behind his seat. The delivery service was only available at lunchtime, which was all that any of them could handle for the moment, especially now that the Babylon was closing later and later. As the summer months opened up, the afternoon tea-farers prolonged their ecstasy by turning their pots of oolong and jasmine mint into early dinners, driving Marjan to bursting point as she rushed around preparing double, triple batches of everything.

By June, school had broken up for the summer and Layla was able to help full time in-between play rehearsals, waiting on the busy tables and cleaning up in the kitchen. Sharing the work-load helped a great deal in easing the tension between Layla and an exhausted Bahar and soon the two sisters were back on good terms, their relationship as calm as the lush valley that surrounded them.

June's warm weather had surprised everyone in town. For, although the sixth month marks the solstice, summers in the west of Ireland are usually plagued by heavy, ominous clouds that beat down upon the farmlands with freezing rains. Other counties may be basking in the start of sunny days, but for County Mayo, and Ballinacroagh in particular, June usually just meant more rain. But not that summer. June 1986 brought a sultry, steady sun that reminded a bitter Thomas McGuire of the balmy after-noons in Majorca and left the ladies of the Patrician Day Dance committee in a state of panic as to what to do with the upgraded outdoor heaters they bought only last summer for the usually cold July night festival.

Most Ballinacroagh natives, though, wel-comed the dramatic change in climate, and the exuberant pronouncement of sunshine and flora that came with it. Unnamed buds appeared overnight along ivy-covered walls; plain cottages awoke to bursts of magenta, sienna and lilac flowers that had been slumbering far too long under moss-ridden stones. The soggy grass of surrounding glens rippled with tones of gold, baking in the sun, while the sky over Ballinacroagh took on a shade of untouched blue that previously had been seen only in the cobalt of Pompeii murals. Not surprisingly, this unexpected homage to her Italian homeland gave Estelle Delmonico much reason to rejoice.

Marjan, unfortunately, missed the start of summer's magnificence, as she was too busy filling the daily orders of cherry rice and *dolmeh* that Bahar and Layla delivered at breakneck speed. It was only after the lunchtime rush had passed that she was able to take a quick breather. Leaving the kitchen clean-up to her sisters, Marjan would make her way out into the warm, sunny street, crossing Main Mall towards The Butcher's Block. Leaning against a weathered aluminium poster for Clonakilty Blackpudding on the butcher's brick frontage, she examined what she and her sisters had created.

The café windows stood open on their vertical hinges and the warm afternoon breeze off Clew Bay carried zephyrs of fried cinnamon *zulbia* and cherry preserves, which they had made that very morning. Shoots of the African violets Estelle had given her were finally taking root, their flowers bursting out of two large wooden pots sitting below the windows. The violets fluttered their tiger-eyes seductively in the gentle wind. With her own hazel eyes closed, Marjan could almost imagine that she was back in the afternoon gardens of her childhood home, in northern Tehran.

The Babylon Café. The Hanging Gardens of Babylon. This row of shop fronts, Marjan thought to herself, this Main Mall, was their hanging gardens now; their own small slab of paradise.

Gratitude for life's simple bounties, for the good fortune bestowed upon him, was something that Thomas McGuire, self-anointed nucleus of all that was Ballinacroagh, would learn only too late. Had he not felt the poker of ambition stoke his entrails with such insistence, he would have realised that everything he needed in life was already his – healthy children, more money than he could ever spend, and a randy rhinoceros of a wife who knew how to keep things interesting in the bedroom (with the help of a mail-order catalogue sent to her by Hans, a one-eyed Dutch sex toy entrepreneur). All in all Thomas McGuire was a lucky man, but he was the only one in town not to know it.

It had become obvious to the big bully that his boycott and intimidation hadn't stopped the café from thriving. Most of Thomas's cronies and those indebted to him had steered clear of the Babylon's jasmine-tinged threshold, but there were plenty in town who had not. For some, Marjan's *abgusht* was just as powerful a draw as the knowledge that simply stepping foot inside the café was an act of defiance against Thomas. This subtle rebellion was a sleepier, less conscious reason for the Babylon's success than the obvious beauty of the food, but a powerful cause none the less. The combination of bodily satisfaction and the independence of the soul is hard to beat. Still, Thomas was determined to do just that.

Abandoning his boycott, the town bully decided to return to the thing he knew best (next to disco music): competitive pricing and the ousting of rival businesses through the simple laws of supply and demand. Try as he might, Thomas had not been able to unearth the secret behind the Babylon Café's success. Dervla Quigley's scratchily written daily reports had revealed nothing new and he certainly would never step inside the blasted place to find out for himself. Nor could he send Tom Junior to pick up some *dolmehs* or *chelow* for research's sake – word would be out on the streets within seconds. No, he would have to take his investigation on the road. From Westport to Galway, from Tuam to Killala, he scoured the main streets of towns on the move, trying to decipher for himself why people kept going into the Babylon Café and not the Wilton Inn for their lunches.

Thomas finally found his answer in Galway City's seaside Quay area, where a handful of ethnic restaurants had popped up over the last few years. As Thomas strolled up and down the bustling Quay, past the packed dining rooms of The Real Greek and Dim Sum More restaurants, it dawned on him why the Babylon Café was such a success. The solution had been under his nose all along, really. What Ballinacroagh had been crying out for, what had been lacking from the village all these years, was a bit of the exotic, a taste of the unknown. There was nothing particularly special about this Babylon Café; it had simply arrived at the right time, that was all. Had he not been so busy keeping the whole town plugged with mind-numbing drink, he would have seen it coming sooner himself.

Well, Thomas decided, if it was exotic the village wanted, then it was the exotic it was going to get. But none of this Babylon shite for his hometown. Pushing his distaste of all things foreign aside, Thomas chose to look further east for his newest business venture – to a land of fried pork and surprisingly cheap electronic imports. A place where disco music was still thriving and its people revered tyrannical rulers.

Thomas McGuire decided to build himself a palace, the Tom Tom Palace, Ballinacroagh's very first Chinese take-away.

Patrician Day was still four days away, but already the small town of Ballinacroagh was set spinning on its own exhilarated axis. For the first time since anyone in the village could remember, the streets were packed with an influx of tourists that had in all other years kept to the bigger towns of Castlebar and Westport. Tourism had finally hit the village. Big time.

Stalwart devotees of St Patrick and pilgrims with a penchant for hiking streamed into town by the bus load on Thursday. The religious-minded tourists came from as near as Balla and as far away as Chicago; they meandered up and down humble Main Mall with cameras and Bibles in hand, their mouths hanging open in awe as if they were beholding the relics of some great Mayan city. The excited pilgrims stocked up on bottled holy water and souvenir leather pouches filled with mountain pebbles in Antonia Nolan's religious relics shop, and had their photos taken in front of the weathered St Patrick memorial in the town square.

The Donnelly twins, loitering as usual outside Fadden's Mini-Mart, watched as the tour buses unloaded their cargo of eager pilgrims, many of whom sported sunburnt faces glowing from the combination of miraculous summer weather and the promise of spiritual fulfilment.

'How many minutes would you say, Michael, it'd take someone to notice one of those there buses missing?' Peter smirked, his sly eyes evaluating the line of parked Hibernian Holiday Tours buses.

'We'd be on our way to Dublin before they'd cop on, Peter,' Michael replied, reading his twin brother's crafty mind.

'It's something to think about, all right.'

'That it is.'

Within five minutes the hooligans had telepathically figured out how to hijack a tour bus. They would wait until lunchtime, when all the pilgrims would be packing into the Babylon Café. Michael would lure the driver out of his air-conditioned seat by asking him for directions, and Peter would grab the steering wheel and go. Later, Michael would meet him in nearby Louisburg for the joyride of their lives.

'Think of the crack, Michael! The parties we could have in one of those things!'

'It's a plan, all right. Let's get a drink to celebrate.'

'Paddy's, is it?'

'Na, the Mart for old times' sake.'

Ever since leaving secondary school the month before, the boys had abandoned their beer swapping game, believing the prank to be too childish for them now. Although they still shoplifted from poor Danny Fadden, they no longer replaced the stolen stout with felt IOU notes from Mr Finnegan the leprechaun. This omission had far greater repercussions than either twin could have guessed.

'Hello there, Danny. How's that Finnegan of yours coming along?' Michael stood in front of the counter, artfully blocking Danny's view of the beer shelves where Peter was busy swiping two brown bottles of Beamish.

'Not well, laddie. Not well at all,' Danny

replied sadly. His large glasses were smudged with countless fingerprints he hadn't bothered wiping. In fact, the shopkeeper looked like he hadn't washed himself in days. His meagre supply of hair stood on end and he was wearing his linty Aran sweater inside out.

The truth was that Danny had grown quite depressed in the last month, ashamed of having been deserted by both human and fairy folk alike. It wasn't enough that his wife Deirdre had left him five years ago, but to have his Finnegan leave as well just about pushed the shy man over the edge. Terribly saddened, he wiled away his lonely hours behind the shop counter, poring over tattered history texts and books on Celtic lore, hoping to find some solace in lives more tragic than his own. And, as if he didn't have enough misery in his life, Danny was now being harassed on a regular basis by none other than Thomas McGuire himself. The drinks baron had stopped by the mini-mart twice in three days, the last time with a thick manilla envelope in his hand.

'Twenty thousand. That's a good price I'm

givin' ya, Danny,' he had said, plonking the fat envelope on Danny's counter. 'Three times what this place is worth, you know yerself. I'll leave it with you now but I'll be back soon for yer answer. I've got big ideas for this place.' If Thomas McGuire had threatened to knock his head in with a crowbar, Danny wouldn't have been more frightened. He just stared at the envelope, his quivering lips forming a rejection that never came.

What was he holding on to, anyway? Danny wondered. What was he hoping to accomplish, sitting in this sad excuse for a grocery day in, day out, staring at dusty shelves for a leprechaun who never showed his face? Who was he kidding? As if that sort of magic was meant for the likes of him, Danny Fadden of all people. And now here was Thomas McGuire, wanting to take this heap of rat droppings and wilted vegetable stalls out of his hands, and all he had done was gawk at the envelope in front of him like an eejit.

Well, maybe he would sell the mini-mart, spend his days compiling entries for the fairy encyclopedia he had started writing. Now that sounded like a grand idea, Danny mumbled to himself.

Michael Donnelly shot his brother a worried look. Peter nodded, understanding his silent message of concern. He placed the two bottles of Beamish he had hidden in his trousers back on the shelf and walked over to the refrigerated section. After paying for two Lucozades, the boys said their goodbyes to a crestfallen Danny and walked out on to the busy street.

'Do you suppose it's not having the fairy to look forward to that's got him so down, Peter?'

'I feel like a feckin' eejit, Michael. We're two rotten sods for it.'

'I'll dip into Mam's felt box this very afternoon. We'll get his Finnegan back for him,' Michael decided.

The twins ambled up the rest of the street in silence, each boy blaming himself for taking away Danny Fadden's only companion. By the time they had reached the Ale House, though, they had exhausted their guilt and were ready for a pint. Peter was just about to open the pub door when out flew Tom Junior, thrown in the middle of a grand fight.

A crowd of curious pedestrians quickly gathered around the sprawled figure on the pavement outside the Ale House. One snap-happy pilgrim, a member of the Long Island chapter of the St Patrick's Society, used up half a Kodak roll on Tom Junior's unceremonious expulsion from the pub, catching on camera the young brute's dazed look as he shook his dizzy head and picked his lumbering self off the pavement.

'Fookin' knackers!' Tom Junior yelled, shaking his fists towards the pub door. The pious pilgrims gasped. The Donnelly twins, delighted at the prospect of a mid-morning brawl, stood poised on their tippy-toes with barely contained excitement. But, instead of bulldozing back into the Ale House for a redeeming counter-attack with the unseen assailant, Tom Junior pushed his tank-like body through the wall of gawking tourists and stumbled up Main Mall.

He arrived at St Barnabas's back gate minutes later. Dropping to his knees, Tom Junior crept stealthily behind a hedge of prickly gooseberry bushes, taking care to avoid any branches that might scratch his already tender face. The right side of his jaw still throbbed from where the tinker had punched him, so he peeked with his left eye through the dark green leaves, across the over-grown back lawn, towards the church's side entrance. Most days he would have been well sequestered in his brambly hideout by now, but the bleedin' fight had made him late today.

He needn't have bothered with those tinkers, Tom Junior told himself; he should have let Jimmy throw them out of the Ale House, or better yet, called those two lazy shites at the Garda station to come and collect them, instead of getting his hands dirty on some stinking knackers. But, then again, he couldn't just sit idly by and watch as that lot of drunken trash waltzed into one of his father's pubs as if they owned the place. And how was he to know that one of them was going to come out with a clean south paw from bleedin' nowhere?

A sharp spasm in his right eye made him recoil in pain, and he hissed under his breath. He was going to have a fecker of a bruise come tomorrow. Still, he would have rather taken another stinger to the jaw than miss his afternoon rendezvous behind the church's impressive grove of gooseberry bushes. Leaning forward on his haunches, Tom Junior resumed his close guard over the church, aware that Layla would be stepping out of the door of the Sunday School room at any moment.

Tom Junior had been following Layla's every move for months, ever since his father had given him the job of spying on his brother's romance with the girl. At first, Tom Junior had kept his distance from the couple. In a commando move that he practised many times, he would lie flat on the boggy field adjacent to the cobblestone alleyway behind the café, timing with an army stopwatch the exact minute when Malachy and Layla turned down the side street after school. Pockets of undergrowth in the field kept Tom Junior well out of sight, creating terrific bunkers where he was able to store his spy craft: a Huntsman compass he had bought at Healy's Hardware, a bottle of warm Guinness to quench his thirst and an old pair of camouflage-coloured binoculars that his father had given him for his seventeenth birthday, the year he had seen Sylvester Stallone in *First Blood*.

Disgusting how Malachy cavorted with that Arab girl, with no thought to the damage he was doing to the McGuire name. What was so special about her, anyway? he wondered. Tom Junior had heard the Donnelly twins and some of the younger lads jabbering on about Layla in the pub, as though she was God's gift to men or something. Jaysus. Sure, she was all right looking for a darkie, but he didn't know what all the fuss was about. He much preferred those blonde-haired birds with nipples as pink as they come. And to think that she had taken a fancy to Malachy of all people. Well, that just proved she wasn't right in the head, didn't it?

Tom Junior kept up his vigilant watch in the bog every afternoon. When rehearsals for Father Mahoney's play started in St Barnabas's Sunday School room, he shifted his hiding place to the bushes that bordered the back of the church, waiting until the three-hour practice session ended to resume his covert operation. Using stone walls and bundles of piled-up turf and hay to mask himself from view, Tom Junior would then follow the young sweethearts to Clew Bay Beach, where he had singled out his own private dune for spying. From his sandy fort he was able not only to listen in on the couple's intimate conversations, but to finally appreciate Layla's kinetic beauty. This close proximity to Layla's gazelle legs and glossy black locks was what would finally do Tom Junior in.

The first time Tom Junior smelled Layla's natural cinnamon–rose perfume he staggered back into a razor-sharp patch of nettles near his dune. His entire body felt electrified; his eyeballs and the insides of his mouth sizzled with longing. When the seizure passed, Tom Junior curled up into his own snail embrace, absolutely stunned. The young man found himself crying unexplainable tears that poured from a dark place in his heart. He kept weeping as Malachy and Layla walked back to town, moaning with confused sadness until the sun went down and the moon was pitying him with her full face.

The next day Tom Junior felt hollow inside but also strangely calm. For he finally knew what was wrong with him, why he had cried so hard, so fast. Layla had shown him what he could do, what he could be without the shadow of his father always looming over him. Riding that wave of her glorious perfume over his pain and anger, Tom Junior had seen himself as the conqueror of his father's empire, the rightful heir to the McGuire throne. He should be the undisputed drink lord of Ballinacroagh, not Thomas. With Layla by his side Tom Junior could bring his father to his knees in surrender and finally become his own man.

Loud voices startled Tom Junior from his daydream. He jerked his head up too quickly and accidentally rustled the gooseberry branches. Drawing in his breath, he held his body very still and squinted towards the opened church door. The hairdresser, Fiona Athey, strolled out of the church carrying a massive pink binder and a transparent pencil case full of coloured markers. She was tossing her braided hair from side to side, yapping happily. For a second Tom Junior thought the batty beautician was talking to herself, but then Father Mahoney appeared in the doorway, nodding excitedly. Tom Junior strained to hear a snippet of their conversation.

'. . . used it in the Puck Fair two years ago. Said we could have it for the whole weekend,' Father Mahoney said, beaming.

'An amphitheatre! I still can't believe it! It's absolutely perfect!' Fiona did a quick jig on the path.

'I'll be picking it up from the Arts Centre today. Made out of plywood so it'll need some reassembling. Young Malachy has offered his services,' the priest informed her.

'Would you be wanting to go to Castlebar now, Father?'

Tom Junior winced. There was Malachy, that bastard, walking out of the church door with his arm around Layla. His Layla! That gobshite, Tom Junior muttered lowly to himself. How he would love to bash his head in one of these days.

Tom Junior's bruised eye sent another bullet of pain through his skull as he watched his brother embrace Layla and climb into Father

Mahoney's clunky black 1975 Cadillac Eldorado. His gaze followed her as she waved goodbye to Fiona and walked the length of the square alone, before turning off into a side street that led away from Main Mall towards Clew Bay. Unravelling himself from his leafy hideout, Tom Junior plucked the twigs from his hair and, despite his racing heart, ambled casually up the side street after Layla.

The road was narrow and hilly, flanked by crumbling, three-storey Georgian mansions that had seen better days, when their expansive doors were painted in confident shades of blue, green and red by burgeoning, bustling families. Most of the sad houses were now in disrepair, their lime-stone porticos strangled by impenetrable ropes of creeping ivy, their once grand rooms subdivided into musty flats. Tom Junior climbed the steep hill slowly, keeping a safe distance from Layla. By the time he reached the top, she had already rounded the bend that ran past a number of scat-tered milk farms and was headed straight down to Clew Bay Beach.

Storm clouds were fast gathering over Clew

Bay as Tom Junior mounted the sandy bank. Layla was sitting comfortably on her favourite dune, about fifty metres away from him, her head tilted up towards the changing sky. A gentle current of air carried her intoxicating cinnamon–rose perfume to his hungry heart.

Layla sighed with happy relief. The week had been exceptionally hot, and the Sunday School room, built to withstand treacherous gales and long hours of tedious Bible study, was improperly ventilated for the brilliant summer the town was experiencing. Rehearsing in the sweltering room had proved nearly unbearable, so Layla welcomed the cool caresses of sea breeze on her moistened skin. She checked her watch again, eager for Malachy to finish his errand with Father Mahoney and join her on the beach. How romantic it would be if they were caught together in a rainstorm, Layla thought, hugging herself tightly. Straight out of a movie. Grinning, she looked up and winked at grumpy Croagh Patrick, sharing her fantasy with the ancient mountain.

Seized by a sudden, uncontrollable longing, Tom Junior chose that very moment to expose himself to Layla. He dashed feverishly across the dunes, a deep groan escaping from his churning bowels, and jumped on her from behind. His calloused fingers pulled at her silky blouse and clumsily groped her bared stomach. At first, Layla thought Malachy had turned into a mad animal, but then Tom Junior's glazed eyes and snorting nostrils came into focus. His mutton lips pressed down into her whole face, suffocating her screams. Gnashing hungrily, Tom Junior's teeth tore into the inside of her lip, breaking its persimmon softness. His beefy paw was just reaching under her squirming denim skirt when, out of nowhere, a knuckled fist came crashing down on the left side of his head

Chapter Ten

Fesenjoon

Ingredients:

500g shelled walnuts, chopped
olive oil
1,250g skinless chicken breast, cubed
3 large onions, sliced
6 tbsp pomegranate paste, dissolved in
2 cups hot water
½ tsp salt
½ tsp ground black pepper
1 tbsp sugar
2 tbsp lemon juice

The young tinker girl knocked at the back door at quarter to three in the afternoon. Marjan recognised her as one of the many freckled faces that lingered at the café windows long after other curious schoolchildren had left their mucky handprints behind. The mischievous pack of street urchins, members of the itinerant camp, spent a greater part of their days panhandling with paper cups outside shop doorways on Main Mall. Though never afraid to solicit customers inside the McGuire establishments, for some strange reason the tinkers kept a quiet respect for the Babylon Café and never ventured inside its vermilion walls.

'Hello. What can I do for you? Do you want to come in?' Marjan smiled at the girl standing timidly in her back garden. She was a pale, small-boned child, about nine years old, Marjan guessed; a wisp of a thing with wide-set cerulean eyes and long orange hair that hung in a tangled ponytail down her back. The young girl shook her head and looked down briefly, before bursting into a half-intelligible message.

'Yes bettur git te da water. Better git der quick

now! We've got yer sis der. She'd hurt just da bit, now, so.'

It was enough for Marjan to understand that something was terribly wrong.

Speeding up Main Mall in the green van, Marjan tried her best to make sense of the girl's warbled directions to the tinkers' campsite, while also keeping her own thumping heart from exploding. They finally arrived at Clew Bay Beach, the van lurching into the public parking area just as thunder crackled across the bay. The beach, past the solitary dunes where Layla had been sitting, was filled with summering school-children and the odd Speedo-suited farmer, all burnt to various shades of pink. As soon as the eager sunbathers heard the thunder they scrambled for their unused suntan lotions and crisp bathroom towels, stuffing them under folded arms as they ran for their cars and bicycles.

The young tinker girl quickly led Marjan across a sandy pathway scattered with grass and dulled bottle shards, towards a gravel car park crammed with mobile homes. Marjan briefly scanned the large vehicles before her. Fifty-year-old chrome-hooded caravans sat side by side with last year's sleeker models, confidently equipped with the latest in mobile-home technology. The entire train of caravans was clustered neatly around a communal area consisting of makeshift crate tables and fold-out chairs. Perched on the edge of one white plastic chair was Layla, her black hair tousled and sandy. She was leaning her scratched elbows on her knees as she held a torn piece of tissue to an open cut on her lip. Crouched next to her, and whispering in uncharacteristically angry tones, was Malachy, his usually graceful hands balled into tight fists.

'Layla! What happened to you? What's going on?' Marjan's voice was filled with terror as she rushed to her sister's side.

Layla stood up shakily. 'It's okay. I'm okay. I just—' She broke off, not knowing where to start.

Malachy tried to control his anger, but his voice cracked and skipped octaves as he jumped in to explain what had happened.

'I arrived just after it all. I'll never forgive myself,' he began, his voice heavy with guilt. 'Father Mahoney dropped me off at the beach after we got back from the Arts Centre. Layla wasn't in our usual spot, so I sat on a dune and waited. I thought she might have gone to the toilets near the car park and would be back soon. I can't believe I was so stupid,' Malachy said, shaking his head in utter dismay. He was ashamed to admit it, but at the time he had presumed that one of the tinkers had harassed Layla on the beach and scared her off. Malachy was embarrassed by his assumptions, now that he knew both who had given Layla her bloodied lip and who had saved her from further harm.

Declan Maughan, twice middle-weight champion of the Connaught amateur boxing circuit and chief of the caravan before them, was the man who had rescued Layla from Tom Junior's slobbering assault. As luck would have it, Declan had been just itching for an opportunity to practise the Maughan 'slide and bounce cut', a combination that would surely make his third time on the ropes a charmed one indeed.

Having been ousted from their last three campsites (twice by tractor teams in Donegal and once by a herd of menopausal cows in Galway), Declan had moved his caravan to Clew Bay Beach for the spring and summer seasons, knowing how useful the sand would be for resistance training. Declan had missed his daily beach workout that morning, though, a result of heavy partying with several of the younger men of the camp the night before. The revelry lasted well into the morning, as the whole gang caroused down Main Mall with Guinness bottles held high, bellowing songs of rebellion. And then, of course, there was the fight in the Ale House with those two eejits, those *amadans*, in which, Declan was proud to say, he and his mates had come out the victors before having to make a hasty retreat back to the camp. So, when a still-punchy Declan finally trudged on to the beach that afternoon, the last thing he expected to see was the same gobshite who had picked a fight with him just a few hours before.

He spied Tom Junior grovelling on top of the distant dune, his chunky legs sashaying over the sand like a pig in high heat. Declan slowed down his hoppity jog and squinted into the afternoon horizon. If he wasn't mistaken, that bleedin' bastard wasn't alone. There was a poor girl squirming under him! Declan's sinewy legs sprinted across the sand, flying high over powdery sandbanks and spools of barbed seaweed, landing right behind Tom Junior, on the dune, within seconds.

'I'm going to kill him, Layla. If those bloody guards at the station house don't do anything, then I say we go all the way to Castlebar,' said Malachy. His fists were clenched, his knuckles white as he bit down on his words.

'Where's this man who helped you, Layla?' Marjan said, searching the campsite.

Several tinkers had gathered behind the two teenagers; the impish red-haired girl, Aoife, trailed by a handful of other rascally children, and four gum-clacking, gold-clad women who looked at Marjan with wary eyes. Two older, scruffy men dressed in frayed football shirts sat smoking on chairs near by, but Declan Maughan was nowhere to be seen. He was, in fact, watching the whole scene from his mobile home, the newest and fanciest one on the site, but a debilitating shyness that always overcame him in the presence of strange women kept the caravan chief from stepping outside to claim his heroic deed.

'He's indisposed ri' now. What can I do fer ye?' The biggest woman there stepped forward. Her teased, hair-sprayed blonde helmet reminded Marjan of an overripe kumquat. She had a territorial air about her and was indeed Declan Maughan's older sister.

'I just want to thank him. I can't imagine what would have happened if he hadn't saved my sister,' said Marjan, attempting a smile but managing only a wavering grimace. She could feel her composure beginning to unravel.

Buck up, Marjan, she told herself. Just get yourself back into the kitchen and decide what to do from there. Surrounded by the safety of its warm walls she just might have a chance to make sense of it all.

Bahar locked the café door behind Marie Brennan and Mrs Boylan. After pouring herself a cup of strong Darjeeling tea, she sat down at the kitchen table and replayed Marjan's words in her head.

'Just keep your eye on the *abgusht*, Bahar. Give it a stir, okay? I'll be back soon,' Marjan had whispered urgently, her face a greenish-white as she ran out of the back door.

Had Bahar's hands not been full with Mrs Boylan's order of marinated pepper wrap and red lentil soup, she would have hurried after her sister and demanded an explanation for her stricken appearance. But by the time she stepped out into the cobblestone alleyway, Marjan had already reversed the van and was gone.

Something terrible had happened, Bahar was sure of it. What else could have prompted her sister to run out of the kitchen so hastily, or to ask her to mind the bubbling pan of *abgusht*? Marjan knew how she hated to stand before a hot stove. It was Layla, Bahar told herself. Something bad had happened to Layla.

A tinny sound rang out from the wall behind her. The phone. It was probably Marjan, with the horrible news. Bahar picked up the receiver and slowly brought it to her ear.

'H-hello?' She swallowed hard, a lump caught in her throat.

There was no answer on the other end of the line, just silence.

'Hello? Marjan, is that you?'

She almost didn't hear the low breathing at first. The sound came upon her suddenly, a strange, soft *whoooosshh* like a balloon slowly releasing its air. A deflation of the senses, a deceptively simple expiration that sounded like barely controlled danger. A few seconds later the air spluttered and stopped, ending abruptly in a raspy, almost inaudible grunt. Then silence.

Bahar felt a sharp, painful depression in her own lungs as she stood listening to the void. And then, out of nowhere, she opened her mouth and surprised herself.

'Hossein?' She gulped, the name dropping like lead from her trembling lips. Though he kept permanent residence in a dark place inside of her, months had passed since she had uttered her husband's name. Something in that whispering wind, that creeping *whoooosshh*, had brought him back to her. *Hossein*. The sinister hiss of the middle consonants sent tremors through her entire body. With her hand shaking uncontrollably, Bahar placed the receiver back in its cradle and collapsed into a nearby chair.

A detailed report ensued at the Garda station. Shocked by the news of Tom Junior's attack, Kevin Slattery scribbled Layla and Malachy's accounts in his dusty ledger, while a worried Sean Grogan paced up and down the station's corridor, unsure of how to tackle this new crisis. It would require some serious officiating, that was for sure.

'Rest assured, we'll get to the bottom of this soon enough,' Sean Grogan promised, as he gently ushered the three of them out of the station. 'This here isn't the sort of town where people can go jumping on each other like animals. We're not in Dublin!'

After dropping Malachy off at home, Marjan pulled the van over outside the cobblestone alleyway and turned solemnly to Layla in the passenger seat.

'I want to talk to you about something before we go in.' Marjan's voice was thin and raspy. She paused and looked intently into Layla's eyes. 'I don't think we should tell Bahar what happened to you.'

'Why shouldn't we tell her? I could have been raped, you know!' Layla cried incredulously, twisting her face into a deep scowl.

'I know, *joon-e man*,' soothed Marjan. 'And we'll tell her, eventually. Just not yet. She's only beginning to calm down after the last time you disappeared, and you know how bad her migraines have been. You and I need to protect her sometimes, that's all.'

'But how am I going to explain my lip?' Layla pouted. Her cut lip was clean of blood and sand, but the area around it was swollen and bruised. Bahar would notice it for sure.

'It doesn't have to be a big lie – just tell her that you fell while hiking with Malachy or something like that. Do you understand?' she pleaded.

The younger girl stared sullenly out of the van window, her eyes filled with glistening tears.

'Layla?' Marjan pressed.

'This is history repeating itself,' Layla said

thickly, voicing the words that Marjan was thinking, but could not bring herself to say.

Later that evening, Marjan stood before the food processor in the kitchen. She could hear the bolt on the back gate clanging ferociously in the wind. All of her back garden herbs – the summer savory, the mint and tarragon, were bowing down to the storm that had kept the heavens in a head-lock ever since they returned from the Garda station. Looking at the sky now, thought Marjan, no one would have guessed that the morning had been so cloudless and benign.

Marjan let the food processor run on, its angry steel blades grinding the walnuts to a brown pulp. She added pomegranate paste and cinnamon and allowed the blades to whine for several more minutes before snapping the small machine off. She had to keep her wits about her if she was going to make *fesenjoon*, the invigorating pome-granate, chicken and walnut stew that was Layla's all-time favourite comfort food.

It is the pomegranate that gives *fesenjoon* its healing capabilities. The original apple of sin, the fruit of a long gone Eden, the pomegranate shields itself in a leathery crimson shell, which in Roman times was used as a form of protective hide. Once the pomegranate's bitter skin is peeled back, though, a juicy garnet flesh is revealed to the lucky eater, popping and bursting in the mouth like the final succumb of love-making.

Long ago, when the earth remained still, content with the fecundity of perpetual spring, and Demeter was the mother of all that was natural and flowering, it was this tempting fruit that finally set the seasons spinning. Having eaten six pomegranate seeds in the underworld, Persephone, the Goddess of Spring's high-spirited daughter, had been forced to spend six months of the year in the eternal halls of death. Without her beautiful daughter by her side, a mournful Demeter retreated to the dark corners of the universe, allowing the icy gates of winter to finally creak open. A round, crimson herald of frost, the pomegranate comes to harvest in October and November, so *fesenjoon* is best made with its concentrate during other times of the year.

The *fesenjoon* bubbled happily on the stove, blissfully unaware of the brewing crisis. Even the sweet taste of pomegranate could not cover up the bitterness that had risen between the three sisters. Bahar had been just as distressed about Layla's cut lip as Marjan had anticipated. She gave their younger sister a proper scolding, reminding her of the pitfalls of falling in love, before retiring to her bed with a headache. Layla had opted to lie miserably still on the sofa bed Marjan used as her sleeping quarters, flicking through television channels until she fell asleep with the remote in her hand, a piece of tissue stuck to her lip.

Layla's foreboding words echoed in Marjan's head. *I could have been raped. This is history repeating itself.* It still amazed Marjan how much of the past Layla had retained, especially considering how young she had been back then.

History repeating itself. Was history really that cruel? Marjan didn't know what to think any more. She lifted the lid off the *fesenjoon* and stirred it again. The pomegranate paste had turned the stew a dark maroon, the broth swimming sinfully with a life of its own. History repeating itself. Maybe it was.

Nearly four months after her marriage to Hossein and three days after the momentous Black Friday massacre in Jaleh Square, Bahar had crept into her sisters' Tehran apartment at two in the morning. Using her spare key to get in, she slipped so quietly into the single bed that she had once shared with little Layla, that Marjan did not notice her until the coming of dawn. She had woken up grudgingly with the low light, bracing herself for another day of washing endless dirty dishes at The Peacock Restaurant, only to be confronted by Bahar's soiled body lying in bed.

An ochre and yellow assembly of bruises, imprints of contorted fingers, started at Bahar's neck. A violet of burst veins moved up to her left eye and down the side of her right ear, ending in a torn lobe from which hung encrusted droplets of blood, priceless for their shedding. But the worst damage was what could not be seen, not until Bahar uncoiled her chador, winced out of her long grey skirt, woollen tights and blood-soaked underskirt. Only then did Marjan see the thick baton grooves embossed upon her sister's upper thighs, a serrated ladder that disappeared deep inside her and left unseen wounds in its path.

They packed their bags that very morning.

Out came the two tartan suitcases, bought by their parents at Burberry of London, on that one trip to Europe in the gay 1950s, before any of them were born and the Shah's palaces still gleamed with a thousand brilliant rubies. The bags smelled of uncertainty, of mothballs mingled with the chalky skins of shrunken pistachio nuts. As little Layla lay sleeping in her bed, Marjan and Bahar went quickly to work, rolling up mementos that were too dear to leave behind in chunky sweaters and tube socks. In went their grandmother's samovar, the old photographs, the wooden jewellery box. Clothes, bags of dried fruit, jars of *torshi* and just-made quince and rose-blossom preserves (drenched in sugar, they would provide energy for hard days to come). The last thing Marjan packed was a folder of stacked lined papers, notes and observations of hundreds of recipes, some inherited from her mother, others compiled over the years from her time at The Peacock Restaurant. Recorded in Marjan's precise hand were the jewels of slivered pistachio baklava, the reminders to introduce pitted sour cherries to *albalou polow* before adding the half cup of sour cherry syrup, and a fat botany guide to herb growing she had picked up during her years in the university.

Early the next day, just before morning prayers were bellowed from the neighbourhood mosque, Marjan left the apartment with an envelope of their birth certificates and most treasured documents tucked under a chador she had borrowed from Bahar. She manœuvred her way down archways and dark side streets to Roosevelt Avenue, home of the American Embassy. A fortress wall lined with Marines, the embassy was a clear target of hatred for many revolutionaries. On the north-western side of the cement barrier, a looming teal-coloured gate creaked open only at the behest of its keepers – surly-faced, moustached Iranian policemen who looked strangely alien against the brick and marble façade of the embassy building. The line of hopeful visa applicants consisted mostly of bearded young men sprawled on cheap woven *kilims* and ratty blankets. Spread on the ground before them were the latest leftist newspapers, countless articles forecasting the oncoming revolution, the upheaval of all upheavals that would scald the streets with more young blood.

Praying hard that she would get to file the forms for their American visas, Marjan joined the embassy line on that brisk September morning, but by nightfall the only line that had moved was a steady train of industrious ants on the tall wall overhead. With the Shah's nine o'clock curfew closing in, Marjan was forced to relinquish her spot in line and hurry home empty-handed down Roosevelt Avenue. *I will hit the line at dawn tomorrow*, she decided, as she climbed the dilapidated staircase of the apartment building they had called home for the last two years. Anything to get us away from this living hell, from this Hossein Jaferi, Marjan thought. She was thankful that Bahar had finally come to her senses and left her husband, though she wished her sister's decision hadn't come at such a dear price.

On the tenth floor, Marjan paused to catch her breath, feeling suddenly very weak. She hadn't eaten since the day before, and wondered if Bahar had reheated the pot of pomegranate soup for dinner. Marjan hoped her sister remembered to add the last dash of angelica powder, a good-luck omen, into the simmering pan. Conjuring fortuity was an act of great faith, something they all needed at this fearful moment in time.

The heavy smell of burning pomegranate paste hit her on the twelfth floor, a sad, sweet but also slightly acrid sensation that harks back to the cloistered tang of a mother's womb; by the fourteenth floor it had manifested into a formidable cloud of bitter, mauve smoke. Marjan shielded her stinging eyes with her chador and frantically pushed forward. Gasping, she suddenly stopped short of the apartment door. Splintered and with its golden chain lock broken, the door hung purposelessly off one set of hinges, the wooden frame fanned out in jagged, petrified daggers. She stood in shock before the barbed threshold, unable to move, until muffled screams from inside shattered her trance.

Marjan saw his muddy, green army boots first, then his gaunt profile. Hossein was bent over as if in prayer, his painfully thin shoulder blades grinding together as his head rocked fanatically back and forward. A piercing, mucusy cry came from the far corner of the kitchen. The pot of pomegranate soup was steaming, hissing, its lid lifting off on a crest of creamy, fruit foam as Bahar's small socked feet twitched under Hossein's bony hold. A large object swooped in front of Marjan's eyes and she ducked instinctively to avoid its assault. The descending pendulum, she soon realised, was her own arm, wielding a wooden stake torn from the door frame. As if guided by a force outside her body, Marjan squeezed her eyes shut and planted the wooden stake deep into Hossein Jaferi's leg.

He turned in a slow and silent dance, the same man at whose wedding she had thrown rice, praying hard that it would coat her sister through any hardship. The starkness of his long beard and scaly, balding head terrified her; his pitted facial scars pulsed red with anger.

'You motherless whore!'

Hossein lunged for Marjan with the baton he carried to riots – the jagged wooden wedge still implanted in his leg – just as Bahar scrambled up from the floor and grabbed the scalding pot of soup. Left on the stove for too long, the pomegranate soup had become a pulpy mass, the fructose residue sticking to the pot with a horrible smell. Half of the soup was already burnt to a black sludge, but the rest flowed freely down upon Hossein's head. He fell, his forehead struck by the hot lip of the heavy pan, as a scalding deluge of pomegranate juice engulfed his unconscious body.

A shrill cry from the hallway pulled Marjan out of a black abyss. She burst into the small side pantry and salvaged her youngest sister from amongst the sea of dried fenugreek leaves and clotted *sumac*. She kissed little Layla's face and checked for bruises, thankful to find only tracks of tears and brick-coloured *sumac* stains.

'Get the papers! And the chadors! The curfew cars will be coming around soon,' Marjan whispered fiercely. She turned around to find Bahar shaking like *sholeh zard*, saffron pudding that requires a heavy bowl to contain its almondy, spineless matter.

All the colour had drained from her face and collected at the base of her mottled throat. Bahar's nose was bloody and a piece of scalp tissue hung at a feeble angle from where her husband had pulled her hair out. Hossein hadn't moved from where he had fallen, but Marjan knew their time was short. With Layla spluttering in her arms, Marjan pulled Bahar out of the kitchen and into the small living room.

'Look at me, Bahar!' Marjan held Bahar's chin in her hand and stared into her dazed eyes. 'We have to go now, do you understand? We have to go!' Bahar's eyes did not blink, but kept staring down at Marjan's chest, where a long tear in her chador exposed her white collared shirt.

Marjan saw the blood then. Starting at her armpit, it was spreading rapidly across her breast like a blossoming poppy. There, at the juncture where her arm met her shoulder, stood four inches of splintered wood, embedded when she flew past the broken door frame to save them all.

Chapter Eleven

Migraine Headache Remedy

Ingredients:

> 1 tsp ground nutmeg
> 1 tsp ground cardamom
> 1 tsp ground cloves
> 1 cup warm water

The crisp deeds of ownership lay perfectly flat in front of Danny Fadden. Next to the contract sat the bulging manilla envelope stuffed with twenty thousand and five hundred punts, five hundred more than Thomas McGuire had previously offered. Ballinacroagh's major publican was hoping the unexpected bonus would induce the lonely shopkeeper to hand over his life's work as quickly as possible.

'You sign that contract, Danny, and we'll be having a pint at Paddy's in no time.' Thomas grinned and shoved a fat fountain pen into Danny's pale hand.

Danny stared at the expensive Watermark pen, the kind that important men carried in the breast pockets of their fancy Italian suits. Maybe signing this contract was his ticket to becoming someone important, too. He could invest some of the money in the stock market, and live off the rest until he finished his Fairy Encyclopedia. At the moment, Danny was in the middle of the Ls, having just edited an entry on LEPRECHAUN, the trickster shoemaker who plays pranks on human folk.

Yes, selling the mini-mart to Thomas McGuire might have been the smart thing, thought Danny, had his own leprechaun, Finnegan, not come back to him that very afternoon. Danny had unlocked the mini-mart door after his half-hour tea break and walked in to find two bottles of Beamish missing from the beer shelf. That little scallywag Finnegan had left a piece of emerald green felt and a note in their place: *Hope you didn't miss me, on my holiday, IOU on two stout, till I get me pay. Finnegan.*

'What's the word, Danny? Time to grab the bull by the horns,' Thomas said, gritting his teeth through a forced smile.

Danny reached under the counter, into a shelf where he kept all of Finnegan's notes. He rubbed a piece of felt for courage.

'The thing is, Thomas, I can't—'

Just then, Padraig Carey burst into the mini-mart, soaked to the bone.

'Tom! Tom!' he blurted. 'You best get yourself down to the station! It's Tom Junior!' The councilman's face was red and bloated, his tie flown over his shoulder by the wet winds.

Thomas shot Padraig a dirty look.

'The eejit hasn't rammed his car into a tele-phone pole again, has he? That boy – I'll tell ya, Danny, best stick with girls.'

'The shop's n-not—' Danny stammered on.

'Stay where you are, Danny. We'll have this all signed and sealed soon enough,' Thomas commanded, before stomping angrily out of the shop. 'This better be good, Padraig. Had the deal shut before you opened yer fat gob,' he snarled.

'That's what I've been trying to tell ya. It's bad news, Tom,' Padraig replied.

The two men scrambled into Padraig's tiny Fiat and gunned up rainy Main Mall. On the way to the Garda station, Padraig filled Thomas in on what he had overheard outside the police offices.

'The two of them parked that green van and went inside, with Malachy right behind them! By the time I crossed the square, that Sean Grogan had barred the door. Said there were some "confidential matters" at hand and would I come by later? The bollocks on him, Tom!' Padraig cried petulantly. 'I had to sneak under the window to make any sense of it!'

Thomas's face hardened to stone as he listened to Padraig. Too furious to wait for the councilman to park, he jumped out of the Fiat as it slowed down in the town square. The big bully exploded into the police station, startling Kevin Slattery just as the young guard was making himself a cup of weak tea.

'Kevin, what's this business about my Tom? Where's Grogan? Who's in feckin' charge here, eh?'

Sean Grogan, who was in an adjoining room, quickly tucked away the report of Layla's complaint. He stepped out into the hallway and leaned his arm protectively across the door's threshold, clearing his throat.

'There's probably a fine explanation for everything, Tom. I'll be needing to ask your boy a few questions, that's all. If you could just tell me where Tom Junior is—'

'Am I hearin' this right? You're letting some bloody darkie say what she likes about me and mine? Is that it, eh?'

'Thomas . . .' Sean Grogan could have said more, could have attempted to calm the steaming man in front of him as his position required, but he was enjoying himself too much to stop Thomas's rant. There was no doubt in his mind that Tom McGuire Junior, that dirty sod, had attacked Layla. He had no reservations about locking the boy away in the station's small cell for a whole year, if need be, Sean told himself. No matter who his father was.

'And you, Sean Grogan, yer calling my Tom on it?' Thomas's eyes bulged out of their sockets. He couldn't believe his ears. It was taking all his strength to keep from hitting Sean Grogan in his fat face. And that Slattery, too, thought Thomas, standing there with his mug of tea like the nancy the whole town knew he was.

'The thing is, ah, Tom, there's a witness, so. Nothing I can do about it.'

'Witness? What witness. Who is it?'

'Ah, well now, I can't say. That's strictly confidential, you see.'

'Feck you and yer confidential!' Thomas growled. He turned on his heels, and stomped down the station hallway, knocking Padraig straight into the corridor wall. Pausing at the station door, he pointed towards the two officers. 'You're going to be sorry you did this, Sean Grogan,' he threatened, and thundered out of the Garda station.

A silent Padraig shrugged his shoulders nervously at the guards and followed Thomas to the car. The short councilman knew precisely what side of the plate his meat was on.

Beyond the rain clouds, above the constant peak that he was now beginning to detest, was the constellation Hercules. The star was a consolation to Malachy, as he sifted through his own personal storm.

The young man stooped in his alcove bedroom stuffing his burlap school bag with clothes, while his mother and three sisters lingered on the upstairs landing, watching him with confusion. They were accustomed to seeing Malachy and Tom Junior at ends with each other, but no fight had been bad enough to make one of them want to leave home. Joanne, the youngest of the three sisters, burst into tears when she saw Malachy begin to disassemble his telescope.

'Don't cry, Joanne. I'll be back to visit,' he said, before turning to his mother. 'Are you sure you haven't seen Tom today, Mam? Are you telling me the truth?'

'Haven't seen him since the mornin', Malachy. Maybe that foreign girl there was the one to take him. I heard a few things about those three in that café. I hope you're looking after yourself when you're down that end. Never know what one of them would do if she saw your lovely looks, eh?'

She went to pat him on his head, but Malachy swatted her away. It was the first sign of defiance he had ever shown his mother and it made his head burn with unexpected fury. He was glad he hadn't told her about his relationship with Layla, as he had been tempted to do so many times in the last few months.

'Whatever it is, it can't be that bad. You'll work things out, now,' his mother mumbled vacuously, leaning against his bedroom door. She was decked out in her usual Thursday-night get-up: a black sequined sweater paired with tight stretch leggings that highlighted the grapefruit texture of her cellulite-ridden thighs. Her head was wound up in thick, spongy rollers, which she would prop up against four pillows at night to ensure the next morning's do. Cecelia McGuire never went anywhere without her poodle-like curls.

Watching Malachy now, Cecelia couldn't help musing about her long-ago love affair with Juan Carlos Escobar II. Being the daughter of a late county mayor had assured Cecilia Devereux the choice of Mayo's most eligible bachelors, but she had chosen Thomas McGuire for his ambition and attractive, muscled thighs. Thomas's ambition had its drawbacks, though, as his lonely wife soon discovered, so Cecelia was grateful when Juan Carlos Escobar II's ship came in, that exhilarating summer of 1967. The Spanish sailor taught her words like *amor mio, cariña* and *pasión* while he strummed her inner strings, and although he disappeared before summer's end, he left her with a living, breathing souvenir in the form of Malachy.

The boy stuffed the last piece of clothing, his favourite football shirt, into his backpack and, swinging his telescope case on to one shoulder, lumbered out of his tiny bedroom. Patting a tearful Joanne on the head, Malachy gave his other sisters, Delia and Helen, a silent nod goodbye, determined never to return to his damp, claustrophobic bedroom. At the bottom of the stairs, he stopped and turned back to the four bewildered faces gaping down at him from the landing, his anger softening slightly as Joanne's whimpers grew louder. Just as he opened his mouth to say something reassuring, Thomas McGuire nosed the Land Rover into the driveway, honking the horn madly.

By the time Thomas burst into the house roaring for answers, Malachy had already slipped out of the kitchen door. He looked back one last time at the house of his lonely childhood, before disappearing into the dark forest of the neighbouring fields.

Meanwhile, in the upstairs shoebox of a bedroom she shared with Layla, Bahar lay perfectly still in bed. She had been asleep, caught up in a fitful nightmare, the only dream she ever had, when the smell of cooking pomegranate and flashes of lightning woke her. Downstairs, she could hear the sound of the back door clicking shut. It was probably Marjan, she thought, running out to the shop for a missing ingredient for the *fesen-joon*.

Ripples of pain shot up from behind her ears and washed down the right side of her head to pool in her temples. Bahar turned over in bed and reached dizzily for the small glass jar of brown powder sitting next to her on a wobbly pedestal table. The powder, a mixture of nutmeg, cardamom and ground cloves, was a potent Baluchi remedy that cured mild migraines within minutes of swallowing. Nowadays, though, it took at least six large spoonfuls to ease Bahar's migraines, and even then it was never as effective as the first time she had tried it, back in the Dasht-e Lut desert.

Bahar brought the spoonful of grainy medicine up to her lips and grimaced. She took a deep breath and swallowed all of it in one go, feeling the powder slide slowly down the back of her throat like hot gravel. She could never get used to its harsh taste, its unforgiving texture. Strange, though, she didn't remember the medicine ever tasting so bad when it was administered by the Baluchi women. Even now, deep in the fog of another fierce headache, she could clearly recall their tribal kindness.

The Baluchi women, with their patchwork skirts and sunburnt faces, had presented Bahar with two jars of the headache medicine the morning the sisters had escaped from Iran. After two nights spent with the Baluchi tribe in the desert, they crossed the Pakistan border with the help of an illiterate goat farmer from the nearby town of Zahedan. For a three-pound-sterling charge, he drove them in his dungy truck to The Red Cross refugee camp erected outside the Pakistani town of Quetta. Surrounded by other frightened Iranians on the run, the girls took refuge in the camp for five months before they finally secured visas to the UK.

They arrived at Heathrow Airport to the scrutiny of thick-necked Immigration officers. Interrogations were fired and passports checked, then double-checked, before the three sisters were granted the sweet stamps of entry. The girls stepped out of the grey, colossal airport and straight into the South London concrete block of flats appointed to them by The Red Cross. The Brixton Bay View housed an array of personalities: Castro defectors and disco mavens shooting up under rusty stairwells, drag queens who moonlighted as Avon ladies, and half-naked latchkey kids practising their break-dancing in the car park. Before long Marjan was working as a pitta stuffer in *A Thousand and One Kebabs*, a shish kebab and falafel take-away near Trafalgar Square, while Bahar and Layla rejoined the daily humdrum of school life. Things were going well, despite their meagre existence on oily couscous and fatty rinds of questionable impaled meats. Within four years Bahar had been accepted into St Bartholomew's School of Nursing and Marjan had moved up in the culinary world, working as a sous chef for Plantain, a Jamaican fusion restaurant in the trendier suburb of Notting Hill. Soon they were able to move from the estate to a nice two-bedroom flat in Lewisham, where Layla could play in a cul-de-sac without running across used needles, and where Marjan could encourage a few precious herbs to grow. A place where Bahar could really forget the bruises. But, despite this hard-won tranquillity, it was hard to ignore what was happening in their homeland.

Iran in the early 1980s was suffering the digestive heartburn of a revolutionary feast gone on far too long. Civil war had broken out, pitting militant mullahs against Islamic Socialists, each vying for the seat of power and getting nowhere in the process. Reverberations of the revolution were felt across the saharas, as honey-fed princes in the shaken sheikhdoms of Qatar, Saudi Arabia and Kuwait scrambled to stop their dripping reserves of gold liquid with white robes. And caught in between these upheavals were the young: the thirteen-year-old soldiers who had forsaken puberty for the religious cause. In cemeteries throughout Iran laminated cardboard tombstones declared their short lives, while shrouded mothers mourned the unnatural reversal of time.

Marjan watched the worldwide demonstrations against the growing Islamic regime on the BBC nightly news with a mixture of awe and relief. Thank God they had got out in time, she would tell herself. Bahar, on the other hand, would never sit through the televised images of bombed-out streets filled with men who looked like they could all be Hossein. She wasn't afraid that he might be one of the dead, but rather that he *wouldn't* be among the bodies strewn across their television screen. She never should have believed in such a cause, in such a man. What had made her do so? Bahar could no longer remember the reasons she had given herself or Marjan for marrying into it all, for believing, so whenever Jim Muir's pasty face came on with his nightly reports from Tehran's bloody streets, she would hastily retire to her bed with the headache that was fast becoming her best friend.

Time passed again. Marjan got a new job at *Aioli*, a chi-chi Italian joint in Lewisham, where she befriended the head chef, Gloria, and was able to unburden some of their pain on to her sympathetic new friend. Bahar graduated with top honours from nursing school and started work at the Green Acres nursing home, an occupation that, if it did not provide close friendships, did ease the acute depression she had been suffering under for over half a decade. By the end of 1985, Bahar had returned to stretches of headache-free days and the occasional laughing fit as she and Marjan watched Layla grow up into gawky adolescence. Then, one night in March, just over four months ago, the telephone rang in their Lewisham flat.

Bahar was first to pick up. 'Hello?' Was that an electric shock in her ear as she picked up the receiver or was it the chime of Hades' bell?

'Did you think that God was on your side, Bahar? That I would let you and your dirty sisters make a fool of me?' The voice grated through the telephone lines like sheets of sandpaper. 'I can't even show my face at meetings any more, did you know that? My mother won't leave the house for the shame you've brought our family, you whore. If I were you I'd start praying. Pray for mercy, wife, because the next knock you hear will be mine.' The phone clicked off, so chirpy and correct that it made Hossein's threat sound even more sinister. Bahar stared at the receiver in her hand with disbelief, feeling sick to her stomach. The BBC news was drawing to a close, and Marjan turned to her sister.

'Bahar, who was that?'

Bahar's eyes rolled back into her head. Shadows took over.

Could it be happening all over again? Bahar wondered, wringing the bed sheets in her fists. Had Hossein found her here in Ballinacroagh? Was the eerie, hissing on the telephone line this afternoon another warning perhaps?

And what about Layla's weak explanation later for the cut on her lip? A hiking accident with Malachy. Who knows if any of it was true? Maybe her sisters had not wanted her to know what had happened, what was going to happen, but Bahar had seen it all play out in their eyes. They had wanted to protect her, bless their hearts, but she knew the truth, the real reason behind Layla's bloody lip and the tremor at Marjan's chin. The signs were all there; that silent phone call had been for her.

Bahar sat up quickly in bed. The tribal migraine medicine had worked its magic, dulling her painful headache considerably, but she knew its effects wouldn't last long. There was no time to lose, she told herself.

Layla was still asleep on the living-room sofa when Bahar took the remote control out of her sister's fist. She turned the TV off and pulled the blanket up to Layla's chin, pausing a moment to admire the young girl's beautiful face. She should have been nicer to Layla, more understanding of her needs, Bahar told herself. Layla was only fifteen, after all. Bahar bent down and gently kissed her sister's forehead, then turned and crept towards the creaking staircase. A chill ran down her back as she reached the bottom landing. The kitchen had gone so cold so quickly. Bahar's eyes rested on the pan sitting on the stove. She was right, it was *fesenjoon*.

The pomegranate was calling her back. It wanted her to return, to face up to the pact she had made so long ago, a promise she hadn't kept. There would be no running away this time. Hossein had finally found her.

At midnight, the lights in the café's kitchen could be particularly harsh. Without the comfort of daylight streaming in through the stained-glass window, everything in the room looked grim and strangely utilitarian.

Marjan and Layla sat at the round kitchen table in morose silence. Scattered on the table were trails of brown powder, where Bahar had hastily mixed her special headache remedy before leaving. Marjan absently traced a finger through the grainy remains.

'She must have taken the medicine with her. I can't find the jar anywhere,' she observed sombrely.

'We can't just sit here, Marjan!' Layla jumped up from the kitchen table, determined to do something, anything. After a frantic search of the nearby flooded streets, they returned to the café and sat waiting for over two hours, hoping that the note in front of them was a big mistake, praying that Bahar would realise her folly and come back. She had taken her clothes and personal belongings in one of the tartan suitcases, leaving behind a quick note propped against a yellow enamel jug filled with bluebells:

This is wrong. We've been running because of me.

I can't any more.

Bahar

– I'll call soon. I promise.

'Why is she doing this? I've told her over and over again that we're safe here. There's no way Hossein's going to find us.' Marjan shook her head.

'Call the police again!'

'I have – twice. They just said to wait. She's not considered missing for another nineteen hours, apparently.' Marjan laid her face in her hands. She could taste the gritty spice mixture everywhere. 'I was only in the butcher's for ten minutes, fifteen at most.'

'Yeah, but you didn't find the note until ten o'clock,' Layla said pointedly.

Marjan slowly raised her eyes and met her sister's gaze. Layla's face was filled with disappointment. Layla was right, of course, thought Marjan. She hadn't even noticed the folded sheet of paper leaning against the jug until the *fesen-*

joon had finished cooking and she was getting ready to go to bed. And even then she hadn't known where to search for Bahar. What was wrong with her?

'You're sure Bahar didn't say anything before you fell asleep?' Marjan said.

'No, nothing. She was in the bedroom the whole time. Where could she go, anyway? No one can stay out in this rain for long.' The storm was still lashing out in anger, with spidery electric bolts illuminating the sky above the alleyway. 'Look, just give me the van keys. I'll find her myself!' Layla cried, stamping her foot impatiently.

'No, you're staying right here,' Marjan said, getting up from the table. 'Don't let anybody in, okay?'

Layla nodded, reassured to see her sister in action once again. Her relief was short-lived, however, as a heavy knock sounded at the back door.

'Marjan?' Layla whispered, frightened.

'Shhh . . .' Marjan crept slowly across the kitchen. It was too dark outside to see through the door's glass partition. The shadow of a tall figure moved back and forth across the glass, then there came another booming knock. Marjan's fingers touched the cold doorknob, pausing a beat, before she jerked the door open. In front of her stood Malachy, drenched and dragging his telescope and backpack behind him.

Chapter Twelve

Pomegranate Soup

Ingredients:

>   2 large onions, chopped
>   2 tbsp olive oil
>   ½ cup yellow split peas, rinsed twice
>   6 cups water
>   1 tsp salt
>   ½ tsp ground black pepper
>   1 tsp turmeric
>   2 cups fresh parsley, chopped
>   2 cups fresh coriander, chopped
>   ¼ cup fresh mint, chopped

POMEGRANATE SOUP

1 cup fresh spring onions, chopped
500g ground lamb
¾ cup rice, rinsed twice
2 cups pomegranate juice
1 tbsp sugar
2 tbsp lemon juice
2 tbsp angelica powder*

'I hear the middle one took off at the same time as Thomas's boy. Wouldn't be surprised if she's got her hands on Tom Junior by now.' Dervla pursed her lips over her teacup the next day and scanned the room of women before her. 'They're all sluts – mind now I have to say the word – sluts, and they get what's coming to them. I'd lock up your sons if I were you, Joan,' she warned.

The congregation of sour-faced women, most of whom were regulars to Antonia Nolan's religious relics shop, nodded their heads in agreement. Dervla, happy for such quick compliance, continued to slurp her watery brew. Ballinacroagh's Bible-group members, who gathered every Friday

*optional

afternoon at The Reek Relics, were a complete contrast to the pleasant ladies of the Patrician Day Dance committee. The sanctimonious assembly consisted of the usual spinsters and elderly matrons, but had recently gained younger members in Joan Donnelly and Assumpta Corcoran.

'She had her eye on my Benny, you know,' Assumpta informed them.

'Sure, my boys won't even come home any more. Ever since that hussy started strutting her stuff around the place. They could have been priests, those two. Priests!' Joan protested.

The old biddies nodded simultaneously in a geriatric chorus line. Dervla tisked, tisked and shook her head.

'I'd tell that sister of yours to keep out of that café, Joan. I saw her going in there just this morning. Knocked on the door with Evie Watson at her side. I thought that café was closed for the day,' she said.

'Fiona's never been one for sound judgement. Sure, she's still letting those tinkers in for cuts. Driving out decent business without a thought to myself. And she won't listen. She won't listen,' repeated Joan, feeling the pressure of judging eyes upon her.

All heads turned as the café door opened across the street. Mrs Boylan and two good-willed ladies from the committee emerged, without the large casserole dishes they had carried inside just half an hour earlier. The stinging drizzle had picked up again, and the three elderly women linked arms and ran up the main street like a trio of carefree schoolgirls.

'Did you see that then? Geraldine Boylan taking them her best dishes. Sheer wastage,' said Dervla, spitting out her words.

The Bible-study ladies nodded, although most tried their best not to think of the delicious food piling up inside the Babylon Café.

The café's kitchen was indeed teeming with a vast array of delicacies. Mrs Boylan had made two casseroles of her buttery potato champ and Maura Kinley brought by three loaves of barm-brack, that wonderful medley of marmalade and dried fruits. There was a chunky rabbit stew, moist brown bread, and creamed vegetables, as well as the minestrone Estelle was cooking.

There was nothing like a good bowl of steaming minestrone to put things into perspective, thought Estelle Delmonico. The old widow sat at the kitchen table, chopping carrots into fine slices. She was making the soup for Marjan, who was lying upstairs recovering from the flu – a result of staying up all night looking for Bahar. Marjan had bravely manœuvred the green hippie van in the pouring rain, taking all the main roads out of town, hoping to spot her sister somewhere along the way. But in the end she had come home alone, chilled to the bone and shivering with fever.

As soon as the chunky vegetable soup had finished cooking, the little widow climbed up the stairs, balancing a bowl in her arthritic fingers. She walked into the flat's tiny living space, still surprised at how much it had changed since Luigi had used it as an office. Back then it was filled with yellowing receipt books and boxes of quick-rising yeast. Now there was a small woven rug on the scratched wooden floor, a pretty Paisley coverlet spread over a futon and, sitting on a spare café chair, a second-hand television Marjan had picked up in Castlebar.

Marjan was lying on the sofa, still sniffing and surrounded by crumpled tissues. Though her face was grey and clammy, she looked much healthier than she had the night before.

'Here you go. Some minestrone, yes? Don't get up.' Estelle bent down towards Marjan's open mouth to lovingly administer teaspoonfuls of soup.

'Where's Layla? Is she downstairs?' Marjan asked, before coughing into a wad of tissue scrunched up in her hand.

'Shhhh . . . She is okay. She is with Malachy and Emer. They went to Castlebar today. To look for Bahar. They will find her, you will see,' said Estelle, smoothing strands of hair from Marjan's eyes. Had Estelle borne a daughter, she had no doubt that she would have looked a lot like Marjan. Such a Roman nose, such an Italian complexion. 'Shhhh . . . you go back to sleep, okay?'

Marjan sank deeper into the couch, tears springing up in her reddened eyes.

'What if they don't find her? What if she's gone and they never—' Marjan broke off and looked away for a moment. She hadn't told Estelle much about Bahar's disappearance, only the fib that she had told everyone else who had already paid her a visit: that Bahar had felt so badly about Tom Junior attacking Layla that she had decided to leave town for a while. Marjan knew it was a weak explanation, but the alternative would mean opening up too many wounds.

'I'm sorry. I just don't know if we'll find her. And . . . God—' Marjan surrendered into coughs and tears once again. Estelle shushed her gently and wiped her forehead with her wrinkly fingers.

The old lady's touch reminded Marjan of her mother's caresses. Shirin Aminpour had often lullabied her daughters to sleep with fantastic tales of Scheherazade and her courageous storytelling. On such warm nights, as was the custom in Iran, their whole family would gather on their house's flat roof. Sunken and completely cleared of stones or rubble, the roof was lined with back-to-back rugs and ornate pillows, upon which they would all sleep the humid night away, dreaming of golden arches and flying Arabian horses. Someone always had an instrument on hand, usually a *tomback*, the gourd drum of poets, which would thump, thump, thump to the stories that were being passed around.

Marjan doubled over from the pain of the memory. They were so young then. Nothing to regret. Nothing to run away from.

Estelle sat quietly by Marjan's side, tenderly stroking her hand as the younger woman sobbed her heavy tears.

'You lie down and don't move,' Estelle said, propping several pillows behind Marjan's back.

Marjan marvelled at how their situations had reversed; only a couple of months ago *she* had been the one helping Estelle into bed after her fainting spell.

'You need to rest. No more sadness, okay?'

Marjan nodded tiredly, her cheeks burning with fever.

'Now, open your mouth. This is going to make you feel much better, you will see,' Estelle said gently. She scooped a big spoonful of broth-softened courgette and carrot from the bowl in her hand, offering it with a soothing smile. Finally, she thought, someone to take care of. She was going to look after all three girls from now on, just as a mother should.

Everyone felt the absence of aroma when they stepped inside the café on Saturday morning. The heady steam that always surrounded the golden samovar had deserted its keeper, giving it the look of a barren woman. But for a few stale *zulbia* and a half-plate of almond delights, the pastry counter held only the crumbs of past sweetness, an emptiness that further stressed the importance of their mission.

Father Mahoney led the search party that had gathered in the café's closed front room, outlining his reconnaissance plan like a seasoned general out to conquer.

'I'll take the old Cadillac to the east – Westport, Ballintubber, Claremorris,' he said, unfolding an old, dusty map of Western County Mayo on the long communal table. 'Who wants the coastal road?'

'Evie and I will take it,' Fiona volunteered.

'Fine. Malachy, Layla and Emer can try Castlebar. You'll need a full day for that, I'd say.'

'We only got as far as Bridge Street yesterday,' Malachy said apologetically.

'Right, everyone. We're as good as we'll ever be, so. Time to pull out. Now remember, meet back here at eighteen hundred hours. That's six in the evening if you didn't know. And good luck!'

Father Mahoney attempted a half-salute, but stopped midway when he realised that he was not in a Bob Hope war pic and the troops were in no mood for light entertainment. Nevertheless, the search party rolled out of the Babylon in regimented strides. No one noticed Marjan's pale face watching through the kitchen door's round windows.

It had been just a day since she had taken in Estelle's comforting minestrone soup, but after five healthy bowls Marjan was finally able to walk up and down the stairs without feeling her muscles atrophy. Estelle had stayed awake all night to nurse her and instruct Layla in making the foot bath, a recipe of salt, vinegar and hot water that Marjan had herself made many times when her sisters had fallen sick. Only after she was sure that Marjan was free from the flu's hold, did Estelle let Mrs Boylan drive her home to her little white cottage by the sea. For the first time in the four months they had been in Ballinacroagh, Marjan was all alone in the empty café.

Four months. Marjan backed up against the staircase banister as though propelled by a sudden blast of wind, the magnitude of her swirling emotions momentarily sucking the breath out of her. Resinous grief, the echo of guilt, and yes, simple gratitude. Observing the efforts of the kind people gathered to help them, it was impossible not to feel grateful. After those lonely years of running and barely trusting anyone Marjan and her sisters had finally found a home. A real home. So why hadn't Bahar seen that? Why was she giving up on it all, to go – where?

Marjan sank down into a nearby chair. The kitchen seemed to be suffering from a fast of seasons, looking so desolate in its creaking appliances. She had insisted that Estelle and Mrs

Boylan take home the remaining food, the lovely casseroles and stews cooked by the generous ladies of the committee. The groaning refrigerator was empty but for some ground lamb, three eggs and leftover *fesenjoon*. She should really throw it away, thought Marjan. Start a new batch, maybe some other kind of stew, or perhaps some pomegranate soup. It had been a long time since she made pomegranate soup.

For the first time since December 1981, when he bought Boney M's Christmas album, Thomas McGuire was back in Kenny's Record Shop, thumbing through the latest dance singles with a look of consternation on his fleshy face.

Hi-NRG, *Snap!*, Industrial, In Dub, *Renegade Soundwave*, Techno, House. It was mind-boggling, but according to his teenage daughter Helen, this was the music that everyone listened to nowadays. The new beats were not fit to be called dance music, if you asked him. With their overpowering bass lines and unintelligible lyrics, the whole lot sounded more like a haemorrhoidal computer on its last legs. Nothing like his beloved disco tunes with their dignified synthesizer beats. But, Thomas reminded himself, after seeing how Ballinacroagh had taken to the Babylon Café, he would have to be more adventurous in his choices.

The bar owner stole a peek outside the record-shop window. Although the café was too far down Main Mall for him to see the CLOSED sign on its door, he knew all about Bahar's disappearance. Three days now. Same as his boy Tom, although he for one was sure the two had nothing to do with one another.

He had to admit, thought Thomas, he was proud of Junior. Maybe not for his choices, but for his impeccable timing. With one sweep of his Neanderthal paws, Tom Junior had achieved what Thomas, even with all his influence over the town, had not been able to accomplish in months: that stinking café was finally closed. Good feckin' riddance, if you asked him.

And as for Malachy – that good-for-nothing bastard was no longer his son. Thomas had gone so far as to give his solicitor a call to change his Will, so certain was he of the excommunication.

Nothing and no one, not his wife's mewling pleas, not his youngest Joanne's crying, not even his sister Margaret, with her bullish force, could convince him to go back on his pronouncement. That boy was as good as dead to him.

To satisfy his jivey fingers, which kept crawling over to the 'Disco' section in the record shop, Thomas picked up the first album he saw, The Bee Gees' *Saturday Night Fever*. He paid for a rake of dance cassettes that the puzzled shop boy stuffed into two KENNY'S KNOWS KOOL MUSIC plastic bags, and worked his way down Main Mall towards Paddy McGuire's pub.

Thomas's eye flitted over the café's silent façade with satisfaction. No sign of activity, not even the golden glow he had peeked at that first day. There was only darkness beyond the half-drawn curtains. A slimy round of phlegm flew out of the bar owner's mouth and landed on the pavement between two pots of African violets outside the café's windows. With the expelled spit came a sort of peace that he hadn't experienced since his pre-Turbo Tan days. Back then, everything around him ran like a well-oiled machine and there was no competition to worry about except the one waged in his own head. Why had he doubted the outcome? Thomas wondered. Of course the café wouldn't have worked out; the strange spell Ballinacroagh had fallen under these last few months would eventually have been broken, one way or another. Smug and warm all over, Thomas had his hand on the pub door when he heard his oldest son's voice.

'Dad?'

Tom Junior was standing outside Fadden's Mini-Mart, desperately trying to keep his emaciated knees from knocking against each other every time a gale tunnelled down Main Mall. A long minute passed before Thomas recognised his son, for although he had been away only three days, the boy had experienced a complete and utter metamorphosis. Tom Junior had lost an incredible amount of weight in a short amount of time. Gone was the premature beer belly of too many yeasty pints, replaced now by a concave pit of ribs and wrinkled skin. Instead of his usually fat, puffy jowls, Tom Junior's jagged cheekbones now fell into hollow recesses, while his sunken, saucer eyes were devoid of their usual insolence and cruelty.

'Tom? Is that ye?' Thomas walked towards his son, squinting as though it would help flesh out the carcass staring back at him. 'Get in the pub right now. Do ye plan fer the whole town to have a look?' said Thomas as he pushed his son up the street and into the pub. 'Thought you'd know better than to get yerself back here in a hurry.'

A lone figure occupied the long, oak-panelled bar, slouched over a bottle of Scotch. Thomas immediately recognised him as that drunk of all seasons, The Cat. Had it been any other time, the poor sod would have been thrown out on his sclerotic spine, but at the moment there were more important matters for Thomas McGuire to attend to.

'What happened, son? Thought you'd be in Galway having a laugh for yer old man. What's this, now?' He grabbed a crinkly piece of notepaper from Tom Junior's gaunt fingers and peered at it. Thomas could make out only a few words in the dim pub lighting, but his meaty hands started to shake with anger when he saw his son's sloping signature at the bottom of the page.

'It's my note of apologies. I was going to give it to Sean Grogan to give to the Ara – to the girl there. I shouldn't have done it, Dad,' Tom Junior said, looking down at his dirty trainers.

The apology was genuine, the culmination of three of the longest days of Tom Junior's life. His journey began when he had swallowed a whole bottle of tequila, purchased from the Dew Drop Inn outside Westport, and had ended with Junior squatting in a one-room dust-heap better known as The Cat's mouldy cottage. And all the while, without his knowledge, Tom Junior's insides were being gnawed at by a ravenous tapeworm.

Posing as a tequila worm, the parasite had been biding its time at the bottom of the now emptied Jose Cuervo bottle, just waiting for a healthy farm boy to cross its path. The worm had eventually worked its way into Tom Junior's bland soul, boring deep holes from which his ignorance and pent-up frustration had seeped out. Gone with the unnecessary bulk of fat was the anger that had burned indiscriminately towards all who stood to oppose him, especially his overbearing father. Tom Junior now realised that Thomas had been suffering under similar strains of unfulfilled dreams; and that he had wrongly compensated for his failures by steamrolling and manipulating everyone in his path.

All in all, these three days had been a spiritual fasting for Tom Junior, from which he had emerged thinned and complete, bereft of any desire to rule over Ballinacroagh or his father's weighty legacy.

Thomas, on the other hand, was not so understanding.

'What are you talking about? Have you gone feckin' daft, Tom? Leave this to me,' he said, crumpling the written apology in his shaking hand. 'Get yerself home to yer mother. She's been driving me up the wall with her crying. Go on, now,' Thomas ordered, then added, 'And for God's sake, eat something while you're there.'

'Da . . .'

'What? What, Tom?' Thomas glared at the ghost of his once hardy son. Was it just him or had the whole town gone mad?

'I'm not going home, Dad,' Tom said firmly. 'I'm leaving today. For America. To sort meself out. Find meself.'

There was no denying it: Tom Junior was a changed man, through and through. Two days of squatting with The Cat had done more for his mind and soul than the two decades he had lived under his parents' damp roof.

Tom Junior had met his raggedy alcoholic host in a water ditch, where he had spent his first night on the run from the law. What no one in town knew about The Cat, and what Tom had come to discover, was that the old drunkard was once a well-known philosopher in his native Bulgaria. Growing up in a quiet hamlet near the Balkan Mountains, he had been untouched by the seemingly endless Russian-led coups that rocked the little Slavic country towards the end of the nineteenth century. This quiet existence had allowed The Cat to concentrate on his dissertation paper (via correspondence with Trinity College Dublin) on Kierkegaard and the missing fourth stage in his existential approach. It was a thesis he was working on well into the second decade of the twentieth century when, out of the blue, Bulgaria found itself caught in the international game of war, choosing the wrong side to cheer for. The Cat escaped the fighting for his Irish alma mater, and after several unrequited love affairs in the capital city, soon found himself in Ballinacroagh of all places. And in Ballinacroagh he had come to stay.

When Tom Junior, with his body thoroughly ravaged by the tequila tapeworm, first stepped inside The Cat's one-room, thatched-roof cottage, he was struck dumb by the incredible library amassed before him. Crammed into every corner of the modest space, and piled high in teetering columns, were hundreds of books. Books everywhere. What windows there were had been blocked by barricades of well-thumbed Mills and Boon romance novels (which, if asked, The Cat would vehemently deny were his), and the old philosopher's Louis XIV daybed was raised on a stack of esoteric Egyptian texts, bought from a Berber peddler in Bulgaria. Tradition had given way to innovation when it came to the cottage's floor; the customary dirt ground was paved in encyclopedias, thesauri and dictionaries from every language imaginable, with prominence given to the Afro-Asiatic idiom, which was The Cat's favourite tongue to date.

Never a bright student, Tom Junior felt he had died and landed in his own personal hell. Collapsing on the book-strewn floor, he slept four solid hours that felt like four long years, and awoke to find a stack of feathery paperbacks supporting his neck. Next to him, on a dainty white plate, was a glass of milk and two orange crème biscuits, and in a corner across the room sat The Cat, in one of two rocking chairs, with Samuel Beckett's *Waiting for Godot* clutched in his liver-spotted hands. The old tramp did not look up as Tom Junior made his way to the other rocking chair. He just kept rocking away as he read about his favourite limbo contestants, chuckling to himself over the many highlighted passages.

Thirty-eight hours passed before The Cat ceased his slow rocking, and looked up to find himself under siege in his reading corner.

Stretching from one side of the wall to the other, and cutting him off from the rest of the small room he used as bedroom, parlour and kitchen, was a wall. Four feet high and eight feet across, the wall was made up entirely of books, many of which were The Cat's personal favourites: the entire works of Nietzsche including a frayed edition of *Also sprach Zarathustra*; from Camus and the Absurdists of the theatre (Ionesco, Beckett and that prisoner of life Genet), to the gossamer stanzas of Khalil Gibran, the Lebanese poet with a heart of gold.

Tom Junior had built the wall while The Cat was deep in a mental soliloquy on the meaning of meaning. Assuming that the young lost soul had made a hasty escape, the old thinker was overcome by a great sadness, but after using a wiry finger to nudge a book out of the precariously built barrier, The Cat discovered a new Tom Junior, thinned to the bone but present and more alive than ever. Tom Junior's eyes, encircled in blue-black rings of exhaustion, were nevertheless filled with a renewed sense of being. On his lap sat the opened pages of *The Prophet*, and through his cracked lips came the words he had been reading over and over again:

> It is when your spirit goes wandering upon the wind,
> That you, alone and unguarded,
> commit a wrong unto others and therefore unto yourself . . .

Tom Junior's spirit had come home for a landing. He was beginning to see that his attack on Layla was just the symptom of an even deeper disease. A sickness he would tend to from this day on, starting with his sincerest apology.

'I tried calling the café the night it all happened. A woman answered the phone, but I couldn't find the right thing to say. I don't know, but it was like I suddenly ran out of breath. So . . . so, I hung up. I thought a note would be best.'

'What were you thinking calling those darkies?' Thomas McGuire said, bristling with anger. 'You listen to me, boy, it's taken a mighty hand to get Sean Grogan off me back. I'll not be the one holding me bollocks in all of this, you hear?

Feckin' "find meself"! I'll find ye all right.'
Thomas slammed the crumpled apology note at
Tom's feet. 'You look in on your mam, then get
yer arse down to the Ale House where I'll be
waiting. Don't even think about getting out of
work tonight.'

He stormed out of the pub just as The Cat
awoke from his alcoholic stupor with a loud belch
that told little of the innovative theories running
through his inebriated yet brilliant mind. Jimmy
the bartender grimaced at the soured smell
emanating from the darkened slump in the
corner.

Tom Junior picked up the ball of paper and
smoothed it out so that his words were legible
once again. He hadn't really expected his father
to give the note to the guards, let alone understand the epiphany that would forever mark his
path.

Hoisting a heavy, book-filled satchel (a going-
away present from The Cat) on to his back, Tom
Junior sidled up to the old drunk at the bar.

'Jimmy, take care of my man here,' Tom said.
He slapped The Cat on his hunched back,

330

causing the crinkly old man to double over in a coughing fit. 'Give him all the drink he wants on me. See you, Cat.'

Tom Junior gave The Cat a thumbs-up before slipping a hundred-punt note into his soiled coat pocket. He then walked down to the pub's back room, a cavernous carpeted ground of mismatched tables and chairs all facing a rotting dart board. Pushing the emergency exit door open, Tom Junior stepped out into the wet cobblestone alleyway. He looked both ways to make sure that his father was nowhere in sight, before creeping quietly up to the café's squeaky back gate. There, with bated breath, he slipped his refolded apology note between two of the fence's wooden boards, then turned and left the town of Ballinacroagh for ever.

Moments later, just as Tom Junior disappeared down the alleyway, Marjan walked out into the café's back garden. She knelt down among the dewy, bottle-green coriander and, encircling the stems with her thumb and forefinger, tugged firmly at the herb. She was careful to leave her other hand on the plant's base to protect its roots. The tempest that had raged over three days had decimated her garden, tearing the delicate blue-bells and velvety purple violas that had blossomed in June from their comfortable beds. The dead flowers lay scattered about the garden now, their once vibrant inner petals turned to clomps of rotting brown. The hardy coriander, parsley and mint, Marjan was happy to note, had fared better in the storm. As she pulled the last sprig of tall coriander, she whispered safe keepings so that Bahar would come back home quickly. For this was home, she was sure of that now more than ever.

Marjan walked back into the kitchen with her handful of herbs just as the phone rang. Fiona's bright voice greeted her on the other end.

'We've taped the MISSING fliers on every tree and lamp-post,' Fiona informed her. 'Don't worry, Marjan. We'll find her. There's not many petite, olive-skinned brunettes around these parts. Someone would've noticed her.'

'I hope you're right, Fiona,' Marjan replied, trying hard not to think of the multitude of hiding places in Ireland. Surely the endless green quilted fields, separated by the tidy pilings of rock borders, were ideal coverlets for escape.

After several more minutes of reassuring conversation with Fiona, Marjan hung up the phone and began chopping the parsley, coriander and mint. She mixed the herbs in a bowl with ground lamb, onions and seasoning, the meat squishing between her fingers, feeling like warm mud inviting itself between bare toes on a hot summer's day. The familiar rhythm of mixing was soothing, and by the time she added the meatballs to the pot of hot broth, her hopes were singing once again.

Unlike *fesenjoon*, where the pomegranate taste is equalled out by a robust walnut companion, pomegranate soup relies entirely on the fruit for its inspiration. A shimmering magenta when fully cooked, the pomegranate juice gives the broth a sweet–sour taste, and is usually enjoyed as an appetiser, rather than a main course. There was no other dish with such a perfect balance of *sardi* and *garmi*, in Marjan's opinion; the *sard* pomegranate and coriander equalling out the *garm* lamb and split peas. She wished Bahar could smell it now. She would realise that there was nothing to fear – real or imaginary.

Marjan stirred the luscious waves of pomegranate beneath her and thought about her sensitive sister. Had she done enough to help Bahar? she wondered. She certainly tried to be understanding and protective, Marjan told herself; but maybe she could have tried harder to ease Bahar's painful memories, those headaches that plagued her every day. She knew how hard it was for her sister to trust her surroundings, but had she been as sympathetic as she could have been? Or had Estelle Delmonico's observations been right; was she still playing the mother to her sisters?

Perhaps the little Italian woman was right in her advice; there were some things that were even out of her control. Some things had to play themselves out, burn themselves cold, without her stirring hand, without her help. Because, maybe it wasn't all up to her.

Marjan nodded silently, admitting a welcomed defeat. It was necessary. Bahar and Layla would just have to find their way without her always being there. She just couldn't do it any more. She would have to learn to put her trust in something greater than them all; she would have to just believe everything would work out in the end.

Placing the lid back on the hotpot, Marjan turned away from the stove and exhaled.

Bahar was going to be all right.

Layla was going to be all right.

She was going to be all right.

The lightness of her surrender carried her up the stairs and to an afternoon sleep that was a long time coming. And behind Marjan, left bubbling on the stove for the first time in all her life, was the unattended pot of pomegranate soup.

Like her sister, Bahar too was about to be lifted, rising up to higher grounds. At the moment though, as she looked around her hostel room, hope was the last thing on her mind.

The patch sewn on to one corner of the chequered duvet read PROPERTY OF CASTLEBAR CASTLE, but the chipped plaster ceiling contradicted such grandiose claims. *There is definitely nothing regal about this hovel*, Bahar thought to herself. She still couldn't get used to the springy mattress or the shocking chartreuse walls of the stuffy room, even after three long days. The shag carpet, a psychedelic pattern of orange circles against a dark brown background, still smelled like devilled eggs; and the faded window blinds with their missing slats let in the gloomy grey light far too early every morning. The room's only redeeming factor – a white, Victorian cast-iron fireplace carved with two cherubic angels on either side – was marred by a faded, larger-than-life, portrait of a beaming JFK that hung in a gilded frame over the mantelpiece. The dead president's glazed eyes had followed her as she stumbled into the room that first night, falling straight into the musty single bed in her wet clothes.

She woke up with the worst migraine the next morning. After swallowing eight spoonfuls of the headache medicine she had packed in her suitcase, she pulled a creased piece of paper out of its side pouch and stared at the phone number scribbled on it in Persian numerals. The page had been torn out of an old address book that Bahar had flipped through the previous night, just before leaving the warmth of the café. She found the phone number sitting under the letter J, nestled innocently between the names and addresses of two of Marjan's old schoolmates.

Her plan was simple enough in theory: remove the dangerous element (herself) from the café, book a room at the Castlebar hostel, the same room she and her sisters had stayed in when they first arrived in County Mayo, and call Khanoum Jaferi's apartment in Tehran. Then she would just wait until Hossein found her. Bahar was sure it wouldn't take him long to come to the hostel, especially if he was already in Ireland. She would let him do whatever he wanted with her, take her back to Iran even, just as long as he left Marjan and Layla alone. Yes, it was a clean enough solution, thought Bahar. And it would have worked, had she actually had the courage to make the call. Instead, she had spent the last three days and nights locked away in her hostel room, pacing the expanse of the shag carpet and counting the water spots on the plaster ceiling above her.

Bloody coward, that's what she was. She couldn't even run away right. Can't even go downstairs to the lobby and make a phone call, Bahar thought disgustedly, as she pushed her aching body up from the bed. Casting her eyes down to avoid John F. Kennedy's disconcerting stare, she slowly crossed the room to the fireplace. Using her shoe, Bahar tentatively poked the small pile of turf ash inside the hearth, ready to jump back in case anything moved in the chalky residue. *I could die in here and nobody would notice*, she thought morbidly. Sighing, she stretched her arms wearily across the freezing iron mantelpiece and hung her head.

Her stomach growled angrily. She would have to leave the room sooner rather than later, if only to get reinforcements; the food she had bought the night she arrived at the Castlebar Castle was nearly gone. All that was left was one green apple and a half-eaten packet of biscuits sitting forlornly on the bedside table. Weakened suddenly by the thought of her meagre food supplies, Bahar lifted her head and stepped away from the mantelpiece. She turned around, about to flop dejectedly back on her chequered bed, when her eyes suddenly fell upon several brochures scattered across the mantelpiece. She had forgotten about the glossy leaflets, which the receptionist had handed her along with her room key the night she arrived at the Castlebar Castle. The pamphlets showcased the usual destinations favoured by American tourists: Knock, Leenane, the Aran islands. And Croagh Patrick.

Bahar grabbed the first brochure from the pile: Hibernian Holiday Tours of Croagh Patrick. It contained a garish green and yellow foldout of the mountain with a brief history of St Patrick on one side, and archeological facts on the other. Gift shop hours. Mass times. Pilgrimage season. LET HIBERNIAN HOLIDAY TOURS TAKE YOU UP THE MOUNTAIN!

Hibernian Holiday Tours. It was the same tour bus company that had picked her up on the stormy road out of Ballinacroagh. The Irish bus driver, a portly man with a light case of eczema, had kindly agreed to drop her in front of the shabby hostel in Castlebar, before driving off towards the more expensive lodgings like Mountain Manor on Bridge Street.

'Picking up the Americans at the Manor there. Irish-Americans, they call themselves. Out here to have a look at the Reek. Better off going to the Bahamas, if ye ask me,' the driver had said, before winking at her in the rear-view mirror.

Bahar's heart began to pound furiously. The Reek. Of course. That was it.

She had been spending all this time moving, running, avoiding – but never in the right direction. Not across lands and small seas, not through valleys or shifting deserts, but up. Up! The source of the calling was mysterious; Bahar didn't know where the soft voice in her head had come from, but all of a sudden it was telling her to go up. There was no other way but up.

The flirtatious bus driver winked at her as she climbed up the bus's steep, rubbery steps.

'Back again, I see. I'm not complaining, mind

you. Always happy to see a pretty young face,' he said, throwing her a lop-sided grin.

Hoping to avoid further unwanted attention, Bahar crouched low in her seat. She was thankful that none of the bus's passengers – Irish-American retirees who were retracing their fractioned ancestries – had tried to strike up a conversation with her. The jolly senior citizens were swapping addresses and sharing wallet-sized photos of their smiling grandchildren, and took no notice of the young, dark-haired woman sitting in the front seat. As the bus pulled out of Castlebar bound for the mountain, Bahar kept her eyes glued to the rolling countryside. The rain-soaked heather and forests of oak with their awnings of dark green alder suddenly struck her as very beautiful. Ireland was an enchanting country, Bahar thought to herself.

The Hibernian Holiday Tours bus joined a pack of fifteen other buses in a large car park situated at the eastern base of the mountain. Pilgrims, mostly well-fed Americans with new Nikes and bulging bum bags, spilled out of the tour buses, some whistling sprightly renditions of

'Danny Boy' as they all headed for a small brass and marble plaque erected at the base of the mountain.

'St Patrick,' the tour guide started. 'Patron Saint of Ireland. Tormented visionary. Benevolent missionary. Saviour of the heathen Irish.' She paused, flashing the crowd an ironic smile.

'Battled his own demons when he climbed the mountain. The devils came to him in the shape of blackbirds, shrouding the sky with their dark wings. But Patrick kept on praying, not stopping until the sky shone bright again,' she said, passing around complimentary shamrocks laminated on to small cards. 'There'll be no Mass as today's Saturday, but don't let that stop you from saying your prayers if the need strikes you. I'll be saying my own thanks, now that the storm's gone.'

The tour guide directed everyone to a narrow walkway that zigzagged up the steep mountain. Though a wispy veil of mist obscured the road ahead, and the short, pale grass on either side of the walkway was littered with jagged stones, it did not stop some of the more dedicated climbers from walking with feet bared and souls opened. Bahar trailed behind the tour group, taking her time to breathe in the thin mountain air.

Prayers, the tour guide had said. What sort of prayers could help her now? Bahar wondered. What did she have to be so thankful for? There was no way of undoing what she had done, the misery she had brought on her sisters when she married Hossein. And she was still causing Marjan and Layla pain. Right this very minute, even as she was climbing this mountain. She knew they would be worried sick about her, thinking the worst had happened, but she still hadn't phoned to let them know she was all right. All she had done was run away again.

Bahar shook her head and grimaced. She was always running away. Not once, not one single time had she ever taken responsiblity for her actions, apologised for not listening to her older sister's warnings about Khanoum Jaferi and her disgusting, pock-marked son. Instead she had hidden behind her headaches, forced Marjan and Layla to tip-toe around her all these silent years, as if she was some sort of helpless invalid. Prayers.

She was going to need a lot of prayers, Bahar told herself, as she hoisted her body up onto a granite ledge.

As Bahar reached the last leg of her hike, the steepest, rockiest part of the mountain, a most curious thing began to happen. It seemed that the higher she climbed, the more lucid her thoughts became. She was well ahead of most of the American tourists by now, and had almost caught up with the sprightly tour guide, who had the happy advantage of toned calf muscles and a trusty walking stick. As she scaled the stony mountain path, Bahar found herself suddenly bursting with energy, her morning migraine long gone.

Why, she asked herself, had she assumed that that strange-sounding phone call had been from Hossein? Just because he had found them in London didn't mean that he was going to follow them all the way to Ballinacroagh. And really, if she thought about it rationally for a moment, the phone call in the café could just as likely have been a wrong number or some neighbourhood kids playing a prank. So why had she chosen the worst possible explanation and allowed her headaches and hysteria to fog her judgement? If she wanted to survive, if she wanted to move forward, then she'd have to learn not to believe the worst from situations – or people, for that matter.

Yes, Bahar told herself, she had her own set of penances to pay. She needed to suture that inner, accordioned tunnel that had been battered and left out of tune for so long. Layla had her youthful cinnamon–rose promise and Marjan, the ability to create one spectacular dish after another, but that was their journey, not hers. She didn't know what her strengths were just yet, but she did know they were there to be discovered.

At Croagh Patrick's summit, Bahar stopped hiking and turned around, towards the dazzling blue waters of Clew Bay. The grey clouds were fast departing across the horizon, their liquid wings reflected in the bay below. Climbing this ancient mountain had given her the clarity to claim her ill spirits, she decided. Each rock-strewn step forward had made her feel stronger, as if she was indeed casting off her fear and loneliness, the monsters who had been riding her for such a long time. Just as Saint Patrick had done so many centuries ago, thought Bahar. Whatever miracles that old bishop had performed among these thick clouds, thought Bahar, they were still working their magic on her. Even Hossein could not reach her at these heights.

She stretched her arms and, closing her eyes, drew in a deep, loud breath that made even the more extrovert of the American tourists do a double-take. The sweet innocence of their stares brought a small smile to Bahar's face.

Below on Main Mall, a scowling Thomas McGuire was also experiencing the first of many belated epiphanies. His sense of smell set off the initial alarm.

The burly publican first smelled the soup as he was stomping his way back down to Fadden's Mini-Mart. He had little clue about his own approaching demise. In fact, when he would later recall the whole incident to himself, curled up on the many sleepless nights that would follow him to his dying day, Thomas would swear that it was not the smell that had brought him to the café's kitchen, but the duties of a concerned parent and citizen who had finally had enough. Such, it seems, are the altruistic fantasies of many a skewered, criminal mind.

Thomas never made it into the mini-mart for another round of badgering poor Danny Fadden. Smelling the cooking pomegranate as soon as he stormed past the Babylon Café, he turned and marched back up Main Mall with a renewed sense of purpose. He veered into the alleyway, side-stepping overturned rubbish bins and a pack of rabid cats to reach the café's back garden. Ballinacroagh's beer baron didn't stop to knock on the gate, but chose instead to kick his way in. He raised his foot and was about to karate chop through the gate when he saw the note. It was the same lined sheet of blubbering apologies he had crumpled up not two hours before, Junior's words living on to taunt him once again. With blood pumping in his ears, Thomas shoved the gate open, and stumbled into the café's back garden, trampling the remainder of Marjan's standing herbs with his heavy work boots. The unlocked back door gave way easily to his fist, and he staggered into the kitchen, a place he had secretly dreamed of since he was a little boy, when the Delmonicos still ran their little pastry shop.

Expecting to be confronted by Marjan chopping up questionable chunks of rotting meat and animal parts, Thomas was somewhat disappointed to find the opposite. There were no intestines flying about or globular fish eyes staring back from bloody chopping boards. Before him stood a round table spread with a frilly, blanched tablecloth printed with cherries. A little way beyond, in the middle of the kitchen, was the wooden island, clean but for a bowl of blushing apricots. And on the stove was a bubbling, half-covered silver pot, from which escaped taunting tendrils of pomegranate.

The perfumed fingers reached Thomas's curved chin, tickling his jaws like an animated temptress. Thomas gasped audibly as he stepped back against the wall in horror. Disgusting, what some people would put in their mouths, he thought, feeling dizzier than he ever had in his entire life. His breathing came out in short spats, and his head was swimming. After he had partially regained his composure, he stole another glimpse around the kitchen.

Just look at what those cows have done to his place, Thomas thought to himself. That's right; this was his place, always had been, always would be. Where he was standing now, just under his mud-coated boots, was where the Polyester Paddy's dance floor would have been. Writhing bodies would be commanded to move to fabulous disco beats here, the sexy whirl of a glittering disco ball throwing light prisms around like rainbow confetti. And there, through those doors, there in that feckin' empty place, for God's sake, that's where he'd walk through from the adjoining Paddy McGuire's, taking his time to give his hellos to the couples that would be strewn across velveteen couches and chairs. Black marble tables would stand crowded with cocktails; drinks he had been dying to try out but for those feckers who just wanted stout and more stout in his pubs. Here he would have been able to do it all. He might even have hired one of the O'Reilly girls, the one with the big knockers, to take to rollerskates and bum-filled short shorts, swirling about with her drink orders. Why the feck not? This was his place. This was Polyester Paddy's, where it was all going to happen!

Caught in his disco dream, Thomas twirled over and over again in the middle of the kitchen, hearing the funky music in his head once more as he was blinded by the glittering lights. As if possessed, he suddenly lurched forward towards the stove and the pan of cooking pomegranate soup. But for the red tea towel that Marjan had hung on the oven door's handle, Thomas would have fallen straight into the open flame. Even so, he was only able to hang on to the linen towel for a second before letting go of it on his way down to the cold floor.

The plastic bags of dance albums from Kenny's Record Shop shot into the air overhead. They intersected with the airborne tea towel, spinning in such perfect symmetry that for an instant – that brief suspension of time before his skull hit the linoleum floor and his eyes rolled back –

Thomas was really in his own discothèque; a fabulous place of rocket-propelled fireworks, falsetto voices, and syncopated synthesisers. But, like the era it lived and died in, the disco music came to an end all too quickly, just as Thomas's arteries, strained from decades of pig's blood sausage breakfasts and butter and creamed rashers, clamped shut.

Thomas McGuire's heart stopped the same instant the flying cassettes landed all around him, sounding a lot like the applause of a hundred plastic hands. The copy of *Saturday Night Fever* fell into his open palm, a soundtrack to step over with on his way to a white polyester-suited heaven. The tea towel landed on the stove, erupting into an instant fire ball that bounced up the adjoining wall.

Yes, it all came to a stop for Thomas then, everything but the beat that rose above his mammoth body, beyond the insatiable ambition that had led him through all the wrong door-ways, all the wrong songs. For it was the eternal beat, the endless tune that stopped for no one, not even him.

Epilogue

After Dinner Lavender-Mint Tea

Ingredients:

> 2 tbsp honey
> 3 tsp fresh lavender flowers
> 1 cup fresh mint leaves, chopped
> ½ lemon, cut into thin wedges

Early the next morning, just as the more devout pilgrims reached Croagh Patrick's white church to watch the sunrise, the circus came to town. Quite literally.

A train of four wooden, horse-pulled caravans

rambled through Main Mall, their canvas and patchwork coverings stretched to reveal banners written in fluorescent orange and pink: THE McGUIRE FAMILY CIRCUS.

The McGuire Family Circus was really the linked caravans belonging to Thomas's actor brother Kieran and his troupe of physical story-tellers. The travelling performers parked their train at the far end of the open field, near the pitched tents and fold-out tables of the Patrician Day celebrations. From there the circus troupe showcased their theatrics, an extravaganza of torch jugglers, levitation exhibitions and a hilarious Punch and Judy show. The circus was not only a delightful surprise for the pilgrims and tourists that had gathered in the field after their arduous mountain climb, but a perfect opening act to Fruits of Labour, Father Mahoney's play.

Despite having missed some last-minute rehearsals due to the unforeseen dramas of the week, Fiona Athey's directorial début was a smash hit. Following the fortunes of Gino Pepino, a young apple picker who wakes from an

afternoon siesta to find himself the only male
left in a village of one hundred very hungry
women, the play drew roars of delight from its
large audience. Layla and Malachy proved themselves to be excellent romantic leads and carried
Father Mahoney's delicious romp to a standing
ovation.

Marjan watched the happy priest bite down
on a carrot *torshi*, one of the many pickles he
had consumed from the jar he bought at the
charity table. All of the *torshis* that Bahar had
packed were already sold out, but thanks to a
generous Benny Corcoran, who had loaned
Marjan the use of his bakery kitchen (Assumpta
wasn't talking to him as a result), a panoply of
buffet dishes was available for the picking. The
pots of *abgusht*, trays of feta and mint wraps,
dolmeh and elephant ears were being gobbled up
faster than the beer that kept flowing from free
taps, the only time the McGuire pubs would be
so charitable.

It would have been enough to push Thomas
McGuire back through the gates of oblivion, had
he been there to see it all. As it was, Thomas

was in no position to move a toe, even if he wanted to. He was strapped to tubes and machines that kept him barely alive and breathing, though after hearing what had happened to him in the Babylon Café, he sometimes wished he had died.

Thomas had been legally dead for just over a minute when Bahar, dropped off by the tour bus after her momentous climb, burst into the kitchen with exhilaration that quickly turned to alarm. She forced her way through the pinky-black pomegranate cloud that had filled the entire kitchen, the smoke stinging her eyes and throat. Tongues of vicious orange and black flames darted across the wooden kitchen counter and snaked up the walls above. Panicked, Bahar ran for the stairs to find her sisters, and tripped over Thomas McGuire's lifeless body.

Using her own hot breath to puff out Thomas's chest, Bahar pumped his torso over and over until his heart began beating once again. Thomas started to cough, his eyes blinking open only to fall back into a faint; the shock of finding Bahar in the midst of resuscitating him was too much for the fallen lord of Ballinacroagh to handle.

Marjan, woken up by Bahar's screams, had tumbled downstairs to find her estranged sister hunched over a large man and the kitchen burning before her very eyes. Thanks to the small fire extinguisher Luigi Delmonico had kept in the pantry, Marjan was able to stop the flames from reaching the refrigerator on the other side of the room, choking the fire just as Thomas McGuire spluttered his first breaths back on earth. By the time Marjan knelt down next to Thomas's body with a glass of water, the devastating fire had been quenched.

Dervla Quigley almost fell out of her open window when she saw the lime green hippie van screeching out of the alleyway in the wake of billowing smoke, heading towards the Westport Road with Marjan at the wheel. The old gossip would have keeled over in an instant had she been able to see the van's cargo that day.

Bahar kept a close eye on Thomas's staccato breathing in the back of the van as Marjan drove to Mayo General. A waxy, peach tinge had returned to the bully's flaccid face, but he remained unconscious and his skipping heartbeat was extremely faint. Why *had* he come into their café? Bahar wondered, as she checked Thomas's pulse again.

Marjan thought she had a pretty good idea about Thomas's intentions, until she saw all the dance cassettes piled up into little hills on the kitchen floor. What a strange man, she thought.

Thomas McGuire would never really recover from the heart attack that had briefly sent him to that great big nightclub in the sky. He did his best to forget what had happened in the café, but found peace only after he had paid Estelle the hefty sum it would take to restore the café to its former glory. Though neither guard filed formal charges against him, Thomas McGuire's long stint of tyranny was as good as over. He would spend the rest of his days listening to his dusty collection of twelve-inches and quietly tending to his wife's libidinous needs (for Cecilia became even more enthusiastic in the bedroom after her sons were out of the house), trying hard not to die in the process. And from that Patrician

Day onward, Thomas's sister Margaret took full power of attorney over his business affairs; she acted as both his eyes and ears as she set about fixing the family reputation he had shattered in one fell swoop.

Marjan ambled over to the samovar and poured herself a steaming cup of lavender-mint tea. She and Malachy had carried the big machine out of the café especially for the occasion, using a long extension cord to plug it into the nearby mini-mart's outer-wall socket. Estelle had brought down the mint and lavender from her own small herb garden, and together they arranged the various teacups and sugar spoons for the town's second favourite beverage. The weather was no longer threatening to explode into storms, but it had yet to return to the summer heat of previous weeks, so tea was a particularly pleasant drink that Sunday afternoon.

Taking a sip, Marjan settled into a plastic chair set under a pink and turquoise striped tent. Sitting close by were some of the people who she loved most in the world, as well as some who she would eventually come to call family. Estelle was reclining in one of the plastic chairs, also sipping on the lavender-mint tea while she chatted away with Mrs Boylan about the infinite uses of cold-pressed, virgin olive oil. Seated to the little Italian widow's right were Layla and a skinny young girl with tangled, carroty hair. Marjan recognised the child as the little urchin who summoned her to the tinker camp on that stormy Thursday, only four days ago. The young girl had come to town with the tinker camp, the proud itinerants streaming through the afternoon festivities with their own brand of a good time.

A heroic Declan Maughan claimed a piece of the field near the stage for his caravan, but pretty soon had sauntered over to the pink and turquoise tent with redheaded Aoife, his youngest of thirteen sisters. After a slug of Dutch courage in the form of a Guinness (or two), the boxing champion had seated himself down on a deckchair and promptly struck up a rather passionate conversation about the state of amateur boxing in Ireland with none other than a blushing Bahar herself. Marjan could tell that her sister liked the ruggedly handsome gypsy, despite the fact that Declan was doing most of the talking. Bahar's smile, though quite shy, did not look so different from Layla's own beaming face just about then – hopeful and unabashedly proprietary.

The love between Layla and Malachy was the best kind of ownership, Marjan thought to herself, where the only commodity was the ceaseless flow of affection. The young couple had arrived well after the fire in the café's kitchen died down. They had bypassed the necessary grittiness to find only blackened kitchen walls and a story that, especially for Malachy, was a bizarre one indeed. It was right that they had not been involved in the commotion, thought Marjan. Their destinies required them for greater adventures, unencumbered by needless dramas. She watched Malachy curl his long fingers around a lock of Layla's straight hair, gently caressing it as he mused on the origins of stars. The young astronomer knew that in Aristotelian times the word *comet* was described as 'the length of luminous hair', but that the word eventually changed to signify the orbiting streak that sometimes, just sometimes, flies a little too close to the sun.

But Marjan knew that those two would be just fine. In fact, she thought, they would all be fine. Of course, there was still a lot she and her sisters needed to talk about; too much had been left unsaid since that dark night they left Tehran for good, in the wake of a revolution and a man she hoped would never cross their path again. But that could all wait until tomorrow. For now, she told herself, for now it was enough just to have Bahar and Layla with her, here in this small village called Ballinacroagh, both with sweet smiles on their beautiful faces.

The sun began to set over Clew Bay as Marjan leaned back with her tea to watch members of the acrobatic circus troupe, dressed in jumpsuits of green and gold silk, cartwheel across the modest wooden amphitheatre. The impromptu show was a dance based on the Festival of Lughnasa, that harvest celebration of ancient Celts, which marked their new year. Marjan marvelled at the similarities between this ancient ritual and her own version of the pomegranate myth.

Unlike the Ancient Greeks, for whom the fruit symbolised the inescapable cycle of bitter death, with a remorseful Persephone returning to the underworld for her six months of required winter, Marjan liked to believe the old stories of Persian soothsayers, who held a different vision for the tart fruit's purpose in life. She liked to remember that above all else, above all the unfortunate connotations of death and winter, the pomegranate was, and always would be, the fruit of hope.

The flower of fertility, of new things to come and old seasons to be cradled.

It had shown even her that some of the best recipes are the unwritten ones, the ones that happen when you pour yourself a generous glass of Shiraz *vino*, pop on a soothing Billie Holiday song, and just let the bountiful ingredients lead you. Because, like it or not, life will go on with or without you, forever blooming in someone else's back garden, giving flavour to yet another pot of pomegranate soup.

Yes, that's how she would like to think of that particular sweetness. The myriad seedlings that could only, really, be the flower of new beginnings.

Marjan's Recipe Box

Dolmeh

Ingredients:

> 30-40 canned vine leaves
> 2 onions, chopped
> 250g ground meat, lamb or beef
> olive oil
> 1/3 cup fresh summer savory, chopped
> 1/2 cup fresh dill
> 1/3 cup fresh tarragon
> 1/4 cup fresh mint
> 1/2 cup fresh lime juice

2 cups cooked basmati rice
1 tsp salt
½ tsp ground pepper

Rinse vine leaves and lay aside. Fry onions and meat in olive oil over medium flame until meat is brown. Add chopped herbs to pan and fry for three minutes. Remove from heat. In a large bowl, combine the meat, onion and herb mixture with rice, lime juice, salt and pepper. Lay one vine leaf, vein side up, on a clean surface. Place one tablespoon of rice and meat mixture in middle of leaf, then roll from base up, tucking the sides to form a tight pocket. Repeat until all leaves are stuffed. Line a greased, deep baking dish with stuffed leaves, pour in ¾ cup of water, cover with foil and cook for 45 minutes in oven at 110°C.

Red Lentil Soup

Ingredients:

2 cups dry, red lentils
7 large onions, chopped
7 garlic cloves, crushed
1 tsp ground turmeric
4 tsp ground cumin
olive oil
7 cups chicken broth
3 cups water
salt
2 tsp nigella seeds*

Place lentils in a saucepan, cover with water and bring to a boil. Cook, uncovered, for 9 minutes. Drain and place aside. In a large stock pot, fry 6 of the chopped onions, turmeric and cumin in olive oil until golden. Transfer lentils, broth and water to the pot. Add salt, nigella seed or pepper to taste. Bring soup to boil. Lower heat, cover and simmer for 40 minutes. Fry remaining onion in olive oil until crisp, but not blackened. Add as a garnish over individual bowls of soup.

* ground black pepper may be substituted

Baklava

Ingredients:

> 4 cups brown sugar
> 1 cup water
> ½ cup rose water
> 500g shelled pistachios, chopped
> 500g blanched almonds, chopped
> 2 tbsp cardamom
> 1 tsp ground cinnamon
> 15 frozen filo pastry sheets
> ½ cup unsalted butter, melted

Bring 2 cups of sugar, water and rose water to boil in a medium saucepan. Set aside to cool. Grind pistachios, almonds, cardamom, cinnamon and remaining 2 cups of sugar in a food processor for 1 minute. Set aside. Lay 5 sheets of buttered filo pastry into a greased, 13 x 9 inch pan. Spread a thin, even layer of nut mixture, then cover with 5 more buttered sheets of pastry. Repeat until all mixture is used. Cover with 5 more buttery sheets. With a sharp knife, cut across and diagonally to form diamond shapes. Bake in oven at 180°C for 1 hour. Pour cooled sugar and rosewater syrup over top. Let cool before serving.

Dugh Yogurt Drink

Ingredients:

> 2 cups plain yogurt
> 3 cups mineral or spring water
> 3 tbsp fresh mint, chopped
> 1 tsp salt
> ½ tsp ground pepper
> Mint leaves for garnish

Mix ingredients in a large pitcher or jug. Add ice slowly as you stir. Garnish with mint leaves.

Abgusht

Ingredients:

2 kilos boned leg of lamb, save bone
5 large onions, chopped
1 tsp turmeric
10 cups of water
1 cup yellow split peas
1 tsp paprika
4 tsp salt
1 tsp ground black pepper
5 large potatoes, peeled and quartered
7 tomatoes, sliced

2 tbsp tomato paste
1 dried lime
2 strands saffron dissolved in
7 tablespoons hot water
2 tsp advieh*

Brown meat, 1 onion and turmeric in a large stock pot. Add water, split peas, paprika and bone. Lower heat and simmer, covered, for 2 hours. Add remaining ingredients. Simmer, covered, for 40 minutes. Remove bone. Remove all vegetables and meat and mash them together in a large bowl. Serve mash in a separate bowl alongside remaining broth.

* optional: equal amounts crushed rose petals, cardamom, cinnamon and cumin, mixed

Elephant Ears

Ingredients:

    1 egg
    ½ cup milk
    ¼ cup sugar
    ¼ cup rose water
    ½ teaspoon cardamom
    3¾ cups all-purpose flour
    6 cups vegetable oil

Garnish:
1 cup icing sugar

2 tsps ground cinnamon

Beat egg in a bowl. Add milk, sugar, rose water and cardamom. Slowly mix in flour, kneading into a dough. Roll out on a clean surface with a floured pin until it is paper-thin. Using the rim of a wide-mouthed glass or cup, trace and cut out a circle. Pinch the centre of the circle with your thumb and forefinger to form a bow. Set aside. Repeat until all circles (approx. 15) are done. Heat oil in a deep pan. Fry each ear for 1 minute. Lay pastries on paper towels to cool. Sprinkle with sugar and cinnamon mixture.

Lavash Bread

Ingredients:

> 1 tbsp quick-rising yeast
> ½ cup warm water
> ¼ cup olive oil
> 1 cup milk
> 2 tbsp sugar
> 2 tsp salt
> 4 cups all-purpose flour
> ½ cup poppy and sesame seeds

Preheat oven to 260°C. Mix yeast and water. Set

aside for 15 minutes. Combine yeasty water, oil, milk, sugar and salt in a large bowl. Slowly mix in flour. Knead into a dough. Divide into 3 even balls. Cover with a clean towel and leave to rise for 30 minutes. Roll out one ball of dough on a clean surface with a floured pin until it is paper-thin. Sprinkle with poppy and sesame seeds. Place on a buttered baking tray and cook in oven at 260°C for 5 minutes. Repeat with remaining balls of dough.

Torshi

Ingredients:

2 large eggplants, cubed
500g small cucumbers, cubed
500g carrots, cubed
2 large white potatoes, cubed
8 garlic cloves, peeled
3 cups cauliflower florets
500g pearl onions, peeled
250g green beans
3½ litres white wine vinegar
4 cups chopped fresh herbs

(parsley, basil, tarragon, mint, coriander)
2 tbsp salt
2 tsp black pepper
½ tsp cayenne pepper
1 tbsp nigella seeds
Torshi all-spice mix (½ tsp turmeric,
1 tbsp ground cumin, 1 tsp ground saffron,
1 tbsp ground cardamom, 1 tsp ground
cinnamon)

* makes 5–6 small jars

Wash vegetables and dry well with paper towels.
Combine all ingredients in a large bowl. Ladle
out the mix into sterilised pickling jars. Leave
lidded jars in a dry, cool place for a minimum of
one month.

Chelow

Ingredients:

> 3 cups uncooked, long-grain basmati rice
> 6 cups water
> 2 tbsps salt
> ½ cup olive oil

Place rice in a large bowl and wash under luke-warm water. Drain, then repeat two more times. Bring water and salt to boil in a stock pot. Add clean rice, cover and cook for 30 minutes, or until *al dente*. In another large pot, heat the oil.

Spread an inch-thick layer of cooked rice at the bottom of the second pot. Slowly scoop cooked rice into the pot, forming a pyramid shape so that the top layer is the point. Cover pot and cook on low heat for 30 minutes. Tadig will form at the bottom.

Fesenjoon

Ingredients:

500g shelled walnuts, chopped
olive oil
1,250g skinless chicken breast, cubed
3 large onions, sliced
6 tbsp pomegranate paste, dissolved in
2 cups of hot water
½ teaspoon salt
½ tsp ground black pepper
1 tbsp sugar
2 tbsp lemon juice

Grind walnuts in food processor for 1 minute. Fry in olive oil for 10 minutes, stirring constantly. Set aside. Sauté chicken and onions in a deep pan until golden. Add walnuts, pomegranate juice, and remaining ingredients. Bring to a boil. Lower heat to a simmer, cover, and cook for 45 minutes or until the pomegranate sauce thickens. Serve with chelow.

Migraine Headache Remedy

Ingredients:

> 1 tsp ground nutmeg
> 1 tsp ground cardamom
> 1 teaspoon ground cloves
> 1 cup warm water

In a clean jar or glass, mix spices thoroughly. A soft brown powder should form. Take 1 tablespoon of medicine, making sure to swallow quickly. Wash down with warm water. Repeat, if necessary, every 4 hours.

Pomegranate Soup

Ingredients:

2 large onions, chopped
2 tbsp olive oil
½ cup yellow split peas, rinsed twice
6 cups water
1 tsp salt
½ tsp ground black pepper
1 tsp turmeric
2 cups fresh parsley, chopped
2 cups fresh coriander, chopped
¼ cup fresh mint, chopped

1 cup fresh spring onions, chopped
500g ground lamb
¾ cup rice, rinsed twice
2 cups pomegranate juice
1 tbsp sugar
2 tbsp lemon juice
2 tbsp angelica powder*

In a large stock pot, sauté the chopped onions in olive oil until golden. Add split peas, water, salt, pepper and turmeric, bringing it all to a boil. Lower heat and simmer, covered, for 30 minutes. Add parsley, coriander, mint and spring onions. Simmer for 15 minutes. Meanwhile, roll ground lamb into medium-size meatballs. Add meatballs and remaining ingredients to the pot. Simmer, covered, for 45 minutes.

*optional

After Dinner Lavender-Mint Tea

Ingredients:

> 2 tbsp honey
> 3 tsp fresh lavender flowers
> 1 cup fresh mint leaves, chopped
> ½ lemon, cut into thin wedges

Boil a little less than 2 litres of water. Heat teapot with half of the water. Discard. Fill teapot with honey, lavender leaves, and mint. Add the hot water. Cover and steep for 10 minutes. Serve with a slice of lemon.

Pursuit of Happiness

Douglas Kennedy

Manhattan, Thanksgiving eve, 1945. The war was over, and Eric Smythe's party was in full swing. All his clever Greenwich Village friends were there. So too was his sister Sara – an independent, canny young woman, starting to make her way in the big city. And then in walked a gatecrasher, Jack Malone – a U.S. Army journalist just back from a defeated Germany, and a man whose world-view did not tally with that of Eric and his friends.

Set amidst the dynamic optimism of postwar New York and the subsequent nightmare of the McCarthy witch-hunts, *The Pursuit of Happiness* is a great tragic love story; a tale of divided loyalties, decisive moral choices, and the random workings of destiny.

'A compulsive read'
Kate Atkinson, author of *Behind the Scenes at the Museum*

'This is the novel against which the rest of the year's output demands to be judged'
Express on Sunday

'Kennedy cannot help but write grippingly, and he weaves threads of love and betrayal into a thrillingly masterful ending'
Observer

arrow books

Open House

Elizabeth Berg

'*Maybe Freud didn't know the answer to what women want, but Elizabeth Berg does.*' USA Today

'*You are bending over the dryer, pulling out the still-warm sheets, and the knowledge walks up your backbone. You stare at the man you love and you are staring at nothing; he is gone before he is gone.*'

When Samantha Morrow's husband leaves her and her eleven-year-old son she is faced with the terrifying prospect of having to recreate her whole life. After a few faltering steps she starts to put the pieces into place. She opens her house to a series of lodgers who each in their eccentric way help her to see herself. She fends off her mother, whose idea of getting over a failed marriage is to get a pedicure and get out there dating.

And she makes a friend, King, an MIT graduate turned handyman, who shows her that she has the ability to make her own future and her own happiness . . .

arrow books

We Are Family

Josie Lloyd and Emlyn Rees

1953, and although the coastal village of Stepmouth appears as idyllic as ever, a passionate feud threatens to shatter the small, tight community. Sixteen-year-old Rachel Vale, wilful and unconventional, has fallen in love with the man her brother hates. When the town is devastated by a vast, unstoppable flood, the Vale family is left broken and irreconcilably divided. Or so it seems.

Fifty years later, and Laurie Vale, an only child and aspiring artist, takes a phone call from an aunt she never knew existed, only to discover that everything she ever believed about her family is a lie. As the truth unfolds, the hopes and passions buried in the Vale family's past surface once more. Unknowingly, Laurie has also taken the first step towards becoming ensnared in a complex love affair of her own.

Divided between Fifties Stepmouth and the searing heat of a present day Mallorcan summer. *We Are Family* is a modern family saga which explores the conflicting relationships of two very different generations.

arrow books

Echoes

Maeve Binchy

Growing up in a small seaside town in the 1950s, Clare O'Brien and David Power shout their hearts' desires into the echo cave, praying that their destiny will lead them far away from the town in which they live.

Years later they meet again in Dublin, where David is studying medicine and Clare has won a scholarship to University College. But eventually Castlebay will draw them back and it is against a backdrop of empty grey skies, sea-spray and wind that this drama of ambition, betrayal and love finally reaches its turbulent conclusion.

'A powerful story of love and jealousy'
Sunday Telegraph

'Compulsive reading . . . Ms Binchey has the true story teller's knack'
Observer

arrow books

Firefly Summer

Maeve Binchy

Firefly Summer is the story of four fateful years in the life of a small, sleepy Irish town, and in particular of the family who run the local pub.

Kate and John Ryan have four children, of which the eldest are Michael and Dara, twelve-year-old twins. The small town in which these children are growing up is peaceful and friendly – an unchanging background for a golden childhood and adolescence, where in long, hot summers, Michael, Dara and their friends can fish and swim in the river that winds its slow way through the town, or picnic and play in the ivy-clad ruins of Fernscourt, the great house that burned down during the Troubles.

At first no one in Mountfern has the slightest inkling of what it will mean for their lives when the ruins are bought by an Irish American with a great deal of money in his pocket. Patrick O'Neal's dream is to return, with his two handsome children, to his roots, the village from which his grandfather was once evicted. He will transform Fernscourt into a hotel and a tourist attraction for Americans.

To the people of Mountfern the O'Neill family is seductively attractive, sophisticated – and, although they don't know it, dangerous.

arrow books